"I care."

The words were said without thinking, but he wouldn't have taken them back. He did care. Under the spoiled brat he saw an achingly lonely little girl who'd lost her parents, her grandfather, her world. Somehow he didn't think it had ever quite been put back together again.

His hand slid up her arms, the silk of her shirt sliding smoothly beneath his fingertips. Babs watched him, offering no protest as his hand slid into the thick hair at her nape. Her lashes fell as he tugged her downward.

Sam intended the kiss to comfort, a little human warmth to try to ease some of her pain. He didn't plan on anything more. After all, he admired her guts but he wasn't sure he liked her.

But desire caught him unaware....

FROM THE EDITORS

Dallas Schulze's engaging heroines, charming heroes and lively plot lines always leave the reader wanting more from this talented author. It is our hope that you will read *Lost and Found* with pleasure and leave the story with fond memories in your heart...and with the anticipation of reading another Dallas Schulze book soon!

Other books by Dallas Schulze

HARLEQUIN AMERICAN ROMANCE
RAFFERTY'S CHOICE
A PRACTICAL MARRIAGE
CHARITY'S ANGEL
ANGEL AND THE BAD MAN
A CHRISTMAS MARRIAGE
STRONG ARMS OF THE LAW

HARLEQUIN HISTORICAL
TEMPTATION'S PRICE
SHORT STRAW BRIDE

MIRA
HOME TO EDEN

DALLAS SCHULZE

Lost and Found

HARLEQUIN®

TORONTO • NEW YORK • LONDON
AMSTERDAM • PARIS • SYDNEY • HAMBURG
STOCKHOLM • ATHENS • TOKYO • MILAN • MADRID
PRAGUE • WARSAW • BUDAPEST • AUCKLAND

ISBN 0-373-83421-7

LOST AND FOUND

Copyright © 1988 by Dallas Schulze.

All rights reserved. Except for use in any review, the reproduction or utilization of this work in whole or in part in any form by any electronic, mechanical or other means, now known or hereafter invented, including xerography, photocopying and recording, or in any information storage or retrieval system, is forbidden without the written permission of the publisher, Harlequin Enterprises Limited, 225 Duncan Mill Road, Don Mills, Ontario, Canada M3B 3K9.

All characters in this book have no existence outside the imagination of the author and have no relation whatsoever to anyone bearing the same name or names. They are not even distantly inspired by any individual known or unknown to the author, and all incidents are pure invention.

This edition published by arrangement with Harlequin Books S.A.

® and TM are trademarks of the publisher. Trademarks indicated with ® are registered in the United States Patent and Trademark Office, the Canadian Trade Marks Office and in other countries.

Visit us at www.romance.net

Printed in U.S.A.

Prologue

"I've always suspected that I was adopted. Now I know it must be true. I can't possibly be related to such a collection of half-witted birdbrains!"

"Really, Babette. That's most unkind. I don't think it's the least bit justified, do you, Clarence?"

Clarence Smith nodded his bald head, looking like an occidental Buddha. "Quite right, Bertie. Quite right. Unjustified, Babs. Unjustified."

His great-niece ignored him, as did everyone else in the room. The only person who had paid any attention to Clarence in the past fifty years was his wife, and no one paid much attention to Bertie, either.

Babs focused her attention on the person she knew to be the real culprit. Her aunt Dodie was the only one in the room with brains enough to come up with this half-baked scheme. Dodie Davis met her niece's fiery look without flinching. She'd done what was right, as always.

"Aunt Dodie?"

The older woman imperiously raised one eyebrow. "Don't use that tone with me, Babette. This is no concern of yours."

"No concern of mine? You can't possibly be that stupid."

Dodie bristled, her thin mouth tightening until it almost vanished. "Don't be impertinent."

"I'm too old to be impertinent. I'm being downright rude but it's nothing compared to what I'd like to do."

"I think you're getting a bit hysterical about this, Babs." Her uncle Lionel cleared his throat importantly and then ruined the effect by glancing at his wife as if seeking her permission to speak. When she didn't frown him down, he dared to pull his soft features into a fatherly grimace. "I'm sure once you've had a chance to calm down, you'll realize that you're overreacting and—"

"Overreacting? You think *I'm* overreacting? What do you think Eduardo Stefanoni is going to do when he finds out you've sold him cheap fakes?"

"Reproductions, Babs. They're hardly cheap fakes."

"They're not the originals you promised him."

Lionel stared at her for a moment and then lifted his hand to stroke the neat beard he'd grown recently, thinking it made him look more manly. All it succeeded in doing was making him look like a furry weakling. He glanced at his wife who ignored him, as she'd done for most of their thirty-five years of wedded bliss.

"Er...ah...um."

Babs's brown eyes darkened with contempt. "Hemming and hawing isn't an answer, Uncle Lionel. Did you or did you not sell Stefanoni objets d'art that you claimed were originals?"

"Really, Babette, this is not a court of law. That tone of voice is completely out of place." Lionel subsided gratefully into the background as his niece's demanding look shifted from him to his wife. Dodie was much better equipped to deal with the girl. She was too willful by half. Always had been.

"Believe me, my reaction is restrained compared to what Stefanoni is going to do when he finds out that you've sold him fakes. Don't you know who he is?"

Bertie took it upon herself to answer the question. "He's a businessman here in L.A. I read that in the paper just last week." She looked so proud of herself. Babs wanted to tell her to wake up and smell the coffee. But Bertie hadn't been awake since before Babs was born. There was no sense in trying to change her now.

"Aunt Bertie, Eduardo Stefanoni owns a good portion of southern California. He has strong ties to organized crime. If you had to decide on a life of crime, couldn't you have chosen some nice midwestern banker who was going to hang the paintings in his guest bathroom? The only way you could have chosen a worse person to bilk was if you'd sold the stuff to Don Corleone."

"I don't believe we know Don Corleone, do we, Clarence? Besides, I can't believe that nice Mr. Stefanoni is a criminal. He was very polite. He said he liked my shawl."

Her husband nodded. "Very polite, Bertie. Very polite. But I don't think we could know this Corleone fellow, my dear. I think he's a television person. Don't think he exists at all."

Babs stared at them, wondering how it was possible to be so out of touch with reality and still be alive. They would never understand the dangerous repercussions of what they'd done.

"Give it up, cuz. What's done is done. The artwork is gone. Stefanoni got a great price. We got enough money to hold house and home together for another few months. Everybody's happy."

Babs turned to look at her cousin. Of them all, Lance was the one who suited the magnificent room the most.

How hatchet-faced Dodie and weak-chinned Lionel had managed to produce a son with such Adonis-like features was one of the great mysteries of the Western world. The fact that he had the morals of an alley cat and the ethics of a squid had not yet begun to show on his face. At thirty, he was the picture of masculine perfection. And he knew it.

Having grown up with him, Babs was unimpressed. In her opinion, Lance was the ultimate example of beauty being only skin deep. When you scratched the surface, there was nothing underneath but a vain, shallow man, who spent his time looking for someone else to blame for everything that went wrong in his life. She didn't like him but she was desperate for someone to understand the situation.

"Lance, you've got to know what's going to happen when Stefanoni finds out he's got fakes. The man didn't get where he is by letting people cheat him."

"Don't get so panicky. Who's to say he's going to find out? Besides, what can he do? We told him the sales had to be under-the-table because of Great-grandfather's will. He won't go to the police."

"People like Eduardo Stefanoni do not sit quietly while amateur crooks walk over them."

Lance widened his eyes mockingly. "Why, cuz, how is that possible? He was so nice and he admired Aunt Bertie's shawl."

"He would have admired an old tennis shoe if he thought it would help him get his hands on the Caravaggio."

Lance lifted muscular shoulders in an innocent shrug. "I think you're overreacting. What can he do?"

"He could have you all fitted for cement shoes."

Lance shrugged again and Babs bit her tongue to keep

from shrieking in sheer frustration. How could she get it across to them that this was not something they could sweep under the Aubusson rug and forget? She drew a deep breath and decided to try a different angle.

"I don't understand why you needed the money anyway. When I left for Europe, the quarterly allowance from the trust fund had just been deposited. That was only six weeks ago. What happened?"

"I don't know that it's any of your business. We didn't touch any of *your* money." Lance's beautiful mouth curled in a sneer.

"You may not have used my money directly but you knew that I'd be the one who'd have to bail you out of this mess. Where do you think the money is going to come from to pay Stefanoni back? I'm sure none of you has a dime left."

Her gaze swept the small gathering scathingly. Clarence looked confused and Bertie looked vaguely distressed as if she knew Babs was angry but couldn't quite put her finger on the reason. Dodie's mouth tightened, furious that anyone should dare to question anything she chose to do. Lionel stared at his pudgy hands, clasped over the straining buttons of his vest. He knew that look of Babs's and he didn't want to meet her eyes. Babs's lip curled and her gaze shifted to Lance. His beautiful blue eyes stared back at her, full of malicious amusement.

"What are you going to do, cuz? Throw a screaming fit like you did when you were eight?"

"No, I'm going to do something a lot more effective. You've got ten days to go to Stefanoni and tell him what you've done and give him the Caravaggio and anything else you sold him."

"And then what? Are you going to call the police?"

Her eyes settled on Lance, chill with dislike. Her wide mouth curved in a smile every bit as nasty as his. "I'm going to talk to Finney and explain exactly what you've done."

The mention of the family lawyer had exactly the effect she expected. According to the terms of her great-grandfather's will, if any of the family heirlooms were sold for any reason, the money he'd left in trust for his relatives would be turned over to several charities. If Finney were to find out what had been done, they'd all lose every cent. Except Babs. Her trust fund came from her grandfather and was separate from the others.

The amusement died out in Lance's eyes, to be replaced with an expression that bordered on hatred. Lionel twitched, his pale eyes taking on a frantic look. Dodie paled but she was made of sterner stuff than her husband. Even Clarence looked worried.

"Now Babette, that's not a nice thing to say, is it, Clarence?" Bertie's thin fingers twisted in the yards of fringing on her shawl.

"Not nice, m'dear, not nice at all." Clarence almost managed to sound stern.

"Don't be ridiculous, Babette. You're not going to do any such thing. I forbid it." Dodie's stern words didn't conceal her concern. She knew as well as any of them that her niece was capable of almost anything.

"Bad idea, Babs." Lionel clearly felt obligated to say something.

It was left to Lance to have the final comment. "You're bluffing. You know what would happen if you told Finney."

"I think the terms of Great-grandfather's will were quite specific. You'd lose everything. The house, the money, everything. It all goes to suitable charities. And I don't think any of you qualify.''

''You wouldn't do it because then you'd be stuck with all of us hanging on your pocket.''

Her smile was chill. ''No, I don't think so. I've been paying your way long enough. I'll make sure Bertie and Clarence are settled in a nice little house but that's it. Your father could brush up his law degree and actually try to make a living at something. I'm sure Aunt Dodie could find something to do. And you, *cuz*, you can always become a gigolo. You're little more than that now. Only I'm not getting anything in return for my money.''

Lance jerked upright and took a quick step toward her, his features twisted. ''You little bitch! What right have you got to act like a princess talking to the peasants?''

Babs stood her ground, ignoring the fact that he towered over her by a full twelve inches. ''If I were talking to peasants, I'd be a lot more polite.''

''That's enough from both of you.'' Dodie's harsh voice broke the building tension. Lance held Babs's contemptuous look a moment longer before he looked away. He returned to his position leaning against the mantel, his broad shoulders tight with anger. Babs looked at her aunt, raising one brow in question.

''I'm very serious about this, Aunt Dodie. You've got ten days.''

''I can see that you're upset, Babette, but there's no reason to become hysterical.'' The tone was as close to placating as the older woman could manage. ''Perhaps we were a bit hasty in selling the Caravaggio.''

''The *fake* Caravaggio.''

''The reproduction. However, I think when you consider, you'll see that it's really not worth all this upset.''

''The only good part of this whole mess is that if

Stefanoni takes out a contract, you'll at least be out of my hair.''

"That's not amusing, Babs.'' Lionel ran a finger around the inside of his collar.

"I didn't mean it to be amusing.'' Babs thrust her fingers through her hair, ruffling it into shaggy dark blond waves. "I'm trying to get across to you that this isn't a game. When Eduardo Stefanoni finds out you've sold him fakes, he's not going to say 'They're Malones. I guess they can do anything they want.' He doesn't know a Malone from a chimney sweep. He's going to be angry and he's going to do something about it. It isn't likely to be nice.''

"As I said, perhaps we were a bit hasty but Mr. Stefanoni leaves for Italy in three weeks.''

"Do you think they're not going to recognize a fake Caravaggio in Italy? He was Italian, for crying out loud!''

"Mr. Stefanoni is not the major issue here. You seem to think that we've been demanding too much of you financially. I think when you look at it, you'll see how foolish that is. After all, once you and Lance are married, the money will belong to both of you equally—''

Babs's laughter cut her off in midsentence. "Lance and I married? You've got to be kidding. I thought you gave up that idea years ago.''

"I don't see—'' Dodie began, her mouth tight and her spine stiff as a board.

"No, I'm sure you don't see, Aunt Dodie.'' Babs bit her lip, trying to hold back the laughter. "Let me lay it out for you. I am *never* going to marry Lance. I don't like him and he doesn't like me. Even if we did like each other—which I can't imagine—I'd never marry someone who was prettier than I was and who spends more time in front of the bathroom mirror than I do.''

"Really, Babette—''

"No, don't lecture me anymore, Aunt Dodie. I'm too old to learn respect for my elders.'' Babs glanced around the room, all amusement fading. "I meant what I said. Ten days and then I go to Finney. You'll lose everything.'' She looked at Lance, ignoring the bitter dislike reflected in his eyes. "It just might do you good. Tell Margate that I won't be home for dinner.'' She walked to the door, her steps brisk. "Remember, ten days.''

The massive door shut behind her small figure and the room was quiet. On the mantel the Seth Thomas clock pinged the half hour, breaking the stillness. Those left in the room stared at each other in silence. In their eyes was the dazed look of people who'd survived an earthquake.

"I think she means it.'' It was Lionel who spoke first.

"Mother, we've got to do something about her. If she talks to Finney....''

"I know what will happen if she talks to Finney, Lance.'' Dodie continued to stare at the door.

Bertie fussed with her shawl. "I'm sure Babette wouldn't do anything nasty. She was always such a sweet child. Noisy and perhaps a teeny bit willful but very sweet. Don't you agree, Clarence?''

Dodie ignored the elderly pair. "I'll have to have a talk with her.''

"I don't think talking is going to do any good, Mother. You know what a stubborn little witch she can be. We're going to have to do something more drastic than just talk to her.''

Dodie nodded slowly. "I'm afraid you're right, Lance. We may have to do something more drastic.''

MALONE HEIRESS KIDNAPPED
Police Stumped for Clues

Babette Anne Malone was kidnapped two days ago by person or persons unknown. Ms. Malone was riding near her home in Montecito Monday afternoon, as was her usual practice. Her horse returned to the stables without her. A note was pinned to the saddle stating that the heiress would not be harmed and that a ransom demand would follow. As of this writing, no such demand has been received.

In six months, on her twenty-fifth birthday, Ms. Malone will inherit a fortune estimated to be worth nearly fifty million dollars. The money is part of the fabled Malone empire, which began in the late nineteenth century by Carlisle Malone and continued to grow in the twentieth under the leadership of his son Caldwell, grandfather of Ms. Malone.

In the late 1950s, Malone stock went public and Caldwell retired to a supervisory position, leaving control of the corporation's many interests in the hands of a board of directors.

Ms. Malone's father, Earl, was being groomed for the position of CEO when he and his wife, Lenore, were killed in an auto crash shortly after their daughter's seventh birthday.

Caldwell survived his son by only a few months, and when he died the bulk of his fortune was put in trust for his young granddaughter. His granddaughter's money is held until she marries or reaches her twenty-fifth birthday.

Ms. Malone is the niece of well-known adventure writer Emmet Malone.

The Malone family has offered a reward of fifty thousand dollars for any information leading to the whereabouts of Ms. Malone or her abductors.

Chapter One

"Dammit!" Sam shifted carefully, reaching backward to grasp a long thorny branch and ease its hold on his coat. Despite his care, he heard the nylon rip as the branch came loose and he gritted his teeth against the urge to turn and yank the ancient rosebush out of the ground.

The plant couldn't have made the last few hours any more miserable if it had been guided by a malevolent intelligence. At one time, it had been part of the elaborate landscaping that had surrounded the Empire Hotel in northern Idaho. The hotel had been abandoned a quarter of a century ago and the rosebushes had been left to grow in to a near impenetrable tangle of thorny canes.

Sam eased forward, hoping to avoid any more encounters with the bush behind him. The fact that the plants had provided him cover for the last sixteen hours didn't do much to ease his irritation. Sixteen hours ago he hadn't been cold and hungry. He shifted again and then muttered irritably. The roses might have provided him with cover but they hadn't done a very generous job of it. The hollow he'd found allowed him to watch the ramshackle old building without being seen, but it didn't include room to stretch out.

"I should have been a stockbroker. At least I could

have been comfortable. This is a ridiculous occupation for a grown man. Playing cops and robbers. I should settle down and get a real job.''

He shivered as a chill breeze found its way into the thick overgrowth. He didn't need to look at his watch to know that dawn was not far away. He'd move soon. He flexed his hands inside the warm gloves, his eyes on the hulking old building below.

All in all, he shouldn't complain. It had only taken him a week to find this place. A hunch had brought him here and it had paid off. Shortly before sunset, he'd seen the girl. The elation he'd felt at that moment had worn down during the long cold hours of the night but he was still pleased with the results of the past week's work. Fifty thousand dollars was a lot of money. He could put up with a lot of discomfort to get it.

He waited with the patience of a hunter, studying the terrain that lay between him and the building. He was studying it more in memory than by sight. In the gray predawn hour, the landscape was shrouded in shadows that concealed all but the most obvious features. The old pebble pathway gleamed pale, looking smooth and safe but he knew that it was not as smooth as it looked. Over the years creepers had stretched their way across it, offering to trip the unwary.

He wanted to get the girl out before the kidnappers realized they'd lost their victim. He checked the contents of his pack, making sure that he knew where everything was. His gun was tucked into his waistband, a reassuring pressure against his spine. A hunting knife lay along his calf. He hoped neither one would be needed.

The sun was just beginning to creep over the horizon when Sam left his shelter. It was early May and the air was cold and damp. There was no sign of life from the old building. It looked as if no one had been near it since the last guest left twenty-five years before. But he knew there were at least three people there. With luck, he'd only have to deal with one of them. He hoped she wasn't the hysterical type. If she was, he'd have to coldcock her, and hitting a woman wasn't his favorite way to start a spring day.

He worked his way around the perimeter of the open space that had once been a manicured sweep of lawn. He'd already planned a quick escape route, and he left his pack where it would be easy to find. He hoped they wouldn't need it. He wanted to get in and out without them being any the wiser. With any luck, he and the girl could go straight to where he'd hidden his truck. But it never hurt to be prepared for any eventuality. He stripped off his heavy coat, laying it next to the pack. He flexed his fingers inside the gloves and reached back to touch the reassuring weight of the .45.

In the gray light he was an ominous figure. A black turtleneck stretched across the muscles of his chest and shoulders, disappearing into the waistband of a pair of soft black jeans. Black socks and black tennis shoes completed the dark picture. His hair was as black as the clothes, but when sunlight caught it, there were blue lights in it, a much softer shade than the dark blue of his eyes. But there was no light to soften the darkness of him now.

He drew in a deep breath, measuring the distance he'd have to cross before he reached the shelter of the building. Though the lawn had long since disappeared in a tangle of weeds, the space was still wide open. There was nothing to offer any concealment. There were no lights in the building and the kidnappers had no reason to suspect that they'd been found. They hadn't even bothered to post a guard. Still, crossing that open space was not something he liked. But it wasn't going to get any easier with waiting.

He crouched low, making his body as small as possible before darting into the open. For the few seconds it took him to cross the forty-yard space, he was totally vulnerable, a moving target for anyone watching. He sprinted the distance, deliberately blanking his mind to everything but the need to get into the shelter of the building. If someone was watching, he'd learn it soon enough. Probably in a way he'd rather not consider.

If anyone had been watching, they'd have seen little more than a shadow gliding across the lawn, a darker presence among the shadows already there. Almost as quickly as the eye could register that it was a man, he was gone, disappearing into the darkness that surrounded the big old building.

Sam pressed himself against the rough wood of the wall, his breathing only slightly accelerated. He'd accomplished the first step, but he didn't take time to congratulate himself. The first step was the easiest. The hard part came when he got the girl. So much depended on whether or not he had to take her out as a deadweight. If she could help herself, even just a little, it was going to make his task easier.

He loosened the coil of rope from his belt and stepped away from the wall. Directly above him was the balcony where he'd seen the girl. He was betting that it lay outside the room where they were keeping her. He swung the rope gently, loosening his arm, getting a feel for the weight of it. He moved back until he stood a few feet out from the balcony, once again in the open. He swung his arm once, twice, and on the third swing he let go, feeling the supple nylon slide through his gloved fingers.

He held his breath as the rope sailed upward, pulled by the weight of the grappling hook on its end. The hook went over the edge of the balcony, hitting the wood with a quiet thud that sounded like a gunshot in the stillness.

But he couldn't worry about the noise. He was committed now. He just had to hope that the gods were watching over him. He yanked on the rope, pulling up the slack until the hook caught on the edge of the railing, digging into the wood and gripping. Sam yanked again, leaning his weight into the rope. He knew the rope would hold but he didn't have any such guarantees about the railing. It was old and old wood had a nasty tendency to rot. But there was no give in the rope and he gave thanks that the builders had seen fit to put quality materials into the hotel.

He slid his hands up the rope and tightened his grip. The muscles in his shoulders bulged as he pulled himself off the ground. His feet hooked around the rope, the rubber soles of his shoes gripping and assisting in the climb. He tried not to think about the fact that he was completely vulnerable. If someone chose to take a shot at him, there wasn't going to be a whole hell of a lot he could do about it.

When his hand touched the edge of the balcony, he heaved a silent sigh of relief. He was really going to have to consider changing occupations. Being a stockbroker had its advantages. His other hand gripped the balcony and he pulled himself upward. Just a few more minutes and this was going to be all over but the shouting. With fifty thousand dollars in his pocket, he could consider the advantages of a new career in comfort.

He swung his left leg over the railing. His foot touched the nice solid surface of the balcony—and a figure rushed out of the darkness and slammed into him.

He teetered on the railing, his right foot dangling over the ground twenty feet below. It was only years of living on the edge that saved him.

His left foot braced against the inside of the railing, pushing him forward and away from the drop. He lunged away from the railing and toward his assailant. It was not a graceful maneuver. In fact, it was downright awkward, but Sam didn't care. It got him onto the solid surface of the balcony.

His assailant struggled loose from his clumsy grip and Sam felt the air leave his lungs as a foot connected with his solar plexis. He doubled up but straightened in time to block a second kick that would have forever destroyed his chances of fathering a child. The foot landed on his thigh, drawing a grunt of pain.

There was no time for conscious thought. He was in the midst of a life-and-death struggle. But some instinct held back the blow that would have laid his opponent out flat. Perhaps it was the size of his attacker. The men he'd seen had been average height, whereas this shadowy figure was much smaller. Perhaps it was the fact that the blows, no matter how effective, had not been all that powerful, nor that skilled. Or maybe it was the fact that the figure had made no attempt to call for assistance, as if he had as much reason to keep the battle quiet as Sam did.

Sam didn't have time to analyze his reasons. He'd learned over the years to trust his instincts. His arm came up to block a well-aimed blow that might have broken his windpipe if there'd been more power behind it. Whoever this was, he was planning on killing Sam. He'd had some martial arts training but there was a slight clumsiness to the moves that told Sam the training hadn't been put to daily use.

The figure lunged forward and Sam didn't wait to see what damage was intended this time. His foot swept out in a move so simple it caught his opponent totally off guard. His foot hit just at ankle level, sweeping forward and jerking the feet out from under his attacker. There was a quick gasp and then a grunt of pain as the hard floor of the balcony connected with softer flesh.

The fall knocked the breath out of his opponent and Sam didn't give him time to recover. Within moments, the short battle was over. The struggle was fierce but with the advantage of an extra hundred pounds, it didn't take Sam long to pin the other to the balcony.

Still not a word had been spoken. Sam knelt astraddle his victim and peered down, trying to make out something more than a dark figure. The light was still dim, and with the added shadows on the balcony it was impossible to see anything beyond a vague shape. Yet Sam had an eerie feeling....

"Ms. Malone?" The words were a question, seeking confirmation of his half-formed suspicions. The figure went absolutely still and he could feel the eyes watching him, but there was no sound. "Look, I'm here to rescue you." Still no answer. Maybe she was in shock? "Babette?"

"Don't call me that!" The voice was little more than a hiss, but it was definitely feminine. Sam felt some of the tension drain out of his body. He stared down at her, wondering if she looked anything like the pictures in the paper. The glimpse he'd gotten of her earlier had been from too far away to do anything more than just identify her.

"Are you going to sit on me all day?" The question was asked in an ill-tempered whisper and Sam gave a start, realizing that he still had her pinned down. Muttering an apology, he shifted away from her, climbing to his feet and offering his hand. She disdained his help, standing up by herself.

"Who are you?" There was an imperiousness in the demand that set his teeth on edge. Sam had to remind himself that Babs Malone was probably accustomed to giving orders. Lots of them.

"Sam Delanian. I'm here to…"

"I know. You already said you were here to rescue me." She cut him off without apology. "What took you so long?"

Sam stared at her, feeling his jaw drop slightly. "What took me so long?"

"It doesn't matter now." One small hand came up to wave dismissingly.

"That's very gracious of you." Either the sarcasm went completely over her head or she chose to ignore it. He couldn't decide which.

"Now that you're here, we can take care of these slime balls."

"Slime balls? Take care of them?" Sam wondered if he'd actually fallen off the balcony and had landed in an episode of *Miami Vice*. "What are you talking about?"

"The men who kidnapped me." The husky whisper was impatient, as if she suspected him of being slow-witted. "We can capture them. You brought a gun, didn't you?"

"Yes, but—"

"Good. They're both sleeping downstairs—"

"I don't care if they're sleeping in the attic, hanging by their heels. I came to get you out of here not pull a Rambo imitation."

"You're not going to just let them get away, are you?"

"I'll call the cops as soon as we get to town."

"No. We're going to handle this ourselves."

"Lady, I'm not handling anything. I'm leaving the same way I got here and you can come with me or not as you please."

He took a step toward the railing and his feet tangled in something on the floor. He staggered slightly before regaining his balance. Leaning down, he lifted a length of cloth.

"What's this?"

"The sheets. I tied them together. I was going to use them to climb down off the balcony."

Sam ran the length of fabric through his hands. It fell well short of the yardage necessary to reach the ground. "You'd never have made it."

"I was going to jump the rest of the way."

"Right, and you'd have broken a leg. Besides, surely you weren't going to leave without subduing your captors."

"There's no need to be nasty. Now that you're here, we can take care of them."

"Just how do you think we're going to take care of them?"

"You've got a gun." She seemed to think this one fact explained everything.

"Lady, they've got guns, too."

"Don't call me lady. It makes me feel like a spoiled poodle."

"Well, at least half the description fits." He didn't need daylight to know that she was glaring at him. The impact of the look was palpable.

"Sarcasm isn't going to get us anywhere."

"Neither is standing here arguing. Let's get out of here."

"Why won't you help me capture them? There're only three of them."

"Help you? What are *you* planning on doing? I've only got one gun so unless you've got an Uzi secreted in your bra, I don't think there's a whole hell of a lot you can do to aid this guerrilla attack you want me to launch."

"There're three of them and only one of me. That's three to one and even John Wayne thought twice with those odds."

The veins in his temples stood out with the effort he was making to keep his voice down. When he remembered his concern about her being paralyzed with shock, he wanted to laugh but he knew it would have had a hysterical edge. It was a wonder she was still a captive. If he'd been the kidnappers, he'd have given her back immediately. There wasn't any amount of ransom that was worth coping with her.

"I'm leaving now. Are you coming with me or not?"

"I think you're scared of them." The challenge in her voice made it clear that she expected him to prove his manhood by doing what she wanted.

"You're damn right I'm scared. Only a fool wouldn't be. Now, are you coming?"

What she might have said in reply was destined to remain unspoken. The two of them stood in the doorway that led from the balcony into the bedroom. Directly across the wide room from them was the door that led into the hall. Perhaps the sound of their voices had carried farther than they'd intended or maybe the kidnappers had just decided to check on their captive. They'd never know.

The door opened with a creak of hinges that gave Sam an instant's warning. He grabbed Babs with one hand and shoved her behind him, snatching his gun with the other hand. The bullet shattered the doorjamb next to the other man's head and Sam heard a cry of pain as splinters of wood peppered his face. The man ducked back, jerking the door shut behind him.

Sam turned and grabbed Babs around the waist. "No more arguing. Get down the rope as fast as you can and head due east." If she had a protest, he didn't give her time to voice it. He lowered her over the side of the balcony, waiting only until he was sure that she had a hold on the rope before turning back to the door. He gave her a few seconds to get started down the rope and then fired another shot into the door, just in case they were thinking about trying that entrance again.

He tucked the gun back into his waistband and swung himself over the railing. Grabbing the rope, he slid toward the ground, letting the rope sing through his hands. He hit the ground in a crouch. Sensing a presence behind him, he spun, hands up. Before he could strike, a breathless and all too familiar voice stopped him.

"It's me."

He let his hands drop. "I thought I told you to head east."

"It would have helped if I'd known which direction east was."

The sarcasm was lost in the sudden crack of gunfire. The bullet missed, disappearing in the bushes beyond, but Sam didn't need a stronger hint. He grabbed her arm and ran toward the overgrowth that had shielded him the night before. In the time that had passed since he crossed this space, the sun had slipped high enough to give a weak illumination. It made it easy to see where they were going and he was able to make better time than he had earlier, but it also made it easier to be seen. Twice more, rifle fire split the quiet morning; once the bullet kicked up dirt not two feet ahead of them. That was considerably closer than he liked.

All they could do was keep running. There was nowhere to stop and return the fire. He just had to hope that their luck would hold. And then they were plunging into the overgrown shrubbery.

His pack and coat were laying just where he'd left them and he barely slowed his stride to snatch them up. If Babs thought the pace he set was too fast, he didn't leave her the breath to complain. Over the noise of their passage through the underbrush, he could hear the shouts of their pursuers.

They had less than two minutes head start. It would take the kidnappers that long to rally and get out the front door. The one doing the shooting would have to take a few seconds to explain what was going on. That wasn't going to give them much of a head start. His original plan would have to be scrapped. There was no way they could make it to his truck. They'd have to go to ground for a while.

He dodged around an enormous pine and threw himself into the midst of the overgrown rosebushes that he'd cursed such a short time before. The canes caught at his shirt, tearing loose as he continued forward, dragging his companion with him. He heard Babs gasp in pain and hoped she'd had the good sense to cover her face. He shoved her ahead of him, pushing her to her knees into a small hollow and dropping down beside her. His hand covered her mouth, pulling her close to his body, turning so that he was between her and their pursuers.

Babs's heart pounded in her chest. Beneath her cheek

she could feel the heavy thud of her rescuer's heart. There was something reassuring about that steady beat. She closed her eyes, trying to slow her pulse. His palm was still over her mouth and she twisted her head slightly, trying to dislodge the grip. His fingers tightened for a moment and then slid away, but the arm around her back pulled her closer as if trying to absorb her into himself.

Babs knew what he was doing. This close to the trees it was still more dark than light. The pale blue of her shirt stood out like a beacon while his black clothing blended with the darkness. He was trying to block any possible view of her shirt from outside their fragile hiding place.

He shifted slightly, reaching backward and pulling out his gun. He brought the .45 out, holding it muzzle up, ready to bring it down and fire if necessary. Crushed against him as she was, Babs was mere inches from the weapon. She stared at the cold steel, wondering why she'd never noticed how truly dangerous a gun could look.

She shut her eyes again, turning her face into his shoulder. For the moment, there was nothing they could do but wait. Waiting had never been her favorite occupation. After ten days of sitting in the moldering hotel, waiting for her family to pay a ransom, waiting for the kidnappers to kill her, waiting for something—anything—to happen, this small space of time seemed to pass torturously slow.

Babs concentrated on her immediate surroundings, trying to shut out the sound of the kidnappers blundering around them. His shirt felt soft beneath her cheek. The knit stretched across his chest, letting her feel the bulge of muscle beneath. He smelled of soap and sweat, a combination that seemed uniquely masculine.

He tensed and her body jerked, as if struck, when one of the kidnappers walked within a few feet of their hiding place. The man was so close that she could hear his muttered curses when one of the rose canes caught at his clothing. He jerked loose, stopping less than three feet away to examine the damage to his shirt.

Babs forgot how to breathe. She could see Sam's fingers tighten around the clip of the automatic, edging it downward into a firing position. The kidnapper lifted his eyes from their examination of his torn shirt, but he didn't move on. He stood there, looking around, almost as if he sensed something. Babs shut her eyes. If she didn't look at him, maybe he wouldn't see them.

Just when it seemed certain that they would be discovered, there was a shout from another part of the property. The man turned and ran in the direction of the voice.

For several long moments, it was impossible to move. Sam continued to press her face into his chest, his eyes following the path the kidnapper had taken. Babs had to make a conscious effort to take a breath. When he finally eased his hold on her, it felt almost as if she was losing a part of herself.

"We've got to move. Here, put on my coat. It'll conceal that shirt. You might as well be wearing a neon sign." He shoved the coat into her hands while he shrugged into the small pack.

"Well, excuse me. Next time I'm kidnapped, I'll try to dress more appropriately."

"Next time you're kidnapped, you'd better hope any potential rescuers haven't heard that you've got a temper like a pit viper."

Babs shut her mouth with a snap, shrugging into the coat and zipping it to the throat. It completely covered her shirt. In fact, it almost completely covered her. Her rescuer was studying the area outside the shelter of the roses and she glared at his back.

"Where are we going?"

"I don't know. They're between us and my truck."

"What did you do, park your car in the old lot?"

"I parked it in the woods on the other side of the lot. It's concealed but I don't want to try to get to it with them stumbling around looking for us. We'll move away from it and find some place to hole up until tonight."

"Why did you park your car over there when I was being held in a room on this side of the building?"

Sam didn't bother to dignify the sarcastic question with an answer. His hand closed around her upper arm again. "Come on. Move as quietly as possible."

"Do I look like Hiawatha?"

"That includes keeping your mouth shut." He threw the order over his shoulder as he pulled her forward and out of the rose thicket.

Babs shut her mouth. She knew he was right. She wasn't usually so nasty, especially to someone who'd just helped her out of a very unpleasant situation. It was just nerves. Ten days of wondering if you were about to die was enough to ruin anyone's temperament.

He released her arm as soon as they were out of the tangle of thorny canes and she had the feeling that he was glad to let go of her. The thought irritated her. She studied his back as he walked ahead of her. Funny, she didn't even know what he looked like. She had a vague impression of dark hair and strong features, but nothing definite. He moved like an athlete. Even now, when his stride was tempered by the need for silence, there was an easy swing to his walk.

Sam Delanian. The name didn't ring any bells but then there was no reason why it should. It wasn't likely that her family had hired someone she knew. She didn't know anyone capable of mounting a rescue attempt. Except maybe her uncle Emmet and, as far as she knew, Emmet was in South America somewhere, researching a book.

They didn't travel far but the tension of waiting for discovery made it seem much farther. Babs's nerves were stretched tight with the effort to walk quietly. She'd never realized how difficult it was until now. The man ahead of her didn't seem to give any thought to where he was putting his feet and yet he didn't make a sound. She considered every step and still felt as if she made enough noise for ten people.

When he stopped, she felt clumsy and irritable. She'd had no sleep the night before because she was preparing for her escape. The previous nights had been restless, to say the least. It was hard to relax when you were aware that a man with a gun stood outside your door.

"We'll stay here for the rest of the day."

She looked around but could see no sign of a "here" that looked like a place to rest. "Are we going to squat in the bushes again?" The question held more acidity than she'd intended but she was too tired to care.

The muscles in his back tightened but he didn't turn to look at her. His arm came out, carefully brushing aside some thin bushes. Up a steep slope behind them was a shallow cave, little more than a hollow but big enough to conceal the two of them.

He gestured for her to go in and she scrambled up the incline before collapsing on the rocky floor of the small shelter. For the first time in ten days, she felt almost safe. At least she did until her companion followed her in. Looking up—a long way up—she met a pair of the bluest, most irritated eyes she'd ever seen.

Chapter Two

"You are, without exception, the most obnoxious, spoiled little brat it has ever been my misfortune to meet."

"Well, you're no prince of charm yourself." Babs straightened her shoulders defensively as Sam sank down next to her. The hollow was bigger than it had looked from outside but he seemed to fill it with wide shoulders and long legs.

Babs was uneasily aware that her behavior thus far had been less than exemplary but she felt crowded, physically, mentally and emotionally. The past week and a half had strained her admittedly limited reserves of control and patience.

"If you can't take the pressure, you shouldn't have taken the job."

Sam glanced up from stripping off his gloves, his vivid blue eyes full of annoyance. "What job?"

"This job." One small hand swept out in an impatient gesture. "The job of rescuing me, getting me away from those goons. That job. The one my family hired you to do."

Sam arched one brow as he tucked the gloves into his pack. "Nobody hired me to do anything."

Babs's fine brows, which were several shades darker than her shaggy blond hair, drew together. "If my family didn't hire you to rescue me, what are you doing here?"

"There's a reward. Fifty thousand dollars."

"A reward? You rescued me because of a reward?" Her upper lip quivered in a faint sneer.

Sam's grin held an edge. "That's right. But if I'd known what an obnoxious little pain in the butt you were going to turn out to be, I don't think I'd have done it for twice the reward. As it is, I had to leave a perfectly good rope hanging from that balcony. I may tack the cost of that rope onto the reward. I should have left you with the kidnappers for a couple more days. I bet they'd have been willing to pay your family to get rid of you."

Her eyes darkened to the color of bitter chocolate and her full mouth tightened. "I overheard them planning to kill me as soon as they got their money. That's why I was going to try to escape."

In the moment before she glanced away, Sam saw real vulnerability. A vulnerability that she tried to hide. With a sigh, he reminded himself that she'd been through an awful lot. Being kidnapped and overhearing your own death sentence would be enough to spoil anyone's good temper. He had doubts that Babs Malone *had* a good temper, but he was trying to give her the benefit of the doubt.

"You'd have been as good as dead with those stupid sheets. That trick doesn't work even in the movies."

"Well, I had to try something."

"Yeah, I suppose you did. Lucky I came along. By the way, why did you jump me when I came over the balcony? It wasn't too likely that I was one of the kidnappers."

She shrugged. "I don't know. I guess I've gotten a bit edgy lately."

"Edgy? You damn near pushed me off the balcony. Not to mention the fact that I could have really decked you."

She shrugged again. "Sorry."

Twigs and leaves littered the floor of the cave and Sam began gathering a small pile of them together. He was aware of his companion watching him out of the corners of her eyes and he wondered what she was thinking. He didn't look at her. Right now he had more important things to think about than the moods and thoughts of a spoiled heiress.

"I didn't plan on getting stuck away from my truck like this so I don't have a whole lot with me, but I've got some soup. That will have to hold us until this evening."

"Thank you."

"For the soup? Don't mention it. I could use something myself. Lurking in the roses all night works up an amazing appetite." He dug through his pack, pulling out a lighter, a foldable aluminum pan and some packages of dry soup.

"I meant thank you for rescuing me." Sam glanced up, his eyes meeting hers. He'd never seen eyes quite that color. They were brown but not an ordinary brown. They were the smooth rich color of milk chocolate. Framed by thick curving lashes, they were the kind of eyes a man could fall into if he were susceptible. But Sam wasn't susceptible. Not in the least.

"You're welcome." He picked up the soup packages and tossed them to her, looking away to avoid the seductive pull of her eyes. "Make yourself useful and open these while I start the fire. There's a bit of a breeze and this stuff is pretty dry. I don't think there'll be enough smoke to give us away."

He bent over the small pile of twigs, coaxing them to catch and then feeding the tiny flame until the fire was burning steadily. He poured water out of his canteen into the aluminum pan and set it on the fire. Looking up, he found Babs still struggling with the paper pouches. Exasperated, he reached over and took them from her.

Good Lord. He hadn't expected a pampered woman to be a Daniel Boone in the woods but surely any moderately intelligent individual could open a packet of soup. What did she do when she didn't have servants around to feed her? Starve?

Sam dumped the contents of the package into the simmering water and was about to crumple the envelope when something caught his attention. The white paper was marred by rusty stains, an unmistakable tint. With a curse, he dropped the empty packet and grabbed her hands. Ignoring her attempt to pull away, he tugged her hands toward him, turning them palm up.

In the dim light that filtered into their hideaway, the abrasions on her palms looked angry and painful. Sam sucked in a quick breath in sympathy.

"How the hell did you manage this?" Still holding one of her hands, he reached for his pack and rummaged around until he came up with a tube of antiseptic cream.

"I did it on your precious rope. And don't act like it's any concern of— That's cold!" She broke off in midsentence as the creamy salve hit her scraped palms.

"Sorry." Sam swallowed a pang of guilt. He hadn't considered her unprotected hands when he'd all but thrown her over the balcony. Not that he'd had much choice. With an armed kidnapper just across the room they'd had to make a quick exit, and scraped hands were a lot better than a bullet in the head. Still, he should have considered it once they were out of danger.

He finished applying the salve and wrapped strips of gauze over her palms, cutting through the bandage with the knife that was strapped against his calf. Grudgingly, he upped his opinion of her a notch. Maybe she had a few good qualities besides those incredibly soft eyes.

"There. That should hold them." He released her hands, refusing to acknowledge the way his fingers wanted to linger against her soft skin. "Try not to do any more damage to yourself. I didn't bring much by way of first aid."

"Thanks." Babs watched as he pulled the pot off the fire and tipped the soup into a collapsible cup. Her mouth watered as the scent wafted upward. For the first time in ten days she could eat without the feeling that this might be her last meal. She reached for the mug he was holding out for her and then hesitated.

"What about you? There's only one cup."

"Take it." He pushed it into her hands. "I'll eat after you're done. I'd have brought something more substantial but I figured we'd be on our way to town by now."

Babs sipped at the steaming liquid, feeling its warmth seep into her bones, chasing out the chill that had settled inside her since the kidnapping. She hadn't realized just how tense she'd been until the pressure was lifted. She yawned, suddenly aware of exhaustion creeping over her.

She swallowed the last of the soup, smothering another yawn as she handed the cup to her companion. Sam took it and handed her a light blanket.

"Get some sleep. We can't go anywhere until dark."

Babs took the blanket, her mouth tightening at his tone. She'd never been one to take orders well. A yawn caught her unawares, smothering any argument she might have given him. With a shrug, she unfolded the thin cover and moved farther back into their shelter. Time enough to protest his autocratic tone when she'd had some sleep.

Sam watched her curl up, tucking her hands under her cheek as a pillow. She was asleep almost instantly, her breathing slow and shallow. She'd be out of his hair for a little while at least.

He poured the rest of the soup into the cup. His stomach pointed out that steak and eggs would be more appropriate at this point but he ignored the suggestion. It wasn't the first time he'd gone hungry and it probably wouldn't be the last. Unless, of course, he did the smart thing and got a real job.

He swallowed the last of the soup and set down the cup. If he had a real job, he wouldn't be sitting in this poor excuse for a cave staring out at the Idaho countryside. A wet Idaho countryside. It had started to rain, not a downpour, but a steady mist that coated the landscape in jewellike droplets of moisture.

Of course, if he had a real job, the girl sleeping so peacefully behind him might be dead by now. She'd never have made it off the balcony with those absurd sheets and, if that didn't kill her, her captors apparently would have. She was a spoiled brat but he admired her guts.

Sam leaned back against the rock wall of the cave. With the drizzle outside, he didn't have to worry about the small amount of smoke their little fire created. It would dissipate in the damp air. The chances of the kidnappers finding them were slim to none so he could afford to relax a bit. Most likely, her former captors wouldn't spend much time looking for them. They'd probably cut their losses and hightail it out of the state as quickly as possible.

He fed a few small sticks into the fire. Unwillingly, his eyes were drawn to Babs. She looked very young in sleep. Young and sweet and innocent. Almost childlike. But there was nothing childlike in the full curve of her mouth. Her mouth looked very kissable. A temptation he didn't want to acknowledge.

He dragged his eyes away, staring into the fire instead. She was a job, just another job. Maybe his last. Maybe after this he'd do what any sensible man would have done years ago and he'd go to work like a grown-up.

Babs slept for several hours, making up for the last week and a half when she'd had to wonder if every night would be her last. Sam watched her more than he cared to admit. He dozed off and on, making up for the sleepless hours he'd spent the night before. There was no sign of movement in the damp landscape beyond the cave. Nothing to think about except the future and his companion. He thought about her a great deal more than he thought about his future.

A great deal more than he should have.

When Babs stirred it was midafternoon. Sam glanced up as her eyelids flickered. She stretched, groaning as her muscles protested the hard surface she'd been lying on. Sam tried not to notice the smooth line of her body, the way her breasts pressed against her shirt. She wasn't doing anything to attract attention, which made it all the more irritating to find that he couldn't drag his eyes away.

She opened her eyes and stared at the rock wall above her for a moment. With a sigh, she sat up and Sam wondered if she'd been hoping that she'd wake up and find this all a dream. Who could blame her?

"Did I sleep long?" She ran her fingers through her hair, combing it into place. It was a testament to the skill of her hairdresser that the shaggy, casual cut fell into place, framing her features with elfin charm.

"A few hours." Sam dragged his eyes away, feeding a few twigs into the fire. "You needed the rest and there was nothing else to do."

"Too bad you didn't bring a game of Trivial Pursuit." She folded up the blanket and moved closer to the fire.

"Next time I go on a rescue mission, I'll be sure to include that."

"Do you go on a lot of rescue missions? I don't even know what you do for a living or how you came to find me. You said my family didn't hire you."

"That's right. They offered a reward for information leading to your whereabouts. I figured the reward would be just as valid if I brought you home as it would be if I just found you."

"I'll make sure you get your reward." Irritation laced her husky voice and Sam arched a black brow. Clearly, the idea that he wanted the reward didn't please her.

"Thanks."

They were silent for a moment and then Babs spoke again, her tone determinedly polite. "So, what do you do for a living when you're not finding kidnap victims?"

"I find things. You want some coffee? I've got some instant here."

"Sure." She waited until he'd put the water on to boil before pursuing the conversation. "You find things? What kinds of things and for whom?"

"Most anything for most anybody. If somebody loses something, I'll try to find it for them. Sometimes it's a painting that's been stolen, or a car. Sometimes it's a person they once knew and lost track of. I've even tracked down a couple of missing pets.''

Babs reached for the cup he held out. "You're a private detective.''

"No, not exactly. I don't have the license for it, for one thing. And I don't do divorces or deliver summonses. I just find things. For a fee.''

Babs took a sip of the coffee, her eyes thoughtful. "Doesn't sound like a very reliable way to earn a living.''

"I've done all right. I don't have a family to support so I don't have to worry quite so much about a steady job.''

"So you run a lost and found department.''

Sam smiled, his eyes crinkling. "I guess that's as good a description as any.''

"I still don't understand how you found me. This old hotel is off the beaten track. I'd forgotten we even owned it.''

Sam took the empty cup from her and filled it with the remaining coffee in the pan. "Next time I decide to rescue a kidnapped heiress, I'll have to remember to pack two cups.'' He sipped the steaming brew. "Your uncle told me about this place.''

"My uncle? I thought you said you weren't working for my family. Besides, if Uncle Lionel told you about this place, why didn't he tell the police about it?''

"I'm *not* working for your family. Emmet is the one who told me about this place.''

"Uncle Emmet? Does he know where I am? Where is he? Is he waiting for us? I haven't seen him in months.''

"One question at a time. As far as I know, Emmet doesn't even know about the kidnapping. The last I heard of him, he was somewhere in South America researching a book.''

The excitement faded from her face and Sam was surprised to discover that he regretted its disappearance. Her eyes dropped to the stone floor. He had the feeling she was blinking back tears. The thought bothered him.

"I'm sorry. I wish Emmet was waiting for us."

She shrugged. "It doesn't matter." But he knew it did matter. She looked up, her expression under control. "So, how well do you know Emmet?"

"Not very well at all. We met about a year ago in Mexico. We had a few drinks together and talked quite a bit. He mentioned this place because he was thinking of setting a novel here. He said the family had all but forgotten it but that they'd hate it if he used it in one of his books. I think that was one of the major reasons he liked the idea." He broke off, realizing that his words weren't very tactful.

Babs's grin was every bit as gleeful as her uncle's had been. "He's right. Aunt Dodie would be mortally offended. The thought of Malone property being mentioned in a 'trashy novel' would pucker her up like a prune. I hope he does it."

"He was thinking about it when we talked."

"How was he? For a writer, he's a lousy correspondent."

"He seemed fine. We only spent the one evening together. He was on his way into the jungle the next day and I was on my way home. He's quite a character."

"Uncle Emmet prides himself on being a character." Her face was soft with affection and Sam found himself wondering what it would be like to have that expression turned toward him. "He's the black sheep of the family. Grandfather threw him out of the will years ago because he married an 'unsuitable woman.' It drives the family nuts that he never seemed to mind. He's the only relative I've got who's worth a damn.''

Sam chuckled. ''That's exactly what he said about you.''

Babs laughed softly. ''We always did see things alike.''

Sam dragged his eyes away from the warmth in her eyes and looked out at the cool landscape. Rested and relaxed, Babs Malone was turning out to be a dangerously pleasant companion. Too pleasant by half. The sooner he turned her over to her family, collected his money and got on his way, the better.

''We probably ought to get started. It's going to take us a good half an hour to get to my truck.''

''What about the kidnappers? Won't they be waiting for us?'' She wrapped her hands around her upper arms and stared out, her eyes reflecting her uneasiness.

''They probably left long ago. They must have figured out that their safest bet was to cut their losses and get as far away from here as possible.''

She shivered. ''They sounded pretty serious about killing me.''

''That was when it would serve a purpose. After they'd got the ransom, they'd have had no reason to keep you alive. They can't have any real hope of getting a ransom now, so they have no particular reason to kill you. Unless you could give positive ID on them. Could you?''

She shook her head. ''Not really. They wore ski masks most of the time. I'll never forget their voices but I didn't really see any faces.''

''Well, then, they've got no worries.'' He was replacing things in his pack as he spoke. When Babs didn't answer, he glanced at her. She was still staring out into the early evening light, her teeth nibbling on her lower lip.

"We'll take every precaution just in case but I really think they're gone. Besides, we can't sit in this cave forever."

"I know." But she still looked worried.

"Think of a nice juicy T-bone waiting for you when we get to the nearest town."

Babs smiled but she wasn't thinking about steaks. She was thinking about how determined the kidnappers had sounded. They had wanted her dead. The memory sent a chill up her spine that settled into a lump in her chest.

She watched Sam scatter their fire, carefully stamping out every trace of flame. He looked reassuringly large and solid, and she felt some of the tension ease. She'd only known Sam Delanian a few hours but it was long enough to feel confidence in him. If he thought they'd be okay, she was willing to take a chance. Besides, as he'd pointed out, they couldn't sit here forever.

The rain had stopped, though the air still felt damp and vaguely misty, as if it was reserving the right to rain at any minute. Sam slid down the slight incline outside the shallow cave and then reached back to offer Babs his hand. She took it, feeling his palm engulf her smaller fingers. She could feel his strength in the way he braced her down the slope, the muscles in his arm taking her slight weight easily.

At barely five feet tall, Babs had always been rather defensive about her ability to take care of herself. She didn't want anyone mistaking her for a delicate little flower in need of nurturing, which was how men were inclined to view her, right after they blinked the dollar signs out of their eyes.

But she had to admit that it felt remarkably nice to have Sam's strong hand supporting her. It had been years since someone had offered her a hand to lean on. Of course, she couldn't forget that he was only doing this for the reward. Fifty thousand dollars was a lot of money, especially to a man who earned his living as an adventurer. She'd be foolish to forget just why he was here.

Dusk was approaching but there was still enough light to see where they were walking. Sam led the way through the sparse woods. Once again, he didn't seem to consider where he was stepping and yet he made not a sound. Babs felt as if she might as well be trumpeting their arrival. Her every footfall seemed to echo in the still air. She glared at Sam's black sneakers, wondering if he'd had them soundproofed.

Though he took precautions, Sam wasn't too concerned about the possibility of them running into her former captors. Babs was very concerned. She couldn't forget how cold the men had sounded when they'd talked about killing her. She was, perhaps, the least surprised when their quiet walk was interrupted.

Sam stopped next to a pine tree and waited until she drew level with him. "The road is just up ahead and my truck is parked on the other side. I covered it with some loose brush. Another hour or so and you'll be able to sink your teeth into that steak I promised."

Babs started to smile and then her eyes widened in horror. Her voice locked in her throat. Sam couldn't see what was behind him but he could see her face.

His palm hit her shoulder, shoving her backward with enough force to knock her off her feet. At the same time, he dropped to one knee. The rifle butt that would have opened his skull slammed into the tree instead. The crack as it hit the solid trunk was as loud as gunfire in Babs's ringing ears.

Sam pivoted, still on his knees and lunged upward, his shoulder catching the other man in the belly. Babs scrabbled in the thick layer of pine needles, looking for something she could use as a weapon. Sam's gun was tucked securely in his belt, his knife lay against his leg. He couldn't get to either of them.

Her fingers closed over the end of a fallen branch. She scrambled to her feet, hefting her find. Thick and sturdy, the branch was no match for a gun but it could help to tip the scales in Sam's favor. If only she could figure out whom to hit. In the gathering darkness, it was impossible to tell the two men apart. Sam's black clothes and the kidnapper's looked much the same.

The two men rolled on the ground, their battle punctuated by harsh grunts and harsher breathing. Babs crept closer. Her mouth tasted coppery with fear, a sensation that had become all too familiar since the kidnapping. She barely knew Sam Delanian but he'd gotten her out of the hotel. He'd risked his life to save hers. Whether or not he'd done it for money, the end results were much the same. If he died now, it would be on her conscience. If she survived to have a conscience. Her fingers ached with the pressure of her hold on the branch. Her palms were damp with sweat. If only she could be sure which one was Sam.

One man gained the upper hand. Braced above his opponent, his hands around the other man's throat, he slowly choked the other into unconsciousness.

What if it was Sam being choked? In the dark, the two men were little more than silhouettes. Babs raised the branch over her head, fighting the quivering in her arms, trying to decide whether to strike first and ask questions later. The man on the ground went limp, the battle over. The other man was still for a long moment, his shoulders heaving, his head bent forward on his chest. He seemed to gather himself and Babs tightened her grip.

"Hold it. Don't move or I'll brain you." Her voice shook but she thought she sounded reasonably ferocious.

He turned, ducking automatically at the sight of the branch poised to crack his skull. "That's a hell of a way to thank me for saving your life." The words were breathless, irritated and unmistakably Sam.

Babs's fingers went weak and Sam cursed as he dodged the falling club. "Sorry. I thought you were him."

Sam stood up, running one hand over his face. "I'm glad you waited to find out." He looked down at his vanquished foe.

"Is he dead?" Babs didn't look down. She'd never met a body before and she didn't want to meet one now. But Sam was shaking his head.

"Unconscious. And he'll have a hell of a sore throat for a while." He stooped to pick up his fallen pack and reached for her hand. "Come on. Let's get out of here."

As he spoke, they heard someone approaching from the direction of the hotel. Sam didn't wait to find out who it might be. They didn't have any friends in the area. He tugged Babs forward at a stumbling run, no longer concerned about noise. A few yards beyond where they'd been jumped, they all but fell onto a dirt road. Sam pulled her across and plunged into the scraggly woods on the other side.

He dropped her hand and began tearing at a wall of brush. Babs caught a glimpse of chrome and realized this must be where he'd hidden his truck. She helped him pull the brush away, spurred on by a shout that indicated the unconscious man had been found. The sharp branches jabbed through the thin gauze bandages on her tender palms but she barely noticed the discomfort.

It seemed to take forever but it couldn't have been more than a minute or two before Sam was jerking open the driver's door. Babs started to step up into the cab but Sam's hands closed around her waist, lifting her in as if she weighed no more than a feather pillow. She scooted across the seat as Sam slid behind the wheel and pushed the key into the ignition.

The engine caught immediately. Sam didn't bother with warming it up. He slammed it into gear. Babs banged her shoulder on the door as the truck rocked down the embankment and onto the road. She caught a glimpse of movement from the other side of the road and ducked as light caught on a rifle barrel.

There was a sharp pop and then a loud crack as a bullet hit the rear window. Sam cursed between his teeth, crouching low over the wheel, flooring the gas pedal. The tires spun on the loose dirt and then gripped, and the truck lurched forward. Babs grabbed for the armrest as the movement threatened to send her onto the floorboard.

Several more shots were fired but none of them hit the truck and, in a matter of seconds, they were out of range.

Babs sat up cautiously, reaching for her seat belt as the truck roared down the old road, bouncing in and out of ruts with a fine disregard for the suspension. She glanced at Sam. His face was set, his eyes on the road.

"I told you they wanted to kill me."

His eyes slanted toward her briefly, leaving her with

an impression of blue fire. "Didn't anyone ever tell you that you should never say 'I told you so'?"

There didn't seem to be anything to say in reply so Babs settled back on the not-too-comfortable seat and tried not to think about how close she'd come to dying.

Chapter Three

"Look, if you think I'm going to share a room with you, you're crazy." Babs set her chin stubbornly and stared out the windshield. Sam threw her a look that should have turned her to a cinder.

"Look, there's nothing I'd like better than to stick you in a room by yourself and let the kidnappers take their chances if they find you. They'd have my sympathy. Unfortunately, if the poor devils did succeed in kidnapping you again, there goes my fifty thousand bucks."

Babs glared at him. "All you care about it your damned money."

"That's right."

It was impossible to argue with his flat agreement. Impossible to admit, even to herself, that it hurt.

"I thought you said they'd just cut their losses and leave."

"I also said that they wouldn't try to kill you but those were real bullets." He jerked his thumb toward the neat round hole in the back window. "I just want to be sure you're safe for tonight. Tomorrow, I'll deliver you safely back to the bosom of your family."

"Guarding your investment?"

He ignored her sneering tone. "That's right. Your

family owes me fifty thousand dollars and I may charge extra for the rope I had to leave behind. Not to mention combat pay.''

''You can hardly charge extra for that. You weren't hurt in the fight. Fifty thousand should cover that much at least.''

''I wasn't talking about that little tussle. I was talking about dealing with you.''

Babs opened her mouth, ready to cut him to ribbons with words, but he'd already opened his door and slid out of the truck. She glared after him. Combat pay. She wasn't that hard to deal with. Of course, she *hadn't* been in the most gracious of moods. But then, kidnapping and attempted murder had a way of making her a trifle testy.

Sam opened the office door of the little building and disappeared inside. He was going to rent one room for the night and Babs admitted to herself that she wasn't quite as reluctant as she wanted to be. She didn't like Sam Delanian. He was too pushy, too macho, too sure of himself. But she had to admit—reluctantly—that she felt safer with him around. He'd proven himself capable of taking care of her. Not that she needed anyone to take care of her but it wouldn't hurt to have him on her side just in case.

When Sam came back with their room key, Babs didn't offer any more arguments. He didn't know why and he told himself he didn't care. All in all, it had been one hell of a day. He wanted something to eat, a hot shower and a soft bed, in that order. He wanted Ms. Babs Malone with him so that he could keep an eye on her and, if she didn't like it, well, it was just too bad.

''Why don't you go take a shower and I'll order us a pizza?''

Babs eyed the room's one bed. It was a very large

bed but there was still only one. Sam followed her gaze. For a moment they both stared at the cheap candlewick bedspread.

"Look, don't say anything." Sam's voice held all the weariness he felt. "Just go take a shower. I've got a spare shirt you can borrow if you want to put on something clean. We'll eat and then you can throw a fit if you want."

"I don't throw fits."

"Good. That will save us both a lot of trouble. What do you like on your pizza?"

She dragged her eyes from the bed and looked at him a minute, her gaze speculative. Sam braced himself, waiting for the arguments. She'd never believe him if he told her he'd tried to get them a room with two beds.

"Anything but green peppers. They make me break out in hives. Where's this shirt you said you had?"

Sam didn't know and he didn't care why she'd decided to postpone the argument he was sure was coming. Maybe she was as tired as he was. Maybe she was just trying to keep him off balance. For the moment he wasn't going to look for an explanation. With the bathroom door shut behind her and the shower running, he had some calls to make.

The first and most important was an order for a pizza with everything but green peppers, though the thought of the snotty Ms. Malone breaking out in hives had a certain appeal to it. With food on the way, he dialed the number for the Malone family residence. It wasn't the number that had been given with the reward information but Sam didn't like dealing with a middleman if he could go right to the source. It hadn't taken him long to track down the unlisted number. It paid to have connections.

He kicked off his shoes and lifted his feet onto the

bed, leaning back against the headboard and closing his eyes while he waited for the long-distance connections to go through. This was the last job. He was getting too old for this kind of thing.

"Hello?" The voice was old and quavery.

"Could I speak to a relative of Babette Malone?"

"I'm her aunt Bertie. Who is this?"

"My name is Sam Delanian. I'm calling to let you know that your niece is safe and sound."

"Well, of course she's safe and sound."

Sam hesitated a moment, thrown off balance by the certainty in the reedy tones. "I...your niece was kidnapped."

"That's right." He could have just mentioned that it looked like rain, for all the concern in her voice.

"Well, I've...rescued her and I wanted to assure her family that she's safe and sound." He waited for thanks, possibly sobs of relief.

"Oh, my goodness! You took her from the men who kidnapped her?"

"That's right. She's not hurt and—"

"Well, of course she's not hurt. Oh, dear. Oh, dear, this is terrible. We didn't plan on this at all. Not at all. You'll just have to give her back. At once, do you hear me? At once! This is terrible."

The thin voice babbled on but Sam wasn't listening. He held the receiver away from his ear and stared at it. He was so tired he was hallucinating. That would explain it. Otherwise, it didn't make any sense.

He cut into the flow of fluttering protests. "Ma'am, I don't think you understand. I've *rescued* her. I'm not one of the kidnappers."

"Oh, my. This is terrible. This wasn't the way it was supposed to go at all. Dodie, my dear, we have a terrible problem. There's a man on the phone who says he's rescued Babette. I've told him he'll have to give her back at once."

Sam rubbed his fingers across his forehead. Somehow, he had the feeling he'd lost track of this conversation. There was some vital piece missing.

"Whom am I speaking to?" The new voice was strong and forceful and Sam almost sighed with relief.

"My name is Sam Delanian."

"This is Dodie Davis. What do you know about Babette?"

"I tried to explain to the other lady, I have your niece safe and sound."

There was a long pause at the other end of the line and Sam felt an uneasy tingle start at the base of his spine and work its way up until the hair on the back of his neck was standing on end. Something was not right here.

"I'm afraid you've put quite a crimp in our plans, Mr. Delanian. You see, we paid those men to kidnap Babette."

"*You* paid them?"

"Yes. It was necessary to keep her out of the way for a short time. My niece can be less than cooperative and this seemed the only viable way to accomplish that."

"By kidnapping her?" Sam lowered his voice, glancing at the bathroom door, listening to make sure the shower was still running. "Kidnapping is illegal, Mrs. Davis."

"This was merely a temporary measure. She would have been released unharmed. Perhaps the small fright will make her a bit easier to deal with."

Sam took a deep breath, swallowing his anger. He thought of the disastrously short rope of sheets that could have ended in Babs breaking a leg—or her neck. He thought of the way she'd trembled against him when they'd hidden in the roses, waiting to be discovered. He might find Ms. Malone more than a little difficult to deal with but that didn't mean that he would condone kidnapping as a disciplinary measure.

"Mrs. Davis, your niece overheard the kidnappers planning to kill her."

"Nonsense. She's always had an overactive imagination."

"The bullets they fired at us were quite real."

"Perhaps they were only trying to do their job. I'm sure they had no intention of hitting either of you. They were probably afraid that they wouldn't get paid if you took my niece away from them. They're quite right. I'm certainly not paying full price for a job only half-done."

She sounded as if she was talking about having her carpets cleaned.

"Those bullets could have hit your niece as easily as myself."

"You must be mistaken. The instructions were quite clear. They were to hold her for two or three weeks until they were informed that it was safe to release her." As far as Dodie Davis was concerned, that closed the subject. Sam rubbed his fingers over his forehead, trying to piece together some logic in all this insanity.

"Why did you want to keep her away?"

"That's not your concern. Quite frankly, Mr. Delanian, I'm more than a little annoyed with your interference but it can't be helped now. It will mean a great deal of money to you if you simply finish the job you interfered with. Keep my niece away from home for a few more days and we'll pay you ten thousand dollars."

"But if I return her right away, the reward is fifty

thousand.'' The silky anger in his voice was lost on Dodie.

"Greed is a most unattractive attribute, Mr. Delanian.''

"Kidnapping isn't the most appealing habit around, Mrs. Davis.'' He let that sink in before speaking again. "I'd like to speak to Emmet Malone. Maybe he can make some sense of this idiocy.''

"Are you acquainted with Emmet?'' Sam savored the hint of uneasiness in her overbearing tone.

"Intimately.'' He let her digest that exaggeration for a moment. "Is he there?''

"I'm afraid not. We tried to reach him but he was out of the country. I realize that this may seem unreasonable to you, Mr. Delanian, but the family really had no choice.'' Her tone was as placating as it was likely to get. Clearly, this was not a woman accustomed to explaining herself. That she was attempting to do so now was an indication of how important this whole mess must be.

"I'm sure, even in your short acquaintance with my niece, that you must have some idea of how difficult she can be. We could negotiate your fee. But it's very important that Babette be kept away for a few more days.''

"I'll be in touch.'' Sam hung up the phone without waiting for a response. If Babs had grown up with that pedantic voice droning at her, it was no wonder she'd gone a little overboard in the defiance department.

He closed his eyes, willing away the headache that throbbed in his temples. It was lack of sleep. That was why none of this made any sense. Or maybe some strange Idaho bug had bitten him and none of this was really happening. He was actually still lying in the middle of the rosebushes delirious with fever.

That explanation was surprisingly appealing. This had started out to be a simple rescue mission. Simple, straightforward, with minimal danger. Instead, he'd been attacked by the victim he'd come to rescue, shot at, jumped in the woods and he'd lost a perfectly good rope and the back window in his truck. After all that, he should have been able to just sit back and relax and collect his fifty thousand dollars. Nothing was working out the way it was supposed to.

The bathroom door opened and Sam sat up. "How is the shower?"

"Fine." She was still toweling her hair but she'd put on her own clothes again. "Does the phone work? I ought to call my family."

"I just called." Sam hoped he didn't sound as uneasy as he felt. "There…ah…there was no one home."

Emotion flashed into her eyes and, for just an instant, she looked young and vulnerable and hurt. Then she shrugged and glanced away. "I thought they might have had someone there to answer the phone at least but I suppose that was pretty stupid. There's no love lost between us anyway."

Sam didn't say anything. He knew, maybe better than she did, just how little love lost there was. But he wasn't going to say anything until he'd had a chance to think this through.

Babs toweled her hair some more and then shook it back, finger combing it into tousled waves around her face. "You know, I was thinking about it. There's really no reason for us to spend the night here. We could get started now and I'm sure we could get to an airport by morning."

"No. I mean, I don't think that's such a good idea. You've had a rough few days and, God knows, I could use a decent night's sleep. We can start out in the morning.''

''I don't particularly want to spend the night in this fleabag with you. I hate to be blunt but there it is.''

''It's not my idea of heaven, either, but it's the most sensible thing to do. We're both beat and neither one of us is familiar with this area. In the morning, we'll be rested and we can get directions from someone.''

Babs stared at him, her jaw set. Sam stared back, his expression calm. For a moment, it looked as though she was going to push the issue and he had visions of sitting up all night guarding the door to make sure she didn't sneak out. With a shrug, she capitulated.

''Okay. We'll leave first thing in the morning.''

''First thing.'' He stood up and stretched. ''Did you leave any hot water?''

''There wasn't any to start with but there's still plenty of lukewarm.''

''If I go take a shower, can I trust you to be here when I come out?''

She arched a brow, clearly disliking the idea of anyone telling her what to do. ''And if I refuse to promise?''

''Then I'll just have to take you in the bathroom with me and tie you to the sink.'' He smiled but there was something in his eyes that made her wonder if he wouldn't do exactly what he'd threatened.

''I promise I'll still be here when you get back.'' He looked at her for a moment as if weighing whether or not to believe her, and Babs's chin tilted. She was not accustomed to having her word doubted. He made up his mind abruptly.

''Fine. There's money on the table to pay for the pizza. I'll be out in a couple of minutes.'' He disappeared into the bathroom.

Babs sat on the edge of the bed. She was safe. She let the thought sink in. Really safe. Sam Delanian might be an overbearing pig but she didn't doubt that he could take care of her. If nothing else, he'd protect his fifty thousand dollars. Funny how that hurt just a little. After all, he didn't know her. There was no reason why he should see her as anything more than a means to get the reward. Heaven knew she ought to be accustomed to people seeing dollar signs when they met her.

She shrugged, tossing the towel over the back of the cheap vinyl chair that was the room's only furniture besides the bed and table. Tomorrow, she would see the last of Mr. Delanian. He would take her home, deliver her into the bosom of her family and disappear with his money. The thought should have made her enormously happy. The hollow ache in the pit of her stomach must be caused by hunger.

By the time Sam finished his shower, Babs was well into her second piece of pizza. She glanced up as he stepped into the room and waved an expansive hand at the enormous pizza box that took up a good portion of the bed.

"Not bad for a hick town. They must have an Italian cook."

"The name of the place is Harry's."

"Well, whatever their name is, it's good pizza."

"Right now even bad pizza would taste good." Babs was sitting cross-legged at the head of the bed. Sam sat down at the foot, grabbing up a paper plate and selecting a slice of pizza dripping with cheese and mushrooms. "If I never spend another night crouched in the bushes, it will be too soon."

"Did you spend all night out there?"

"Uh-huh." He nodded, his concentration on the food.

"You must have really wanted that reward." He glanced at her, catching a momentary vulnerability in her expression.

"I wouldn't have left a dog with kidnappers. But there's no denying that the thought of fifty thousand dollars made last night's sojourn in the rose patch a little easier to take."

Of course, there was no telling now if he'd ever see that fifty thousand. After his conversation with her family, he wasn't sure what he was going to do with Babs. It was too bad he didn't know how to get hold of Emmet. From what he'd seen so far, Emmet might be the only sane member of the Malone family.

The pizza was devoured, the box stuffed in the trash can, leaving them with nothing to do but go to bed. Sam stretched, swallowing a yawn. A bed had never looked better. Glancing at his companion, he saw the doubtful look in her eyes as she looked from him to the room's one bed.

"I'm not going to offer to sleep on the floor," he told her bluntly.

"I didn't ask you to. I'll sleep in the chair."

"Well, you can suit yourself but I think you'd be more comfortable in the bed. You can sleep under the sheet and I'll sleep on top of it. Quite frankly, I'm too beat to care where you sleep. The offer of a shirt still stands. It would be more comfortable than sleeping in your jeans."

Babs looked at him, then at the chair and then at the bed. Sam was ignoring her, apparently uninterested in her decision. She glanced away as he tugged the snug black turtleneck off, revealing a lot of tanned skin and rippling muscles. The sight brought a funny little quiver to the pit of her stomach.

Too much pizza. That's what it was. She'd simply eaten too much and her stomach was feeling a bit out of sorts as a result. It didn't have anything to do with the mat of black hair that covered his chest then tapered down to a narrow line trailing across his flat stomach before disappearing into the waist of his jeans.

He unbuckled his belt and then reached for the snap on his jeans before glancing at her. Babs looked away quickly. Not that she'd really been looking at him. She couldn't care less what he did.

"Have you made up your mind? If you're going to use my shirt, why don't you change in the bathroom? By the time you're done, I'll be in bed."

"I don't care if you strip naked in front of me. I'm not a prude." Did that sound nonchalant enough?

"Maybe I am. Are you going to sleep in the bed or are you going to sit up all night protecting your maidenly virtue?"

She shrugged. "I think I'm safe enough with you. Like you said, I'll be more comfortable in the bed. I always sleep on the left side."

"Tough. Tonight you can sleep on the right." He lifted a hand, stopping her furious protest. "I want to be closest to the door. On the off chance that someone tries to sneak in during the night, I think it would be a good idea if they ran into me first."

Babs swallowed her protest, throwing him an irritated look. Did the man have to be so damn reasonable? "Guarding your reward?"

"You got it. Not to mention my professional pride. Imagine how embarrassing it would be if they kidnapped you back after I went to all the trouble of rescuing you. Now, are you going to go change or not?" He reached for his zipper and looked at her, one brow raised.

Babs snatched up the shirt he'd offered her earlier and stalked into the bathroom, wishing she were five foot nine so that she could stalk properly. At five foot nothing, a stalk was inclined to look more like a stomp.

When she cautiously opened the bathroom door a few minutes later, it was to find the room in darkness. She peered around the edge of the door, waiting for her eyes to adjust to the dark.

"It's safe. I'm modestly covered."

"It doesn't matter to me. I just didn't want to trip over anything in the dark."

She snapped off the bathroom light and cautiously made her way across the room, bumping her knees into the foot of the bed. Trailing one hand on the bedspread, she walked around it until she reached the pillows. Crawling beneath the sheet, she held her breath, overwhelmingly aware of Sam's long body only inches away. True to his word, he was on top of the sheet but the thin cotton didn't prove much of a barrier.

If he decided he wanted to change the rules there would be little she could do to stop him, but she wasn't afraid. At least she wasn't afraid that he'd attack her. She wasn't quite sure what label to put on the vague fluttering in her stomach. Too much pizza, too much tension since the kidnapping—those were acceptable explanations. She didn't want to look any further.

"Good night." Sam's voice coming out of the darkness was both unnerving and oddly reassuring.

"Good night." She had to clear her throat to get the words out, aware that her voice was even huskier than it usually was.

Despite the day's sleep, Babs was tired. It didn't take long for the lumpy mattress to lure her into sleep.

Beside her, Sam lay awake, listening to her quiet

breathing. The neon light outside flashed on and off, creating patterns on the wall opposite the bed. He stared at the wall, all too aware of the warm body lying just inches away. She was spoiled and demanding but he had to admire her guts. A lot of people would have fallen apart under the stress of the past ten days.

But her guts was all he admired. Beyond that, she wasn't his type at all. He preferred tall, leggy brunettes. Short, curvy women with shaggy blond hair and eyes the color of a Hershey bar were not his style. It was a good thing, too. He had a feeling the next day or two was going to be difficult enough without the added complication of being attracted to Ms. Babs Malone.

Chapter Four

Babs woke slowly the next morning, reluctant to abandon the pleasant dreams that lay just beyond the reach of her memory. The bed felt warm and safe. She stirred, snuggling closer to the source of that warmth, surrounded by it. It had been a long time since she'd felt so cared for. There was a vague rumbling beneath her ear and she frowned, poking at her pillow.

"Careful. Puncture wounds are dangerous." The quiet words evaporated the last of her dreams. She opened her eyes and stared sleepily at the broad expanse of muscles that lay in front of her nose. No wonder the pillow had felt so hard. Her hand lay a few inches away, looking pale and fragile against all that tanned skin. She moved her hand, combing it through the mat of hair, feeling it curl around her fingers.

"Puncture wounds aren't the only thing that's dangerous." A much larger, harder hand came up to cover hers, stilling her sleepy movements. "I don't think you're going to respect me in the morning." The voice held quiet humor and Babs tilted her head back.

Sam's eyes were only inches away, bright blue, alight with humor and something else that she couldn't quite define. His lean jaw was stubbled with two nights' growth of beard, giving him a piratical look that suited him.

She blinked and then blinked again, awareness trickling into her sleepy brain. She closed her eyes but, when she opened them again, he was still there. Very large, very masculine and *very* close. She swallowed, becoming aware of just how close he was. She was plastered against him, her leg thrown over his hips, her head on his shoulder. The sheet was still between them but it was a fragile protection at best. Never in her life had she been so aware of the differences between men and women. She was surrounded by his masculinity, swallowed up in it.

"What do you think you're doing?" The indignant protest lacked force. It was hard to be forceful when you were practically draped over a man.

"*I'm* not doing anything." The look Sam gave her was full of innocence. "*You're* the one who moved to my side of the bed."

"I told you I always sleep on the left side." It was a weak excuse but the best she could come up with on the spot.

Sam's eyes were bright but he was kind enough not to challenge her. "That must be the reason."

"Of course it is. What else could it be?" It was also difficult to put contempt in her voice when she was vividly aware of the warmth of his skin under her hand.

"If you don't move, I might begin to wonder just what else it might be." The wicked laughter in his eyes made Babs realize that she was still draped across his body like a piece of wet silk. With a muttered comment that Sam was wise enough not to ask her to repeat, she rolled away, refusing to admit—even to herself—that she felt any reluctance to leave that warm body.

She swung her feet to the floor and stood up, hoping that the warmth in her cheeks wasn't translated into a flaming blush. It was one of the curses of her life that her skin flushed at the least provocation. She moved around the bed without looking at Sam again, snatching her clothes off the chair.

"I'm going to go get dressed. The sooner we get out of here, the sooner I can get home." She shut the bathroom door behind her.

Sam sat up against the headboard and stared at the closed door. His shirt had never looked half so good on him as it did on her. For such a shrimp, her legs were surprisingly long and very nicely shaped. The blue cotton that looked so utilitarian on him clung with remarkable faith to every curve of her softer body.

He muttered a curse and swung his legs off the bed. He only noticed such things as a matter of interest. He reached for his jeans and thrust his legs into them. No one had ever said that Babs Malone wasn't an attractive woman but she definitely wasn't his type. Not his type at all. It wasn't just physically either. She had a temper like a wolverine. It would be foolish to lose sight of that.

Besides, even if he was attracted to her—which he wasn't—right now he had other things to think about. Like how to tell her that her own family had arranged for her kidnapping.

He was no closer to an answer when Babs came out of the bathroom. Neither one mentioned the way they'd been pressed together when they woke up but neither of them could think of anything else. Sam looked at her, clad once more in her own jeans and pale blue silk shirt, and he remembered how soft and warm she'd felt against him. Babs didn't even have to look at Sam to remember the crisp feel of his chest hair beneath her fingers, the warmth of skin under her cheek.

"Ready to go? I figured we'd get started right away and then have some breakfast on the road somewhere."

"Sounds good to me." Babs made a production of looking around the room to make sure nothing had been forgotten.

"I already threw the pack in the truck." Sam waited until Babs left the room before shutting the door, making sure it was locked.

Yesterday's misty rain had disappeared, leaving the Idaho skies as bright a blue as a freshly washed dress. The sun shone with gentle spring warmth, drying up the puddles. It was a picture-perfect spring day. The small town was peaceful and quiet, there was nothing to disturb the perfection of the scene.

None of which explained why Sam felt an uneasy itch in the palms of his hands. He looked around carefully, seeking something to explain the uneasy feeling but there was nothing. Still, the feeling remained and he'd learned to trust that itch. He was suddenly very glad he hadn't decided to eat in town. He wanted to put some more distance behind them before they relaxed.

"Let's go pay our bill and get out of here."

"I'm just as anxious to be rid of you as you are to be rid of me." Babs's words held an edge of hurt and Sam opened his mouth to explain that wasn't what he meant. He shut it without saying anything. How did he tell her that he was uneasy because his palms itched? She'd think he was crazy.

They paid the bill and Sam asked about the best route to the nearest airport. The motel's proprietor showed only the most cursory of interest in last night's guests but Sam didn't feel any easier.

Sam had parked the truck in back of the motel, wanting to keep it out of sight of the road. Walking back along the length of the motel, his eyes shifted from one potential hiding place to another. His instincts were insisting that danger lay nearby but there was no hint as to the direction from which it might come. He didn't have to wonder long. It was right in front of them.

Stepping around the corner of the low building, they came face to face with four men who did not look as if they were out for a Sunday stroll.

"There she is. Grab her."

Sam thrust Babs behind him, shoving the truck keys into her hand. "Run." He glanced back to see that she hadn't moved, her wide eyes fixed on the men forming a rough half-circle in front of him.

"Run, dammit!"

She looked at him and he wished he could take the terror out of her eyes. "What about you?"

"I'll be okay. Get the hell out of here."

She looked at him a minute longer and then turned and sprinted back the way they'd come.

"Go after her, Joe. We'll take care of him." The man who spoke was tall, pale and had the coldest blue eyes Sam had ever seen. He kicked out as Joe ran by him, sending him sprawling but he knew he'd gained Babs only a small headstart. Joe was already scrambling to his feet and the others were closing in. On the theory that offense is the best defense, especially when you're outnumbered, he lunged toward them, feeling his fist connect with satisfying force.

BABS HAD NEVER RUN FASTER in her entire life. The image of Sam facing the four thugs lent wings to her feet. She flew by the dusty orange doors that marked each

room of the motel. Behind her she heard the thud of
heavier feet and she risked a glance over her shoulder.
The man who was chasing her looked determined and
terrifying. Adrenaline pumped harder, giving her an extra burst of speed.

She almost overshot her goal. She'd noticed earlier
that the motel was really two buildings set close together
with a narrow alley between them. It was barely wide
enough for two people to walk abreast but she needed
room for only one. She turned right without slowing her
pace, feeling her tennis shoes slip on loose dirt before
gripping. The second she lost felt like an eternity but
then she was in the alley, her footsteps echoing from the
narrow walls.

The quick turn gained her a few precious seconds as
her pursuer overshot the opening and had to circle back.
Babs didn't stop to look. Her heart was pounding in her
chest, whether from exertion or fright, she couldn't have
said. Her mouth tasted coppery. The keys bit into her
tender palm but she didn't notice the discomfort. She
skidded out of the alley and ran for Sam's truck. Somewhere in his pack was his gun. She'd seen him put it
there this morning.

Her fingers shook, costing her precious seconds as she
struggled to fit the key in the lock. Behind her, her pursuer left the alley and ran toward her. Babs's breath left
her in frantic sobs but the door opened at last. There was
no time to find the gun, no time to run. He was right on
top of her. She spun around, the door between them. She
would never forget the way his face was contorted with
anger, the look of triumph that lit his eyes. His arms
were coming up, reaching for her as he slowed down for
the last few feet that separated them. She was trapped
and he knew it.

Babs shut her eyes and shoved the door open. There was a sickening crunch as the heavy metal slammed into a human body. She opened her eyes at the instant of impact, seeing the stunned disbelief in his eyes just before the door hit him, the frantic attempt to back away. But his own momentum carried him forward into the swing of the door. He dropped like stone. The door quivered a moment and then began to fall shut. Babs caught it automatically. She refused to look at the man on the ground. She didn't want to know if he was dead.

She climbed into the truck and reached for Sam's pack, forcing herself to think only of the next step. The gun lay on top, tucked into its holster. Her hands were steady as she pulled it free, flipping open the chamber to make sure it was loaded. It was.

Her knees were shaking as she stepped around the side of the building. Even before she could see them, the awful sound of fists connecting with flesh told her that the fight was still in progress. Outnumbered three to one, Sam was still on his feet but barely. His back was pressed against the wall of the building, his fists still up but his breathing was painful to hear.

Babs drew a deep breath and brought the gun up. "Freeze!" Her voice quavered and cracked but it was loud enough to get their attention. All four men turned to look at her.

"Babs."

"Good God, it's the girl."

"She's got a gun."

"She doesn't know how to use it."

"I wouldn't bet on it." Babs's thumb pulled down the hammer. In the quiet morning air the click was ominously loud. She stared at them over the steel barrel, hoping her eyes didn't reflect her uncertainty. She knew how to shoot a gun but she'd never fired at a living thing.

For a few seconds it was a standoff. The kidnappers might be reasonably certain that she wouldn't shoot but they weren't ready to gamble their lives on it.

"Look, lady, you don't want to shoot anyone. Why don't you give me the gun." One of the men started forward and Babs tightened her hold on the gun, feeling trickles of cold sweat start down her spine.

"I'll shoot if I have to."

"Hey, what happened to Joe?" It was one of the other two. The man who'd been edging toward her stopped, his eyes narrowing. Sam edged along the wall, keeping an eye on the men.

"He's out cold in the parking lot." Babs could only hope she sounded a lot tougher than she felt. "Can you make it to the truck?" she asked Sam while still keeping her eyes on the trio.

"Sure." Sam laughed, the sound choking off on a gasp of pain. "Hell of a rescue, Babs."

"Thank you."

She backed away as Sam came even with her. Risking a quick glance at him, she had to stifle a gasp of dismay. He was upright but she had the feeling it was sheer will-power keeping him that way.

"This isn't over yet." Her eyes met those of the man who was apparently the leader. They were cold and mean. She hadn't seen his face but she knew his voice. This was the man she'd overheard casually planning her death. Staring at him over the barrel of the revolver, she knew that he wasn't going to give up.

She backed away until she could see the truck out of the corner of her eye. The man she'd hit with the door was still lying on the concrete. She had no idea if he was alive or dead. At the moment, she couldn't afford to care. Sam pulled open the driver's door and slid in, ignoring the limp body.

Babs took one last look at the three men in front of her and then backed toward the truck. They followed but kept a respectful distance as long as she held the gun. She stopped next to the driver's door.

"I'll drive." She kept her voice low and her eyes on the men she was holding at gunpoint.

"I'm supposed to be rescuing you."

"You're in no condition to drive."

There was a moment's silence and then Sam heaved an irritated sigh. "I hate it when you're right." There was a pause and then his voice came again. "Reach back and hand me the gun. I'll keep an eye on our friends while you get in the truck."

The awkward exchange was made and Babs scrambled up into the seat. Sam leaned behind her, his arms against her back, the gun steady. The engine roared to life and Babs threw the truck into reverse, backing out of the parking place. She thrust the gearshift into first and put her foot down on the gas.

"Careful. This isn't Indianapolis." Sam turned to look out the back window. "They're running for their car. They didn't even check to see how good old Joe was. What did you do to him?"

"I hit him with the door." Babs tapped the brakes in token respect to the stop sign and pulled onto the highway. "I may have killed him." She was aware of Sam's eyes slanting toward her.

"I doubt it. Even if you did, I wouldn't waste too much time feeling guilty about it. You can bet he wouldn't have lost any sleep over killing you."

"I suppose."

Sam twisted to look out the back window. "They're following us. What the hell!" He grabbed for the armrest as the truck skidded into a right turn and shot down an alley barely wide enough to avoid scraping the paint.

"I've got to lose them." Babs spun left out of the alley. Sam closed his eyes as she made another squealing turn that threatened to overturn them.

"Look, don't get us killed. The idea is to avoid getting killed."

"Don't worry. I took a stunt-driving course a couple of years ago."

"Oh, great. Every bone in my body is broken. There's a car full of goons on our tail who'd like nothing better than to break a few more. And I'm stuck with someone who's had driving lessons from some suicidal maniac who tries to kill himself for a living. Just great. Look out! Didn't you see that car?"

"I saw it. I didn't hit it, did I?" She appeared to feel that was answer enough. Sam shut his eyes again. There were times when it was best not to face danger head-on.

The truck squealed around a corner, throwing him against the door. He swallowed a groan of pain, convinced that every breath was going to be his last. What did a few more bruises matter when he was going to die? Another quick turn and then they picked up speed. Sam opened his eyes, wondering if she'd speeded up because they were going the wrong way down a one-way street. From what he'd seen of her driving style so far, that seemed a likely explanation. They were on the highway. Wide open road stretched out in front of them.

"Great place to hide. They'd never suspect us of leaving town." He hurt in too many places to put much sarcasm behind the words.

Babs glanced in the rearview mirror. "I think I lost

them a couple of turns ago. Besides, we couldn't dodge them in that little town forever.''

"True." Sam leaned back against the seat. She looked at him, her eyes dark with concern.

"Are you all right? Do you need a doctor?"

He shook his head and then wished he hadn't. It hurt to move. In fact, it hurt to breathe. "I don't need a doctor. Just get us someplace where I can lie down and I'll be fine."

"You look awful."

"Thank you." His tone closed the conversation.

Babs drove in silence, watching the rearview mirror for any sign of pursuit, stealing glances at her silent companion. She didn't know if he'd fallen asleep, passed out or just didn't want to talk. Whichever it was, it left her with quite a few questions she didn't have answers for.

What she really wanted to do was find a nice quiet corner and cry herself to sleep. Maybe when she woke up this whole thing would turn out to be an extended nightmare. Of course, if it was a nightmare, then Sam Delanian didn't exist. Glancing at his still figure, she discovered that she wanted him to exist. She didn't want to wake up and find that she'd dreamed him.

She bit her lip, focusing her eyes on the road again. It was stress. That was what made him so oddly appealing. He'd saved her life and it was only natural that she would be grateful to him, but that's all it was. It had nothing to do with waking up in his arms this morning; or the way his eyes could laugh when the rest of his face was still; or the way his muscles rippled beneath his skin; or the thick lock of hair that was inclined to fall onto his forehead, filling her with an urge to push it back. She was grateful to him, that was all.

It was almost noon when she drove into a town considerably larger than the one they'd left behind. She pulled into a motel, parking the truck in back of the building where it couldn't be seen from the street. Not that it had done them a whole lot of good the last time but it was a simple precaution.

Sam roused when she shut off the engine, dragging himself into a more upright position and looking around, his eyes glazed with pain. "Where are we?"

"I don't know. Some town a couple of hours away from the last one. I'm going to get us a room."

"Okay." He caught her hand before she could slide out of the truck. "Be careful." His eyes held hers for a long steady moment. For some reason, Babs felt breathless. She nodded and slid out of the truck without speaking.

Twenty minutes later she was back with a room key. When she opened the door of the truck, Sam didn't move and, for one awful instant, visions of fatal internal bleeding flashed through her head.

"Sam?"

He twitched and opened his eyes, staring at her blankly for a moment. "You don't have to whisper. I haven't died."

Babs flushed. He'd read her thoughts with unnerving accuracy.

"I've got us a room."

"Good." He pulled himself into a more upright position and Babs found herself wincing for him. "No one recognized you, did they?"

"Why should they? I've never been here before." She put her hand under his elbow, bracing him.

"Your picture has been in every paper in the country."

"It was probably a bad likeness."

"Actually, it wasn't all that bad." He grunted as his feet hit the ground.

"I'm surprised Aunt Dodie didn't give them my high-school graduation picture." Babs slid her arm around his waist, urging him forward.

"What's wrong with your high-school graduation picture?" The irrelevant conversation distracted him from the ache that seemed to have invaded every bone in his body.

"I looked like I had just swallowed a tablespoon of alum. My face was all squinched up." She fumbled with the room key for a moment before getting the door open. Sam stepped forward as she found the light switch. He stumbled slightly on the doorjamb and Babs threw her arm around his waist, feeling his groan more than hearing it. "Let's get you to a bed."

Sam said nothing as she guided his stiff footsteps to the nearest bed and eased him down on it. His breath left him on a long sigh of relief. He caught her hand when she would have moved away. Babs stared down at him, caught by the brilliant blue of his eyes.

"I'm supposed to be rescuing you, remember?"

He looked terrible. There was a scrape high on one cheekbone, his nose was swollen, his lower lip was badly split. He looked like a man who'd been in a fight with a Mack truck and lost. Funny how her heart seemed to skip a beat when she looked at him. She smiled, the shakiness of it reflecting her own tension. Without volition, her fingers reached out and smoothed back the heavy lock of black hair that curled against his forehead.

"Consider it a fair trade in the rescuing department."

Sam gave her a half-smile, his battered face stiff. "I guess I don't have much choice, do I?"

"None at all."

Chapter Five

The sound of his boot heels hitting the polished parquet echoed in the huge hallway. At another time, Emmet Malone might have paused to exchange stares with the portrait of his grandfather that hung on one wall, dominating the entryway. The resemblance between the two men was strong. Stubborn chins, gray eyes that held a little too much restlessness. It amused Emmet to know that, of all Carlisle Malone's descendants, he was the one who looked the most like him. It amused him because it galled the rest of the family and anything that shook them off their stuffy little perches, even for a moment, was worth a laugh.

But he wasn't thinking about familial resemblances at the moment. At the moment, he was thinking about his niece—the only person in his entire family he felt was worth a plug nickel. His brother's only child was the one reason he even bothered keeping in touch with the rest of his family. Now she'd been kidnapped and he wanted to know why no one had felt it necessary to inform him.

He crossed the hall with quick strides, waving off the butler who'd heard the door open and scuttled into the hallway, still shrugging into his jacket. The sight of the man annoyed Emmet. Not that he had anything against him personally. It was what he symbolized: a clinging to a way of life that was dead and gone, never to return.

He shoved open the library door, knowing the family would be gathered there in this predinner hour. It was another of the senseless traditions that had driven him to leave home at an early age. The San Andreas Fault could open up and swallow the entire city of Los Angeles but the Malone family would still meet for their predinner drinks and "conversation." In his experience, the conversation was inclined to consist of various family members sniping at each other.

Just as he'd expected, they were all gathered in the huge room. At his entrance, conversation stopped dead and they all looked at him. Emmet took his time, allowing his gaze to move from one to the other without speaking. He might have opted out of running the family holdings but he knew the value of intimidation and he used it now.

His cousin Dodie sat on a delicate Queen Anne chair, her too-large frame looking at odds with the exquisite furniture. Lionel was buried in an enormous leather chair that dominated him, not so much physically as mentally. It was a sad commentary that Lionel Davis was incapable of dominating anything, including a piece of furniture.

Their son, Lance, leaned in his favorite position against the mantel, his chiseled profile shown to good advantage. Emmet felt his upper lip quiver. Of all of them, he despised Lance the most. From the time he was a boy, he'd opted for the easy route, living off the trust fund, never bothering to do a day's work.

Bertie and Clarence sat side by side on a sofa that matched Dodie's chair, their elderly faces turned toward him with matched expressions of surprise and vague alarm. As usual, neither of them had much idea of what was going on.

Emmet let his presence sink in, drawing out the moment until the tension in the room could be felt. And then he smiled. Not the wide grin his friends might have recognized but a predatory, ominous smile reminiscent of a tiger eyeing a particularly juicy native.

"What a surprise to find you all here." He shut the huge door behind him and walked into the room, stopping in the center of the vast sea of Persian rug that covered polished maple flooring.

"Emmet. Er…ah…nice to see you. It's been a while." That was Lionel—as usual trying to pour oil on water already far too turbulent for weak stomachs.

"Emmet." Dodie nodded her head regally but not before he'd seen the flicker of uneasiness in her eyes.

"Well, if it isn't the great white hunter. Brought back any new trophies?" Lance swirled his cognac.

"Careful, Lance. Sneering will give you wrinkles. And when all you've got is your face, you'd better take good care of it." Lance's mouth tightened and his eyes spoke his dislike but he didn't say anything more.

"Look, Clarence, it's Emmet." As usual, Bertie was a few beats behind the rest of the world.

"I see that it's Emmet." Clarence's tone held an edge of temper, like a grumpy old dog whose nap has been interrupted just so he could shake hands with someone.

"Aunt Bertie, Uncle Clarence. I see you haven't changed." Emmet's smile lost some of its edge when he looked at them. Somehow, the world had lost track of Bertie and Clarence and he had a feeling it was far too late to try to bring them up-to-date now. He turned his attention to Dodie, his eyes chill.

"I read in the newspaper that Babs has been kidnapped."

"That's right. It's a terrible thing. We've all been very traumatized by this."

"I think it's strange that I had to find out about my niece's kidnapping through the newspapers." He crossed over to the bar. The quiet tinkle of ice hitting a glass sounded loud in the stillness. He poured a healthy dose of Chivas Regal before turning to look at his family, leaning one hip against the maple of the bar. "Don't you think it's strange?"

"Naturally, we wanted to get hold of you but we were under the impression that you were off on some trip to the Amazon or the Zambezi or some such place."

"As a matter of fact, I was rafting on the Colorado."

"There." Lionel's voice expressed his relief. "You see, we couldn't have gotten in touch with you there. Don't imagine they have phones in those raft things, do they?" His smile faded under his wife's withering glance.

"Did you even try to contact me?" The silence gave him his answer. He took a swallow of his scotch, letting the silence stretch. "Have they made any demands yet?"

"Who?" Lionel stared at him, his eyes reminding Emmet of a trapped rabbit.

"The kidnappers. Who else would I be talking about?"

"Oh, the kidnappers. Of course, of course."

"Of course. Have the kidnappers made any demands?" Emmet spaced the words clearly, sensing an undercurrent he didn't understand.

"Why should they make demands? They were very well paid." Bertie tugged at her shawl, tangling the long fringes, her soft brow puckered in a frown.

"What?"

"What Bertie means is that they are undoubtedly *expecting* to be very well paid." Dodie jumped in, speaking just a little too quickly, a little too loudly.

"I don't think that's what Bertie meant at all. Was it Bertie? Just what did you mean?"

Bertie stared at him, her eyes reflecting her uneasiness. "Mean? I don't know what you mean 'what did I mean.' I didn't mean anything at all. Nothing. I don't think."

"What's going on?" He pinned Dodie with a sharp look. She met his eye without flinching.

"I don't know what you mean. The kidnappers haven't made a demand yet so, really, we don't know much more than what you read in the papers."

Emmet looked around the room. They were hiding something. He could smell it. The question was: what was it? And he knew exactly how to find out. There was always one weak point in any wall. His eyes settled on Bertie and his smile made her give a vague squeak of dismay.

It took him less than five minutes to get enough out of Bertie so that Dodie had to give up and tell him the whole story.

"We really had no choice. When Babette threatened to talk to Finney, we had to stop her. You know the terms of the will, even though you were cut out of it." Dodie looked at him, as if expecting him to agree that they'd done the only logical thing.

"So you had her kidnapped. You've let her think that she's in the hands of criminals who may kill her whether they get the money or not."

Dodie shifted uneasily beneath the building anger in his voice. "We were all upset by the thought that Babette might suffer some worry but she really left us no choice. Naturally, we instructed the men we hired to treat her well.''

"Well, that was gracious of you. Very Malone, Dodie. The Malones are nothing if not gracious. They may stab you in the back. They may mooch money from you. But they're ever gracious.''

"Really, sarcasm is un—''

"Shut up.'' It was probably the first time in her entire life that anyone had told Dodie to shut up. She gaped, her mouth dropped open and she stared at her cousin, looking like a carp thrown up on dry land.

Emmet ignored her. He stalked from one end of the room to the other, needing some outlet for the rage that bubbled inside him. He kept thinking of how frightened Babs must be. His niece was a gutsy little thing but kidnapping was enough to make anyone nervous. He spun around, staring at his family. They stared back, with varying expressions of uneasiness.

"The problem with you people is that you're a bunch of parasites. Not one of you has ever done a decent day's work. You hung on Great-grandfather's coattails and then you hung on Caldwell's. Funny, he was quick enough to boot me out of the family for marrying the wrong woman but he never had the sense to throw all of you out on your butts. Not one of you is worth spit. Babs is the only member of this family that's worth a thing but she's got one weak spot.''

He paused, his eyes pinning each of them in turn. None of them quite met his eyes. "She's kindhearted. I told her to cut you loose years ago but she wouldn't do it. She said you needed her. Hah! You never gave a damn about her unless you needed money.''

His fierce gaze settled on Dodie. "When Earl and Lenore died, you took a frightened little girl and tried to regiment her into your ideal of a Malone daughter and you've never forgiven her for being too damned strong for you to break.

"Well, you've pushed too far this time. Babs should have gone to the police. I'd like nothing better than to see the whole lot of you in jail."

"Jail!"

"Now, really, Emmet."

"What does he mean, Clarence?"

"Emmet, my dear fellow, I really think perhaps you've misunderstood our motives." For once, it was Lionel's voice that prevailed above the babble. No one could have been more surprised than he was. "I mean, no one meant Babette any harm. No harm at all. Besides, she's not even with the men we hired anymore."

"Then where is she?"

"Er...well, actually, we're not quite sure of that. A gentleman called and said he'd rescued her. He said he was a friend of yours. A Sam Delanian?"

"Sam has her?" Emmet's frown lightened a fraction and Lionel dabbed at his forehead with a linen handkerchief.

"When did you talk to Sam? Where is Babs?"

"Your friend called yesterday."

"So where are they? They should have been here by now."

Dodie sniffed. "Actually, I suggested to Mr. Delanian that it might be quite profitable for him to keep Babette away for a few days."

"You bitch." The flat words had more impact than if he'd shouted them from the rooftop. Dodie blanched, her eyes dropping away from the contempt in his. Lionel stared at his hands. Lance looked as though he might say something and then changed his mind and continued to stare broodingly into the empty fireplace. Bertie and Clarence looked confused, as usual.

"If she's with Sam then he'll take care of her. God knows, she's safer with him than she is with the lot of you."

He turned his back to the family and picked up his Scotch and downed it in a gulp, as if to wash a nasty taste out of his mouth. It was Lionel who broke the tense silence—more afraid of what Emmet might do than he was of his current anger.

"You're...ah...not thinking about calling the police or anything hasty like that, are you? I mean, it would be best for everyone if we kept it all in the family. Scandal and all, you know." His voice trailed off, his eyes shifting nervously when Emmet turned to look at him.

"I don't really care what's best for the family. As far as I'm concerned, nothing would make me happier than to see all of you rotting in San Quentin. It's too bad they closed Alcatraz."

Lionel paled and dabbed at his forehead, his hand shaking. Emmet let the silence stretch, giving them all a chance to think about what he'd said. Even Clarence and Bertie looked worried.

"No, I'm not going to the police." His upper lip lifted at the visible wave of relief that ran through the room. "I'm not doing it for your sakes or the sake of 'family.' I'm doing it for Babs's sake. This would cause a hell of a scandal and she'd be right in the middle of it."

"If she hadn't been so unreasonable about the paintings, none of this would have been necessary. In a few more days, Mr. Stefanoni will be going back to Italy and this will all be settled."

Emmet barely looked at Lionel. "If you weren't so

damned stupid, you might be dangerous. This whole plan goes beyond dumb to downright insanity. Do you really think Stefanoni isn't going to figure out that you sold him fakes? He's not going to be amused. I'll go talk to him and see if I can pull your fat out of the fire this time but only for Babs's sake.''

He walked to the door and opened it before turning to sweep them all with one last contemptuous look. "You'd better hope to God that nothing happens to her or I'll fit you all for cement boots myself."

He stalked into the hall, almost running over the butler who was on his way in to announce dinner. Emmet threw open the front door and stepped out into the fresh air, drawing in a deep lungful. God, he felt as if the very air in that house was tainted. He stared at the evening sky, thinking about his niece. Thrusting his fingers through thick gray hair, he walked down the steps. She'd be all right. Sam Delanian was a good man. He'd take care of her.

"OUCH! DAMMIT, THAT HURTS."

"Don't be such a baby." Babs dabbed the cotton swab gently on the scrape that skidded along his rib cage.

"It's easy for you to say. No one is dropping battery acid in your open wounds."

She ignored Sam's muttered complaints. "Do you think any of your ribs are cracked or broken or anything?" She sat back on her heels next to the bed and looked at him, her eyes dark with concern.

"My ribs are just fine except they hurt like hell."

"Maybe we should find a doctor. If you've got a broken rib…"

Sam opened his eyes and looked at her. "Babs, my

ribs are not broken. They're not even cracked. Believe me. I've had cracked ribs before. I'm bruised and that's all.''

She looked doubtful, her slightly gamine face puckered with worry. Sam surprised himself by reaching out to touch his fingers to her cheek. ''Don't worry about me. My pride is hurt more than anything else.''

Babs leaned her face into his hand for just an instant before drawing away and turning her attention to the scrape on his cheekbone. ''But you were terrific. If it hadn't been three to one, you'd have demolished them.''

Sam laughed, the sound ending in a groan as his bruised ribs protested. ''You were pretty terrific yourself. You looked like you knew what you were doing with that gun.''

''I do. Uncle Emmet taught me to shoot when I was twelve.''

''Remind me to thank Emmet.'' He sucked in his breath as the antiseptic burned. Babs stopped and looked at him.

''Does it hurt terribly?'' Sam stared into her eyes, feeling as if he could drown in their chocolate depths. She was so close. Her fingers on his cheek felt cool and soothing.

''It doesn't hurt at all,'' he lied, still looking at her.

''You know, you really were magnificent.''

He smiled, his battered face protesting the movement. ''All I did was get beat up.''

The moment stretched with neither of them quite willing to break it. Something indefinable hovered in the air—awareness, attraction, desire—things neither of them wanted to acknowledge. Babs wondered how it was possible for his eyes to be so blue. It was like looking at the ocean, full of depths, full of promise—and dangers. Outside the motel, a car door slammed and they heard the shrill voices of children as a family arrived. The sounds broke the strange tension and Babs looked away, staring at the first-aid kit as if seeing it for the first time.

"Good thing you had this in the truck." She busied herself with packing everything away, making sure every item was in precisely the right place. That done, she stood up and looked around the room.

"At least we've got two beds tonight." At Sam's comment, her gaze settled on him and then skittered away.

"I've been thinking about it and I think I should call my family. Someone is bound to be home by now and I ought to let them know that I'm safe. As soon as I tell them where I am, they can send someone to come up and get us."

"I don't think that's such a good idea." Sam dragged himself upward until he was more or less sitting, his back braced against the headboard.

"I'll make sure you get your money, even if you don't officially deliver me." Her voice held more than a hint of resentment. Sam thrust his fingers through his hair. Maybe he should have told her the truth last night but it had seemed like such a good idea to think about it.

"It's not the money."

"I thought that's what you were in this for. I mean, after all, that's why you rescued me. You don't have to feel guilty about it. You did a job and you should get paid for it."

"Would you shut up for a minute?"

Babs stared at him, opened her mouth and then shut it again. Sam waited to be sure that he had the floor.

"I lied to you last night. I *did* get through to your family."

"You talked to them? Why didn't you tell me? What did they say? Who did you talk to?"

He stared at her, wondering just how to phrase what he had to say. How did you tell someone that her own family was part of a kidnapping plot? He ran his fingers through his hair again, his gaze wandering over the room, searching for inspiration.

"I…talked to your Aunt Bertie and your Aunt Dodie."

"God, you got the full works, didn't you? From airhead to hardnose all in one conversation. What did they say? I don't understand why you didn't tell me about this."

He reached out, catching her hand and tugging until she sat down on the edge of the bed next to him. He kept hold of her hand, meeting her eyes with his and hating what he had to say.

"Your family paid those men to kidnap you."

The words came out stark and unadorned but there was no other way to say it. She stared at him, her eyes going from questioning to blank disbelief in an instant. She started to speak, words of denial pushing to get out and then saw the regret in his eyes. She looked away but not before he saw the hurt that darkened her eyes to almost black. Her lower lip quivered for an instant before being caught between her teeth. She stared at the cracked green lamp that sat next to the bed. Her fingers stiffened in his and then drew away. She didn't get up but he could feel her pulling away, drawing into herself, shutting the door on the hurt.

She shrugged. "I suppose I shouldn't be surprised. We had quite a dustup a few days before the kidnapping.'' She was silent for a moment. ''You know, we've never been close but I didn't think... I mean, I'd never have expected this. Not really anyone's idea of a happy family, are we?'' Her laugh cracked in the middle but the set of her chin forbade him to offer her comfort.

Sam stared at her helplessly. He could feel her pain as if it were his own. He wanted to say something, offer some consolation, but there was really nothing to be said.

She straightened her shoulders, her chin setting. When her eyes met his, they were a little too bright but the glitter in them defied sympathy.

''Damn them. I know exactly what this is all about. Damn them. Damn them. Damn them. I spent a week and a half thinking I was going to die at any minute.'' She shot to her feet, her hurt and anger too great to allow her to sit still. ''They've gone too far this time. I've made excuses for them before but this time they've gone too far. They had no right. No right at all.'' Her voice broke and he thought he saw her chin quiver before she looked away. Her spine was rigid, her small frame taut with pain.

''Babs, I—''

''Well, they're not going to get away with it this time. I'm going to rub their noses in this one. And they've seen the last penny they'll ever see from me. Let them learn to live on their own money. Are you up to traveling?''

''Why?'' Sam had a sinking feeling that he knew exactly why.

''Because, if we get started right away, I can be home by late tonight. Nothing would make me happier than to roust the whole rotten bunch of them out of bed and tell them they just killed the bird that laid the golden eggs.''

"I don't think that's such a good idea. After our encounter with those thugs this morning, there's a good chance they're still looking for us and I don't think they're going to be any friendlier."

Babs waved her hand dismissively. "They aren't that serious. My family may have wanted me out of the way for a while but they don't want me hurt. Those men have been well paid to make sure I'm okay."

Sam closed his eyes, feeling every ache in his body throb in sympathy with the headache that was starting behind his eyes. Babs was pacing back and forth and he could all but see the wheels of her mind turning. She wanted revenge. He couldn't blame her for that. To be honest, he wouldn't have minded a bit of healthy revenge himself. But they had to be sensible.

He opened his eyes and looked at Babs and gave a silent sigh. Somehow she didn't look in a sensible mood. Her steps carried her from one wall to the other. Her eyes glittered with anger and her lips moved occasionally, as if she were rehearsing diatribes that would leave her family in shreds.

"Babs. The bullets those men were firing were real. They could have put a hole in one of us as easily as the window. I think something is going on here that we need to think about a little more carefully." He might as well have been talking to himself.

"If you're not up to traveling, would you mind if I borrowed your truck? I can send someone for you first thing in the morning. You'll be all right here alone, won't you?"

"As a matter of fact, I *would* mind if you borrowed my truck. I don't need you to send someone for me in the morning and I have no intention of spending the night here alone."

She barely glanced at him. "Then I'll call a cab or rent a car. I can't just sit here."

Sam reached out, catching her wrist and pulling her to a stop. She tugged on her hand, her eyes wild with hurt anger. Sam ignored her attempts to get loose and pulled her down onto the bed next to him, waiting until her eyes met his.

"Listen to me. You're in danger. Whether you want to admit it or not, those men are playing for keeps. They're not boys out for a romp in the park. They're professionals. They were trying to kill me this morning and I think they might have killed you.

"Now, if you take one step out of this room, there's not a damned thing I can do to protect you. I'm just too beat. But I promise you this: If they don't get you first, I'm going to beat the holy hell out of you when I catch you."

She stared at him, her eyes startled. "You really mean that, don't you?"

"Every word."

He waited, knowing that if she decided to leave, he'd kill himself following her. She didn't say anything for a long moment, her eyes searching the blue of his. To his surprise, her chin quivered slightly and her eyes filled with bright tears.

"No one has ever cared enough to threaten me."

The absurd statement should have made him laugh. Instead, it caused a sharp catch in his chest. Odd that he knew exactly what she meant. His face softened and his hand gentled on her wrist.

"I care." The words were said without thinking but he wouldn't have taken them back. He did care. Under the spoiled brat, he saw an achingly lonely little girl who'd lost her parents, her grandfather, her world.

Somehow, he didn't think it had ever quite been put back together again.

His hand slid up her arm, the silk of her shirt sliding smoothly beneath his fingertips. Babs watched him, offering no protest as his hands slid into the thick hair at her nape. Her lashes drooped as he tugged her downward.

He intended the kiss to comfort, a little human warmth to try to ease some of her pain. He didn't plan on anything more. After all, he admired her guts but he wasn't sure he liked her.

Her mouth was surprisingly soft and warm. Her hair slid through his fingers like watered silk, heavy, rich, inviting. The texture of the kiss changed almost without him realizing it. The fullness of her lower lip invited the touch of his tongue. Her mouth opened almost shyly to his. He brought his other hand up, flattening his palm on her back, feeling the ridge of her spine through her shirt.

Desire caught him unaware. He tasted the softness of her mouth and he wanted more. Her hair swung forward as she leaned above him and he wanted to feel it against his chest. Her breasts pressed ever so lightly against him and he wanted to feel their weight in his hands.

His hold tightened on her, his tongue thrusting past the barrier of her teeth to tangle with hers. Her response was tantalizingly shy but hungry. The combination only made him want her more.

He lifted her, drawing her closer and his battered body protested. He groaned involuntarily and Babs jerked away, her face flushed, her eyes bright with some emotion he couldn't quite read. She looked at him and then away.

"You ought to get some rest." She stood up, smoothing her palms over her jeans, looking anywhere but at him. "Are you hungry?"

"Starved." Sam's tone said that he wasn't talking about food and her flush deepened.

"I'll see what we can get by way of take-out."

"Does this mean you're not going to try to leave tonight?"

She glanced at him, her expression unreadable. Sam held his breath, waiting for her answer.

"I'll stay. Maybe you're right about those men really trying to hurt me. Besides, I couldn't leave you here alone."

Sam didn't care why she stayed. All he cared about was that she'd be reasonably safe for tonight. In the morning he'd have a better idea of what their next move should be. In the morning his desire for her would be an obvious case of propinquity.

In the morning a lot of things might happen.

Chapter Six

When Babs awoke the next morning, Sam was already up and more-or-less dressed. He'd only managed to shrug into half his shirt and he was muttering to himself as he fished around for the other sleeve. She lay still, watching him. During the night the bruises on his ribs had turned a rather colorful shade of purple, but they did nothing to detract from his smooth tanned skin and corded muscles.

His searching hand found the sleeve and he shrugged into the other half of the shirt, his movements stiff. He turned, as if sensing that she was awake. Their eyes met, sleepy brown and electric blue. Unspoken lay the memory of the kiss they'd shared. Unconsciously, Babs's tongue flicked out, wetting her lower lip in a nervous gesture. Sam's gaze flickered to her mouth, and was as warm and potent as a kiss. The tension stretched between them.

Sam was the first to break the silence. "How did you sleep?"

Babs dragged her eyes from his, sitting up in bed and shoving her hair out of her eyes. "Okay, I guess. How well are you supposed to sleep after finding out that your own family had you kidnapped?"

''I don't know. You'd probably have to ask Emily Post.''

He fumbled with the buttons on his shirt, his bruised hands awkward. Babs swung her legs out of bed and stood up, tugging uneasily at the bottom of Sam's shirt. Funny how it had seemed to be a perfectly adequate covering until now. She hovered next to the bed, torn between her common sense, which told her to go put on her own clothes, and her compassion, which urged her to help him with his buttons.

''Here. Let me help you with those.''

Sam watched her, his eyes wary as she crossed over the few feet that separated them and pushed his hands aside. Her fingers brushed against the mat of black hair that covered his chest. Babs fumbled with the buttons, feeling as clumsy as he had been, only she didn't have the excuse of bruises. She could feel his eyes watching her and it brought a deliciously nervous feeling.

''You really aren't very big, are you?'' They were so close that his breath stirred her hair.

''Five foot and a half inch.''

''A half inch?''

''Well, it may be only a quarter but I like to give myself the benefit of the doubt.'' She slid the last button through the proper buttonhole and looked up at him, her smile mischievous. ''When you're short, you've got to take advantage of every fraction.''

''I can imagine.'' Sam murmured the words, his eyes on her face. Her hair was tousled wildly around her delicate features, she didn't have on a trace of makeup, she was wearing a wrinkled shirt that was miles too big for her and he couldn't remember when he'd seen a more attractive woman.

He reached up to brush her hair back, seeing the way

her eyes widened at the casual gesture. One of her hands still rested against his chest. The light pressure seemed to leave an imprint on his skin.

He dropped his hand, stepping away, feeling as if he were backing off from temptation. "The water at this motel is a lot hotter than the last one. At least it was half an hour ago."

The hint was impossible to ignore. Babs turned and picked up her clothes, feeling half hurt and half relieved. Sam Delanian confused her. He brought out feelings in her that Babs didn't understand and wasn't sure she wanted to face. Maybe some of the confusion would wash away in a hot shower.

If the shower didn't solve all her problems, it did leave her feeling better able to face them. The way Sam made her feel was perfectly understandable when she put it in context. The man had saved her life more than once. It was only natural that she was grateful. But it wouldn't do to confuse gratitude with anything else.

When she stepped out of the bathroom, her hair fell in shaggy waves around her face, her expression was set with determination and her clothes were as neat as was possible, considering she'd been wearing them for several days. She was ready to face the world, her family and Sam Delanian, not necessarily in that order.

The television was on, the sound of bells and whistles announcing a game show even before she saw the picture. Sam was sitting on the edge of the bed, his eyes on the screen but his thoughts clearly elsewhere. He glanced up as she stepped out of the bathroom, his eyes sweeping over her. Babs had to remind herself that the funny little blip in her heartbeat was caused by gratitude.

"We'll do some shopping today. We both need a change of clothes." He reached out and snapped off the television in the midst of some woman's screams of ecstasy over a prize she'd just won.

"I have plenty of clothes at home."

"We're not heading back to Montecito. At least not quite yet."

"Why not? I think it's time I faced my family. I don't want them thinking they can get away with kidnapping me every time I threaten to do something they don't like."

"Just what did you threaten to do?"

Babs hesitated, all her aunt's training telling her that you never discussed family matters with outsiders. But then, Sam could hardly be called an outsider. She sat down on the other bed, studying the worn carpet under her feet.

"They sold fake works of art to Eduardo Stefanoni." She hurried the words out, not looking at him.

There was a moment's silence and then Sam whistled, a long, low sound of disbelief. "From what I've heard of Stefanoni, he's not the type to shrug that off."

"No. I didn't think so either. My family can be... rather naive." She felt herself flushing, embarrassed by what her family had done, humiliated by the need to try to explain the unexplainable. How could she tell him that her family thought that being a Malone gave you the right to do anything you wanted and the rest of the world just had to like it?

"Downright stupid might be a better description." Sam was more blunt.

Babs nodded unhappily, wishing she could argue. "I didn't find out until after the sale had gone through and I tried to explain to them that Mr. Stefanoni was not going to be happy but I don't think I got through to them."

"So why would they have you kidnapped? I don't see what good that would do them."

She scuffed her foot on the carpet, still without looking at him. "I think they wanted to keep me out of the way until Stefanoni goes back to Italy. They had some idea that once he took the paintings back to Italy, he wouldn't find out they were fakes. I told them that if they didn't go to Stefanoni and tell him what they'd done and give him the real paintings, I was going to talk to Finney."

"Who's Finney?"

"Finney, Finney, Finney and Smythe? He's the first Finney. They've been the family law firm for ages. Practically since time began."

"So what would Finney of Finney, Finney and Smythe do?"

"You forgot a Finney. Under the terms of my great-grandfather's will, if the family sells off any of the art he bought back in the dark ages, for any reason except starvation, the entire estate will be broken up and given to charity. The paintings they sold to Stefanoni were copies of works that my great-grandfather bought. If Finney finds out what they've done, under the terms of the will, it might be enough to break up the estate, especially if they had to give the real things to Stefanoni."

"But why would you risk going to Finney? You'd lose everything, too."

"No. My money comes from my grandfather and it's separate from the rest of the family money. I've received an allowance from it since I was a child and on my twenty-fifth birthday, I inherit the whole thing." She sounded depressed by the idea and Sam wondered what it would be like to have so much money that the thought of it was depressing.

She heaved a sigh and looked at him. "You see why I have to go back right away."

"No. Actually, I see just the opposite. There was more to this than just kidnapping you to keep you out of the way. It may have started out that way but somewhere along the line things changed. Those men yesterday were trying to kill me and you overheard them planning to kill you. That's more than your basic kidnapping."

"There must have been a mistake somewhere." Her eyes were dark with distress and Sam had to suppress the urge to sit down beside her and put his arms around her and tell her that everything was going to be all right.

"Maybe. But, until we find out whose mistake it was, I think we should lay low and think about our next move. I don't know about you, but I'm not all that fond of getting beat up and shot at."

Babs stood up and shoved her hands in her back pockets, her back to him. "You think my family wants me dead, don't you?" Her voice was low and strained, the attractive huskiness deepening.

"I don't think anything at all right now. All I know is that we ought to find out what's going on before we go waltzing into a potentially dangerous situation. We need someplace where it will be safe to stay for a few days and give the whole situation some thought."

She didn't say anything for a minute and he stared at her silently, knowing how hard this was for her. He was asking her to trust him, to do what he thought was best. He was also asking her to accept the possibility that she might be in danger because of her family. After a long moment, her shoulders lifted in a shrug and she turned to face him, her face set.

"All right. I'll go along with this. For a while anyway."

Sam nodded, accepting her decision calmly, as if he'd never had any doubts about her seeing it his way.

"Okay, the first thing we need to do is get some clothes and then find some transportation."

"What's wrong with your truck?"

"The guys who kidnapped you obviously know what it looks like. I want to find someplace to hide for a few days and I don't want them picking up our trail. The truck would make it too easy."

Babs sat down on the edge of the bed, her brow wrinkled as she considered the problem. "Why don't we just buy another car?"

Sam stared at her. In one sentence, she'd summed up the gap between them. For Babs Malone, buying a car was no big deal. She probably didn't give it much more thought than he'd give to buying a new pair of shoes. The reminder of their differences was irritating.

"There's only one problem that I can see with that."

She looked at him, eyes wide and questioning.

"Money. Cars cost money. Generally lots of it. I didn't bring that kind of money. Hell, I don't even *have* that kind of money."

"That's no problem. I can just call up my bank and they'll transfer the money to a bank here and then we can buy a car." She was clearly pleased with having found a simple solution to their transportation difficulties.

"Sure. Great idea. We're trying to lay low and keep out of sight. Every fruitcake in the country is looking for you for that fifty-thousand-dollar reward. So you're just going to waltz into the local savings and loan and announce that you're the kidnapped Malone heiress and you'd like to have a few thou transferred from your bank account and could they arrange it please?"

Babs flushed at the bite in his tone and drew herself up a bit stiffly. "Fine. You're so brilliant. You think of something."

"Thank you, I will."

The silence that settled over the room was thick with indignation. Sam looked at her and then looked away. She looked like a child who'd been unfairly punished. Her chin was set but her eyes held an edge of hurt. Not that it was his problem. He hadn't done anything out of line. Nothing at all. He glanced at her again. She was staring at her fingernails with such an air of deliberate unconcern that he almost smiled.

"Oh, hell. I'm sorry. I shouldn't have snapped like that. We've got enough problems without snapping at each other."

She looked at him from under her lashes, judging his sincerity. She must have been satisfied with what she saw because she smiled shyly and shrugged. "I suppose it was a pretty dumb suggestion."

"Just a little naive." His smile took any possible sting out of the words.

"What about a credit card? We could rent a car with a credit card." She looked so pleased with herself that Sam hated to discourage her. He shook his head.

"Credit cards leave a paper trail. Since we don't know what's going on, I'd rather be as inconspicuous as possible."

"Oh." She frowned and Sam forgot to do anything more than watch her think through their problem. She shoved her fingers through her hair, pushing it back off her face for a moment. The instant she released it, it fell back, framing her eyes in a way that he was beginning to find irresistible.

She smiled suddenly, her eyes meeting his delightedly. "You could steal a car. You know how, don't you?" It didn't seem to occur to her that he might be insulted by her assumption that he knew how to steal cars. He grinned, unable to resist the image of her creeping along behind him while he jimmied locks and hot-wired cars.

"As a matter of fact, I do know how to steal a car but I don't think it's such a good idea."

"Why not? Those thugs wouldn't be able to trace it and you said we needed transportation." The illegality of it didn't seem to occur to her.

Sam's grin widened. "The police frown on such things. I have a feeling your family wouldn't be too thrilled to get a call from the local jail to come and bail you out."

Babs stared at him for a moment and then her eyes began to sparkle with pure mischief. "I hadn't thought of the police. It would almost be worth getting arrested just to see Aunt Dodie's face."

"From my one brief conversation with the woman I can understand your sentiments, but I don't think stealing a car is a good idea."

"Well, then what *are* we going to do?"

"I don't know yet. First thing, let's check out of here and see if there's someplace we can pick up a change of clothes and then we'll go get some food. By that time, I'll think of something."

They checked out of the motel and drove Sam's truck to a shopping area on the outskirts of town. Shopping on a budget was a new experience for Babs. Sam handed her fifty dollars and told her to make it cover everything she needed. She'd never owned a blouse that cost less than fifty dollars, let alone a wardrobe that might have to last several days.

She studied the money in her hand and looked after Sam who was striding into the men's department. She felt an odd surge of possessive pride when she noticed the way women's heads turned to follow him. Shaking her own head, she ventured into the new world of budget clothing.

Half an hour later she met Sam in the front of the store, justifiably proud of her efforts. She was wearing a new pair of jeans and a lavender cotton blouse that she'd found on sale, and her sack contained another pair of jeans, two T-shirts and some underwear. They weren't the personally tailored garments she was accustomed to but she didn't mind. She felt remarkably adventurous and self-sufficient.

Sam grinned at her glowing face before taking the bag from her. His grin turned into a laugh when she held out her hand to display the eighty-seven cents that remained of the fifty dollars he'd given her.

"Remind me to introduce you to my mother. The two of you can swap notes about bargain hunting."

"What's your mother like?" Her voice held a wistful note and he wondered if she was thinking about her own orphaned state. How much did she remember of her own parents?

"She's great. You'll have to meet her one of these days. Are you hungry?"

"Starving."

"We have to conserve money but we can afford to indulge in a hot breakfast if you don't order steak and eggs."

"I promise to restrain myself."

The tiny café was at the very edge of town. It was a little too late for the breakfast crowd and too early for the lunch crowd. A few customers were finishing their meals, lingering over cups of coffee. The waitress wore a bright pink uniform and had hair to match.

Sam and Babs ordered breakfast and ate without talking much. Babs was concentrating on her food and Sam was racking his brains to figure out where they could go and how they were going to get there.

"...hate to have to haul back an empty truck."

Sam stopped chewing, his complete attention on the conversation at the table behind him.

"Yeah, that's too bad. Still, it'll make the going a bit faster."

Going? Going where?

"Where you headed this time, Frank?" It was as if Frank's companion knew how much Sam wanted that information.

"Sacramento. Got a load of books to pick up. Somebody died and left all their books to a little place in Minnesota—their hometown or something."

Sam finished chewing and swallowed, reaching for the biscuits that sat in the middle of the table and stuffing them in his pockets.

"What are you doing? I was going to eat one of those." Babs gave him an indignant look.

"Later. Finish your coffee."

"What's the hurry?"

"I've figured out how we're going to leave town but we've got to hurry."

He gulped down the last of his coffee, thinking wistfully of thermoses and picnic baskets. Still, he'd done without hot food before. Hopefully, his companion could learn to do the same, at least for a while. He took some cash out of his pocket and hastily counted out enough to pay their bill, recklessly adding a tip when he didn't

have the right change. Maybe the waitress could get a
new dye job. They didn't have time to wait for change.

Babs was still chewing when he stood up, taking her
arm and dragging her from the booth to hustle her out
of the café. Throwing a glance over his shoulder, he saw
the two men in the booth behind them exchanging chit-
chat with the waitress while they paid their bill.

"Where are we going?"

"Sacramento. Ever been to Sacramento? Great
place." He still had her arm, towing her behind him as
he headed for the midsize truck that was parked next to
the building. There was only one. It had to be Frank's.
He threw up a quick prayer of thanks that the rear of the
truck was in shadow.

"Why are we going to Sacramento?"

"Why not?" He dragged her around the back of the
truck, muttering a curse when he saw the padlock on the
back. Still, all was not lost. He dropped Babs's arm and
dug his wallet out of his pocket, pulling out a thin metal
strip.

"What are you doing?" Babs automatically dropped
her voice to a whisper, throwing a quick glance around
as if expecting to see the SWAT team coming at them.
"I thought you said you didn't want to steal a car."

"I'm not going to steal it. We're going to catch a ride
in it. Ah-ha." He grinned as the lock sprang loose. The
door squealed as he pulled it open and he winced, hoping
Frank wasn't going to come running.

"Hurry up."

Babs stared at him as if he'd gone mad. "We're going
to ride in that? Why?"

"Because it's free and no one will ever expect us to
do something like this."

"They won't expect us to do something like this because it's crazy.'' She gave the dark interior of the truck a dubious look.

"This is the best plan. Honest." Sam didn't give her time to argue any more. She squeaked as his hands closed around her waist and he lifted her into the truck, climbing in immediately after her as if he were afraid she might try to escape.

Babs turned to protest but he was already pulling the door shut. There was a row of windows high up on either side of the truck, just enough to give them a dim light. Sam turned and grinned at her, his teeth gleaming white in the darkness.

"Isn't this great?"

He held up his hand, listening intently. Babs winced as they heard a door slam at the front of the truck. Moments later, the engine roared to life. There was a grind of gears and then she pitched forward and would have fallen flat on her face if it hadn't been for Sam's quick reactions. Braced for the movement of the truck, his arms shot out and caught her. For an instant, she was crushed against his chest and she couldn't have said whether it was his nearness that made her breathless or her near fall. He set her back on her feet, keeping his hand under her elbow until she had her balance.

"This is something you'll be able to tell your grandchildren about."

She looked around the dusty, unprepossessing interior and then looked at him, her expression unenthused. "Sure. If I live to have any."

EMMET KNOCKED ON THE DOOR and then looked around. The house was small but beautifully kept. The lawn was neatly trimmed, and tidy flower beds flanked the porch. Settled in the midst of a modest neighborhood in Santa

Barbara, the white-and-blue home could have served as a setting for *Father Knows Best*.

Footsteps on the other side of the door drew his attention back to the reason he was here. It had been three days since Sam had called the Malone mansion. No one had heard a word about Babs since. If any one of the family had heard from the men who'd been hired to kidnap her, they weren't talking. Visiting Sam's mother was a far-out chance but Emmet didn't want to overlook any possibility.

The woman who opened the door suited the house. Her face held a soft prettiness that immediately made him think of warm hearths and leather chairs. Her eyes were a clear blue, paler than her son's but no less striking. Her hair was a silvery shade of gray that might have looked cool on another woman. On Cecily Delanian, it looked warm and inviting.

Unconsciously, Emmet straightened his shoulders and smoothed the unruly iron-gray hair that had never been quite tamed.

"Yes?" Her questioning tone made him realize how long he'd been standing on her doorstep staring at her.

"Mrs. Delanian?"

"Yes. Have we met?"

"No. I'm a friend of your son's."

Her face paled delicately and she lifted one hand to press it against her chest. "Has something happened to Sam?"

"No, no. As far as I know, he's fine." Emmet thrust his fingers through his hair, ruining any pretense of neatness. "Actually, it may have been stretching the truth a bit to say that I was a friend of his. We've only met once, in Mexico. But we sort of got to know each other pretty well and… Well, to be honest, I really need to know where he is." He stopped, aware that he was stumbling badly. He looked at her, his expression rueful. "Do you think I could come in and we could talk?"

Cecily studied him for a long moment, her eyes thoughtful. Emmet resisted a surprising urge to shuffle his feet and tried to look as honest and upright as he could. It wasn't easy when you'd spent thirty years adventuring. He would have had an easier time looking just what he was—a little rough around the edges.

"Come in. I was just making a pot of coffee." She unlatched the screen and pushed it open.

Emmet wiped his feet on the mat and stepped into the small hallway. The house seemed to envelope him in warmth. From the polished plank floor to the quiet print of the wallpaper, it spoke of home and hearth. He noticed the house only peripherally. His eyes didn't shift from the slim figure in front of him. She was wearing a pair of lavender slacks and a pale gray shirt. It was simple, appropriate for a day at home and remarkably attractive.

"Sit down. I'll pour some coffee." Emmet settled himself at the oak pedestal table. The kitchen was large and cheerful, big windows letting the spring sunshine spill through.

Cecily set a steaming mug of coffee in front of him. "Would you like a sweet roll? I baked them yesterday. They're Sam's favorites and he'd said he might be home yesterday."

"Thank you." Emmet took the proffered plate with the sticky roll and set it next to his coffee. He waited until she'd seated herself across from him, her hands cradling a warm mug.

"When did you hear from Sam last?"

"A week or so. Is Sam in trouble?"

"No. At least, I don't know."

"You're Emmet Malone, aren't you?"

"Oh, Lord, I didn't introduce myself. My mother is probably spinning in her grave. She never did have much luck drilling manners into me."

Cecily waved her hand. "Don't worry about it. I recognized you from the picture on the back of your books. Sam didn't tell me he'd met you."

"Well, the circumstances were a little peculiar. We were both in Mexico and there was a small altercation. We had cause to assist each other and we spent a bit of time talking."

"Why are you looking for Sam? Does this have something to do with your niece?"

"Yes. Anything you know would help."

She drew her finger around the edge of her cup, her eyes on the aimless movement. "He told me he was going to find her, that he thought he knew where she was. Like I said, he thought he'd be home yesterday."

"He didn't call you?"

"No. But that's not unusual. Sam doesn't check in with me unless he's going to be gone a lot longer than he expected. You're obviously concerned. Do you have reason to think there's been some problem?"

"Not exactly." Emmet studied her face, wondering just how much he should tell her. But there was no real question in his mind. Those clear blue eyes demanded honesty. "It's a complicated story and I'm afraid my family comes out of it looking less than good." He told her the whole mess, starting with the sale of the phony paintings, through Babs's threats, to his family's insane plan to kidnap her and then what he knew of Sam's phone call.

"There's been no word since then. If anyone has

heard from the kidnappers, they're not telling me. I don't think they'd dare to conceal a call from Sam or Babs. The only thing I know is that he had her and she was apparently all right but there's been not a word since.''

''You must be very worried about your niece.'' Cecily got up and brought the coffeepot over to the table, filling his cup, her expression full of warm sympathy.

''She's the only one of the whole family that's worth a damn, including me. She's such a gutsy little thing, has been since she was a baby.''

''It sounds as if the two of you are very close.''

''I suppose we are. If you knew the rest of the family, you'd know it was self-defense. They're all a bunch of worthless parasites. Not that I'm much better. The ultimate example of the Peter Pan Syndrome at work.'' He lifted his coffee cup in mocking salute.

''I think you're being a bit hard on yourself. Your writing doesn't sound like a man who's refused to grow up.''

''You've read my books?''

''Several of them. I particularly liked your nonfiction book about the destruction of the Amazon rain forests. It was quite eloquent. I don't know why Sam didn't tell me he'd met you.''

Emmet stared at her, feeling an odd catch in his chest. ''I don't know why he didn't tell me he had such a lovely mother.''

Cecily's eyes met his and her pale skin flushed a delicate shade of pink. She smiled. ''If you want another cup of coffee, you could just ask. You don't have to flatter me.'' She looked away and then looked back, her smile taking on a shy edge that he found wholly charming. ''If you'd like, you're welcome to stay to lunch. Perhaps Sam will call while you're here.''

"I'd like that. I would like to know that Babs is safe."

She reached across the table and touched his hand gently. "Sam will take good care of her. Try not to worry. He won't let anything happen to her."

Emmet turned his hand, clasping her fingers lightly, feeling a soothing warmth extend from the casual touch. "I hope you're right."

"I am. Just you wait and see. They're probably both safe and warm in a nice hotel somewhere while Sam decides what to do about your family. I bet they've ordered a nice hot lunch. You'll see. Sam will take good care of your niece."

Chapter Seven

"This is, quite possibly, the most miserable excuse for a vehicle I have ever seen in my entire life." Babs was more resigned than angry and Sam threw her a quick smile.

"You've just never ridden in the back of a truck before. Actually, this isn't bad at all."

"Have you made a habit of hitching rides in the backs of moving vans?"

"No. But I've done it once or twice and this one isn't bad. Look, we've got all the luxuries of home. Blankets, windows, a roof to keep off the rain and I've even got some food. I picked up a few things this morning while you were shopping, not to mention the biscuits I took from the café."

"Don't mention them. Please." The dim light was enough to show him that she looked a little green around the edges, and he gave her a sympathetic grin.

"You'll get used to it. It's like sailing. It just takes a few minutes to get your sea legs."

She threw him a sour look. "I'm a lousy sailor."

"Come on. Sit down and lean your head back. If you talk to me real nice, I'll give you a bottle of Perrier. That'll help settle your stomach."

"Don't even say the word stomach." But she let him settle her onto a stack of furniture pads and leaned her head against a higher stack. Sam dug around in his pack, coming up with a familiar green bottle. He pried off the lid and handed it to her. It was still cool and she had to admit that the dry, fizzy taste of it felt good in her stomach.

She leaned back, feeling the queasiness subside. Looking around, she was struck by the humor of the situation. She giggled and Sam looked at her, one black brow raised in question. She raised the bottle in a mocking salute.

"This is probably the first time in the history of the company that Perrier has been consumed in the back of a moving van by two people who are on the run from they don't even know what. Perhaps I should write the company. They might want us to endorse it."

"I don't know. I have a feeling this isn't quite the image they're going for. I can't see yuppies responding to this picture."

"I disagree. I think it has a certain charm. I'd have to have my hair done, of course." She reached up, pulled one side of her hair back and looked haughty. "How's that?"

Sam nodded, his expression solemn. "I think I see it now. Yes, you're right, this is definitely the image they need."

She let her hair fall, her laughter clear and ringing in the hollow confines of the van. "You know, I have to admit, you do know how to show a girl a good time. I haven't known a dull moment since we met."

"I could say the same about you. You started out by trying to shove me off a balcony and then I got shot at, spent the day in a cave, was attacked in the woods, got a bullet in my truck, was beat up in a parking lot and had to pick a lock to get in here. Yes, I would have to say life hasn't been dull with you around.''

"Are all your cases this exciting?"

He winced. "Don't call them cases. I told you, I'm not a detective. I just find things for people. And no, they're not all this exciting. Usually I manage to avoid getting shot at. Sometimes I don't even get beat up.''

"Sounds like a dull life.'' She took another swallow and handed him the bottle, unaware of the unconscious intimacy of the gesture. Sam looked at her and then lifted the bottle to his mouth, taking a drink. He grimaced and handed it back to her.

"That stuff always tastes like Alka-seltzer.''

"Why did you buy it if you don't like it?''

"Because I figured you would like it.''

"Because I'm rich?'' She grinned. "Your prejudices are showing. Actually, I have even been known to drink tap water.''

"No!'' Sam's voice expressed complete disbelief as he dug around in the pack and pulled out a can of Coke.

"Really. You know, growing up rich isn't quite like most people think. I bet you think it was terrific.''

"I suspect it had its ups and downs.'' He held the Coke at arm's length and popped the top. It foamed up and ran down the sides of the can, dripping onto the dusty floor.

"More downs than ups, I think.''

She drew her knees up to her chest, her body swaying with the movements of the truck.

"I used to wish I'd been born without any money.''

"Believe me, that has its ups and downs, too.''

"I suppose. But it would have been nice to have had a nice normal family with a mother and father and maybe a brother or sister. Someone to talk to. You know, just like *The Brady Bunch* or *Eight Is Enough* or one of those shows.'' She shook her head and drank the last of the Perrier, tucking the bottle into a fold in the moving pads.

"I guess real life is never that neat and tidy."

Sam took a sip of Coke, watching her, seeing a loneliness that made him want to comfort her. "It must have been really tough losing your parents like that."

"It was. I was with them, you know."

"No, I didn't know."

"I was in the backseat asleep. I don't remember the crash, of course. I just remember waking up all of a sudden and knowing something was terribly wrong. The whole front of the car was destroyed. The roof had been crushed and I was trapped on the floor of the back. I kept calling my parents. They didn't answer and I think I knew they weren't going to answer ever again."

She wrapped her arms around her knees, hugging them against her chest, her face still. "I screamed and screamed and screamed. Actually, it's pretty funny because the only real injury I had was my vocal cords. I strained them. That's why my voice is so raspy. They said it was a miracle that I was alive but I didn't feel very miraculous. It took me years to get over the guilt that they'd died and I hadn't."

Sam stared at her, the soda forgotten in his hand. He wondered how many people had ever seen through the tough exterior to the frightened little girl beneath. He had the feeling not many people had bothered to look. It shamed him to think that he, too, hadn't really looked below the surface of the "spoiled brat."

"I think it's natural to feel guilty when someone you love dies. It must be a lot harder when you're a child."

The words sounded shallow. He wanted to say something that would ease her pain forever but that wasn't possible.

"Yeah. Well, I got over it eventually. I'm afraid I wasn't a very attractive child, though. I used to throw the most awful screaming fits. When I think about it, I almost feel sorry for Aunt Dodie. My cousin Lance was a sneaky little weasel but, on the surface at least, he was a perfect child. I don't think Dodie knew what to do with me."

"What did she do?"

"Ignored me, usually. If she had company, she'd shut me in my room until I stopped screaming and then she'd come in and explain how that simply was not 'acceptable behavior for a Malone.'" Babs laughed. "I'm afraid I've been a terrible failure in her eyes. I never have learned how to be a Malone."

There was a sharp pop and Sam realized that his fist had been gradually tightening around the can he held. Now one side bent sharply inward. He stared at the can, counting slowly to ten and then to twenty. In those few light words, he saw a frightened, lonely child—her world in pieces around her—and an emotionless woman who couldn't be bothered to give her any of the love she was crying out for. If he'd disliked Dodie Davis before, he conceived a positive hate for her in that moment.

"So, what was your childhood like? How did you get into running a lost and found department?"

He glanced up, hoping the light was dim enough to conceal the rage he knew must be in his eyes. Babs was still sitting with her chin resting on top of her updrawn knees, her hair framing her face in heavy waves. She looked like a pixie, her delicate features shadowy.

Sam shrugged. "Not much to tell. I had a disgustingly

normal childhood. My parents created a home right out of *Leave it to Beaver*. My mom is a born homemaker in the truest sense of the word. I went to school, got a degree in history and discovered that there isn't a whole lot you can do with a history degree but teach. I didn't want to teach so I had a variety of odd jobs for a while. Gradually, I got into finding things for people.''

"Seems an odd thing to do—find things for people. How do they find you? An ad in the Yellow Pages?''

"Word of mouth, mostly. They know someone who knows someone who knows me. Sometimes I find them. People put ads in the classifieds when they're looking for someone or something.''

"How do you go about finding things? How did you find me?''

He shrugged, uneasy with the topic. "Luck, I guess.''

"Luck? It seems like it's got to be more than luck for you to stumble over that old hotel like that. I mean, there are a million places they could have taken me. How did you know it was that one?''

Sam took a swallow of his drink, stalling for time, wishing he could find a way to avoid the question. But, looking into Babs's bright, curious gaze, he knew there would be no avoiding it.

"I look at a map and sort of get a feeling.'' He said it casually, as if it were the most normal thing in the world.

She stared at him, her eyes intent in the dim light. "You looked at a map and figured out where I was?''

"Well, not exactly. I got a feeling of where you were but that only pinned it down within a couple of hundred miles. Then I came up here and drove around. I remembered your uncle mentioning the hotel and it seemed like a good place to take an heiress if you were going to kidnap one. Pretty simple, really.''

"Simple? I don't think so.'' She stared at him, fascinated, and Sam shifted, looking around for a distraction. Unfortunately, in the back of an empty moving van, distractions were not easy to come by.

"You're psychic.''

Sam winced at the pleased announcement. He usually didn't have to explain how he'd gone about finding something. Most clients were simply delighted to have their property back and they didn't care how he'd gone about getting it. On the rare occasion when someone did ask, he usually managed to mutter enough mumbo jumbo so they thought they knew how he'd done it, even if they couldn't have explained it. Babs's reaction was precisely the reason he avoided talking about his methods.

"I'm not psychic. I just have a knack for finding things.''

"Sure. You looked at a map and knew within a hundred miles or so where they'd taken me. The police obviously didn't know it. That's more than a knack. You're psychic.''

"No.''

"Yes.''

"No.''

They stared at each other for a moment and then Babs shrugged. "Have it your way. You can call it anything you want but you and I both know it's true.''

Sam drained his Coke and crumpled the can with a satisfying crunch. "You're like arguing with a mud fence.''

"I'm afraid I've never argued with a mud fence. Are they always right, too?'' Babs looked at him, her face the very picture of polite inquiry. Reluctantly, Sam laughed.

"No, they're just very stubborn. And they don't change their minds."

"I'm perfectly willing to change my mind when I'm wrong. But I'm not wrong this time."

"Psychic is not a word I'm comfortable with. I have a knack—a gift, if you want to get maudlin about it. Some people know when it's going to rain—I know where lost things are. It's not a big deal."

"It must be neat to find things that people thought they'd never get back."

"I suppose that's one reason why I keep doing it instead of getting a real job. There's nothing like handing some little kid his lost dog and watching his face light up." He grinned. "Of course, the pay on that kind of job tends to be a little chancy. Jawbreakers and marbles don't pay the rent. But every once in a while someone asks me to find a stolen car or some lost jewelry and I charge a hefty fee for those jobs."

"Am I the first person you've found?"

"No, I've located a couple of runaways and once I found a little boy who'd gotten lost."

"I bet his parents were thrilled to get him back."

"They were pretty happy."

"Must be nice to have someone who's happy to see you come home safe and sound." The wistfulness in her voice captured his emotions, reminding him that no one seemed to care whether or not she came back.

"I bet Emmet is worried sick about you." It was a weak offering, since for all he knew Emmet didn't even know Babs was missing. But he couldn't stand the loneliness in her eyes.

"If he knows about it. He's out of the country quite a bit, you know."

"Well, you must have friends who are worried about you. A boyfriend?" Funny, how unpalatable that thought was.

Babs shrugged. "No one close. People always talk about money opening doors but it closes quite a few, too. You never know whether someone likes you for yourself or for your money. Usually it's the money. You certainly wouldn't have come looking for me if there hadn't been a reward offered."

She said it without malice but Sam winced anyway. He wanted to tell her that he would have looked for her anyway, but it would have been a lie. He'd been motivated by the money. Just like everyone else she knew.

"What about the people you work with? You must have friends there. Or don't you work?" He arched one brow, challengingly, wanting to shift the tone of the conversation.

Babs wrinkled her nose, acknowledging the challenge. "Wouldn't you just love to find out that I'm like the lilies of the field—I toil not and neither do I spin."

Sam grinned. "Only if the shoe fits."

"Well, it does and it doesn't. I don't work a nine-to-five job. It would be a little silly to pretend I needed to. I do quite a bit of volunteer work, though."

"Arranging flowers at the hospital."

"Sometimes. I also spent two months in Ethiopia working with famine victims. I've done quite a bit of work with the Red Cross in different parts of the world. It sounds pompous, I suppose, but I kind of feel that when you've got as much money as my family does, you should do a little something to help other people with it."

"You could donate money. No one would expect you to get involved personally."

She shrugged uneasily. "I guess. It's more satisfying, though, when you can feel like you actually made a difference personally."

Sam watched her, trying to imagine her in dirty khakis giving aid to victims of disaster. It wasn't as hard as he thought it would be. He was discovering that there were several sides to Ms. Babette Malone. It was a discovery he didn't entirely welcome.

"I'm starving. What have we got to eat?" Babs's question put an end to the uncomfortable conversation— uncomfortable for both of them.

Isolated in the back of the moving truck, they might have been the only two people in the world. There was no one else to talk to, nothing else to do. It created an odd feeling of intimacy, a closeness that made them feel as if they'd known each other for years rather than a few short days.

"Looks like it's getting dark."

Sam glanced up at the windows. The light had been fading so gradually, he hadn't really been aware of it. Babs's comment made him realize that it was getting difficult to see inside their moving hideaway.

"We'd better figure out where we're going to sleep tonight. Looks like our friend plans on driving straight through."

"Well, he stopped long enough for lunch," Babs grumbled.

Sam grinned, remembering her exasperation when he'd refused to let her leave the truck except for a quick trip to a service station rest room. He didn't want to risk their being left behind—not when he was running out of money. As it turned out, they'd have had plenty of time to get a meal but there'd been no way of knowing that. So they'd sat in the back of the truck, which was growing uncomfortably warm, and waited for their unwitting host to return.

"The poor guy had to eat."

"Considering how long he took, he must have eaten enough to feed an army."

"He's a big guy."

Whatever Babs might have said was lost in a series of sneezes. The truck hit a bump, throwing her off balance and Sam caught her arm, holding her steady until the fit eased. It was the second time in the last hour that she'd had a sneezing fit.

"Are you catching a cold?" He reached out to put his hand on her forehead but she pulled away.

"It's just the dust in this truck. I think I'm allergic to packing blankets."

Sam didn't insist on checking for fever. He wasn't sure he'd be able to tell anything anyway. Their close confines had done nothing to cool the ache that had begun with last night's kiss. He gathered a stack of packing blankets and spread them out in a makeshift bed, trying not to think about spending yet another night sleeping with Babs only inches away.

She wasn't his type. He kept telling himself that but it didn't seem to help. Somehow, over the course of the last few days, his type seemed to have changed. Big brown eyes and a slim little frame were beginning to look more and more appealing.

It didn't matter how many times he reminded himself that it was just their proximity—or the differences in their life-styles. He tried remembering his first impressions of her as a spoiled rich brat, but now what he saw was a frightened woman who'd been willing to risk her neck to try to escape.

He thumped the packing blankets with unnecessary vigor, too aware of Babs just a few feet away. He wanted her. He allowed the thought in. He wanted her. In fact, he ached with the wanting. But that didn't mean he was going to do anything about it. Not only was it bad policy to get involved with a client, it wasn't smart to get involved with a woman who was rich enough to make Fort Knox look like a coin collection. Besides, she was too vulnerable, too dependent on him. Only a scoundrel would put the moves on a woman in her position.

He poked his foot into the stack of blankets. Too bad he was such a nice guy. Scoundrels had all the fun.

He turned, forcing what he hoped was a normal smile. Whatever he'd planned to say was forgotten when the truck hit a deep rut. Babs stumbled and Sam reached out, catching her close, bracing his feet apart to take her weight.

She was such a lightweight against him. Sam shifted his hold to her waist, intending to set her away. Somehow, his hands lingered, feeling the warmth of her skin through her shirt. Babs tilted her head back, looking up at him. The light had almost disappeared, replaced by the occasional flash of brilliance as they passed a street lamp. In the darkness, her eyes were deep, mysterious pools full of secrets and promises. Her mouth was soft, inviting. An invitation he couldn't quite resist.

Her mouth felt as soft as it looked. Her hands quivered against his chest but he could only guess at the emotions that caused it. It was a monumental effort to stop with a simple kiss. He wanted more, so much more. His mouth drew away from hers reluctantly and he stared down into her eyes.

Now was the time to make some light remark, some casual comment that would ease the tension. He'd say something witty and urbane and they'd both be reassured that a kiss was nothing much these days, nothing much at all.

He opened his mouth—and the truck hit another rut. This one felt as if the left side wheels had just fallen into the San Andreas Fault line. Sam's hold tightened on Babs and he heard her soft gasp as his feet shot out from under him and they tumbled onto the thick mound of blankets he'd so carefully stacked.

Babs landed on top of him, her slight weight pressed along his body. In a passing flash of light, Sam saw her eyes, wide and startled. All thoughts of casual comments slid from his mind. She felt so right against him, so dangerously, wonderfully right.

His hand slid up her back, his eyes never leaving hers. He held his breath, waiting for her to object, knowing he'd die if she didn't want him as much as he wanted her. His hand clasped the back of her neck, her hair sliding like watered silk over his fingers.

Babs quivered and he paused, trying to read her expression in the light of passing street lamps. But he didn't need to see her face. Her hands moved up his chest to rest on his shoulders and it didn't take any urging from him to bring her face down to his.

This kiss was different from others they'd shared. This time the passion was in the open. He wasn't offering her comfort or companionship. He was offering pure masculine need, a hunger for her. Her breath left her on a sigh as his lips opened, his tongue sliding between her teeth to stroke sensuously over hers.

Sam kept one hand at the back of her head and slid the other down her back to her hips, pressing her closer, letting her feel the pressure of his need. She tensed for a moment, as if half-frightened, and then her body went limp against him, her mouth softening magically. Sam felt her total acceptance sweep over him, blowing the flame of his need even higher.

He groaned low in his throat and rolled so that she was beneath him, pinning her to the thick padding, making her his willing prisoner. Her fingers slid through his hair, pulling him even closer, her body arching into his.

"I've wanted you forever." The words breathed out against her cheek as he moved to taste the delicate shell of her ear.

"You've only known me a few days."

"Forever. I've known you forever." Sam's fingers slid open the buttons on her shirt, tugging the fabric loose from her jeans and spreading it beneath her. His mouth slid down her neck, tasting the frantic pulse that beat in the hollow at the base of her throat. Babs gasped as his hand slipped inside the lace of her bra, cupping her breast, his thumb teasing a dusky nipple to life.

She went rigid when his mouth replaced his hand. Sam hesitated but she seemed to be holding her breath, waiting. His tongue flicked out, stroking around her nipple, dampening it before his mouth closed around her, suckling gently. She arched, her hands drawing him closer, telling him without words just how she felt. He clasped her waist, feeling the satin of her skin, warm beneath his hands—warm and supple. He wanted to feel that skin against his, wanted to feel every inch of her.

Babs mumbled a protest when he drew away from her but he was already pulling her with him, tugging the opened shirt off and tossing it aside. Her bra followed but when he reached for the snap of her jeans, she stopped him, her hands reaching for his shirt. The message was clear.

He grinned and held his arms out to his sides. Babs concentrated on his shirt, sliding each button loose, baring his chest by inches. The feel of her fingers brushing so lightly against him, the scent of her hair, everything about her combined into a haunting image that Sam knew he'd never forget. Never.

The shirt was open at last and she slid her hands inside, tilting her head back to look at him as her palm settled over his heart, feeling the strong beat of his pulse. Sam reached out to cup her face, staring into her eyes, wishing he could read her expression more clearly, half-afraid of what he might see there.

He kissed her, a long drugging kiss that left them both breathless and aching for more. His hands fumbled with the snap of her jeans, feeling the silky skin of her stomach jump beneath his touch. He slid his hands inside, cupping her buttocks, drawing her onto her knees facing him.

A street lamp flashed by illuminating them in a stroke of white light. Two figures, one slim with pale skin a soft contrast to the harder, darker planes of her companion. Her lover. She leaned closer, her hands linking around his neck, her breasts brushing against the dark hair on his chest. Sam groaned. His knees were braced apart to compensate for the sway of the truck; he drew her against him, cradling her between his thighs, tantalizingly close and yet apart.

Her head fell back, an invitation that was impossible to resist. His teeth nipped the taut cord of her neck, tasted the incredibly soft skin of her shoulder and then found the gentle weight of her breast. Babs whimpered, a quiet sound in the back of her throat. Her hands opened and closed on the hard muscles of his shoulders, telling him without words just what his mouth was doing to her.

He eased her back, sliding the jeans down, his hands shaking as he stripped the last of their clothes away. He lay next to her, his thigh pinning her hips, his mouth catching her soft gasp of pleasure as their bodies touched.

Sam kissed and stroked her, his hands exploring her body, learning it through touch, reining in his burning need, feeling her skin grow hot beneath his hands. Her legs shifted beneath his, her body arching in an age-old invitation. It was more than Sam could resist.

He shifted, lifting himself above her, settling between her thighs. A light flashed by, giving him a glimpse of her. Her eyes were wide in her flushed face, glittering with a need that she only half-understood.

He pressed into her, hearing her startled gasp as she felt the weight of him. He eased forward, giving her time to adjust. His body screamed with the need to bury himself inside, to take what was so clearly his alone.

He felt his arms tremble as the softness of her belly met the tight muscles of his. Never had he felt so complete, so whole. Babs lay still beneath him but he could feel the tension that quivered through her, the trembling need for something she didn't understand.

He began to move, grinding his teeth together, drawing on every bit of control he'd ever possessed. She gasped, her fingers digging into his waist. Hesitantly, she echoed his movements and Sam thought he'd surely explode. He picked up the pace, feeling her tremble beneath him. She whimpered, her movements becoming more frantic.

He felt her fear as the tension spiraled higher, felt her

trying to draw away, frightened by the precipice that loomed ahead.

"It's okay, baby. Let it go." He whispered the words, his voice hoarse.

"I can't. I can't." Her words reflected her growing panic.

"I've got you." She shook her head, her body quivering on the brink of something that would surely tear her apart.

"No."

"Yes." He reached beneath her, his palm spanning her buttocks, drawing her upward, letting her feel his demand. His insistence.

The movement left her no choice. She arched, her eyes wide with startled wonder as his movements threw her into the vortex she'd so feared. She spun into a million pieces, only the weight of Sam's perspiration-slick body keeping her from dissolving completely. Her nails bit into his back, seeking something to cling to in a world suddenly, deliciously mad.

She heard his groan and felt the heavy pulse of him as he joined her in the whirling pleasure. For an instant the pleasure was so intense it frightened her, but Sam held her close and she knew he'd never let her get lost.

The slide from the peak was long and slow. Sam stroked her trembling body, dropping kisses across her flushed face, murmuring soft words of praise. He made her feel warm and loved, a feeling she'd known all too little of in her life.

She yawned, feeling exhaustion slip over her like a heavy blanket. She struggled with it, trying to keep her eyes open. There were things that needed to be said. But Sam kissed her eyes shut, the rough brush of his cheek soothing and homey.

She yawned again, vaguely aware that Sam was pulling a blanket over them. He held her close, settling her more comfortably against his shoulder. In all her life, Babs had never felt safer nor more loved.

She slid into sleep on the thought that nothing would ever be the same again. Nothing.

Chapter Eight

When Babs awoke the first thing she noticed was that the truck was no longer moving. The second thing she realized was that she was alone. Not only in the make-shift bed but in the truck. Sam was gone.

She sat up, feeling a surge of panic which was quickly followed by a rush of relief. She wouldn't have to face him. At least not yet. She'd have some time to pull herself together, if that were possible. Last night had been shattering in more ways than one.

Babs rested her face on her updrawn knees, drawing in a deep breath and releasing it slowly. Never in her life had she let someone get so close, so quickly. It wasn't just the physical aspect of it that had shaken her, though God knows that had been enough to rock anyone. It was the emotional closeness that had her shaking.

Never before had she opened herself up like that, let herself be so vulnerable. She'd learned early in life that it didn't pay to be vulnerable. It had been a hard lesson but she'd learned it and lived by it. And now, in the space of a few short days, she'd let so many barriers crumble. She'd let Sam through the protective walls she'd built over the years. She'd let him waltz right into her life with barely a token resistance.

Babs lifted her head and looked around the dim interior. Her entire world felt tilted, shifted somehow and she couldn't quite see the new patterns. With a muffled sob, she reached for the stack of clothes that Sam must have gathered for her. Her face flushed as she remembered the night before. They certainly hadn't bothered with folding anything. Sam had obviously been up for quite a while. Long enough to dress and leave. It had been nice of him to fold her clothes and put them near the makeshift bed but Babs didn't feel gratitude. It made her uneasy to know that he'd been up and about while she was sleeping. He'd probably looked at her. What had he been thinking?

Her fingers knotted in the sturdy fabric of the jeans, her eyes panicky. It was too much, too soon. She didn't want him so close. She didn't want to let anyone that close. It opened the way for too much pain.

Babs stood up and began dressing, her movements uncoordinated as she struggled into the jeans and blouse. Forgotten was the foolish pleasure she'd felt from buying the simple garments. All she wanted now was to cover herself and get out of the truck. She paused, her fingers shaking on the buttons of her shirt. The truck seemed to be spinning around her and she closed her eyes, breathing deeply. After a while, the feeling passed and she finished dressing.

She listened for Sam's return, wondering what she was going to say, wondering what he was going to say, wondering if she should just leave and make her own way home. At the moment, her fear of the kidnappers ran a poor second behind her dread of seeing Sam again.

There wasn't a chance to find out if she really would have left without Sam because he returned just as she finished dragging her fingers through her hair. Babs spun around as he pulled open the door, flooding the truck with light. Her stomach clenched with tension. She was only marginally relieved to see that it was Sam who jumped into the truck and not an irate owner who'd want to know what she was doing there.

"Good. You're up." He strode across the truck and Babs could only stand there and watch him approach, every nerve in her body quivering. She felt stripped of her defenses, open and achingly vulnerable. She didn't move as he stopped in front of her, cupping his hand around her cheek and tilting her face up for a slow, sweet kiss.

Babs blinked at him as he drew back and looked at her for a moment, as if sensing something was different but unable to put his finger on the source. She dragged her eyes away, afraid that he could read her feelings in her eyes. Lurking behind her uneasiness was a niggling anger. She didn't like feeling this way. She didn't want to feel helpless and vulnerable. It was her fault. All of it. And she resented it.

If Sam wondered about the difference in her, there wasn't time to question it. He bent to pick up his pack. "I hate to rush you, but good old Frank is going to be back any minute and we need to be out of here before he drives off."

"Are we in Sacramento?"

"Nope." Sam jumped off the truck and turned back, lifting his hands. Babs hesitated a moment, uneasy at the thought of him touching her but then she saw the question starting in his eyes. She leaned down, letting him clasp her waist and lift her out of the truck. Right now she couldn't bear questions. Not from him. She had too many of her own that she couldn't answer.

It felt strange to be standing on solid ground again.

She squinted into the weak sunshine, looking around. There wasn't much to see. A stretch of highway was about it. To their left was a sprawl of white buildings and a sign that announced "Truck Stop" in fire-engine-red letters.

"Where are we?"

"A truck stop about ten miles from an old place that my father used to own. We sold it five years ago when he died but I bet it's still there and I'm betting that it's empty." He was leading her away from the truck as he spoke, turning the corner of a building and stopping in its shadow.

"So why are we getting out here? Why don't we go all the way to Sacramento with 'good old Frank'?"

"Because this is perfect. We need someplace where we can sit and think for a little while. I'd like to try to track down Emmet. We need to figure out who might want you dead. My dad's old place will be perfect. It's a farmhouse out in the middle of nowhere. The people who bought it figured property prices were going to skyrocket but they haven't, so it's not likely they've done anything with the place. We can stay there for a while until we figure out what our next move is."

He reached for her hand again but Babs tugged it away, digging in her heels. "Wait a minute."

Sam turned to look at her, too caught up in his plans to notice the stubborn angle of her chin. "What?"

"I think we should discuss this."

"Discuss what?"

"Whether or not this is the best thing to do."

"Of course it's the best thing. What else are we going to do?"

"Just because you thought of it doesn't mean it's the best thing. Who elected you Great White Leader? I think

I should be consulted. After all, it's me someone seems to be trying to kill.''

Sam looked at her, his jaw dropping slightly. He wasn't sure what he'd expected after last night but it certainly wasn't a return to the near hostility that had marked the beginning of their relationship. Anger followed too quickly on the heels of astonishment. Babs wasn't the only one dealing with uncertainties.

''Well, excuse me. If you have a better idea, I'd be delighted to hear it.'' He folded his arms over his chest and looked at her, his expression insultingly polite.

Babs glared at him for a moment and then looked around. He made her feel so damned stupid and it didn't help to know that she was being unreasonable. She knew it but couldn't stop herself.

''Why don't we go into Sacramento with Frank and then find someplace to stay there?''

''Well, the first problem with that idea is that 'good old Frank' pulled out about two minutes ago. The second problem is that we're running out of money. We can't afford to pay hotel bills.''

''All right, why don't we go to the nearest town and I'll wire for some money or for someone to pick us up or something?''

''We've been over that before. We don't know who's trying to kill you. I don't think it's such a hot idea to announce your location to the world. I think we should stay out of sight until we can get hold of Emmet. He's in a position to know what your family is up to.''

''What if we can't get hold of Uncle Emmet? Are we just going to hang out in some godforsaken old house waiting? If he's out of the country, it could be months before he gets back.''

"If we don't get hold of him in a reasonable amount of time, then we'll come up with something else."

"And I suppose *you'll* decide what's a reasonable amount of time."

A muscle in Sam's jaw twitched but his tone was level. "We'll take a vote on it. Now, can we get started? Ten miles is a hefty chunk of ground to cover, especially for someone who's accustomed to traveling in a limousine."

"I'm perfectly capable of walking any distance you care to name."

"Good. Then let's get started."

Babs glared at him, seeking some flaw in his reasoning and finding none. The knowledge only added to her irritation.

"Do you think we could take time to eat something before we start this great trek of yours?"

Sam's eyes glittered bright blue, his irritation rising to meet hers. "Fine. Just remember that our funds are limited."

"I'll try to restrain the urge to order lobster." She bent down and snatched up the small bag that held her clothes and then stalked into the restaurant. Sam grabbed his pack and followed her. Watching the swing of her narrow hips, he was torn between the urge to walk away from Babs Malone and the money, and the urge to find a place to lay her out flat on her back and make thorough love to her. Damn the woman. Just when he thought he had her all figured out, she threw him another curve.

The interior of the restaurant was as simple and unpretentious as the exterior. Scuffed linoleum flooring that had probably started out white was now a vaguely gray shade. Red vinyl booths were set in neat little rows along the windows. There was a low counter with backless stools set on stainless-steel pedestals in the floor. Behind the counter, the cook was visible—a thin, cadaverous man who was a poor advertisement for his own cooking. Waylon Jennings moaned about lost loves from the jukebox in the corner.

It was late enough in the morning that the heaviest breakfast crowd was gone and it was too early for the lunch crowd. There were still half a dozen men seated at the booths. Sam noticed the way the conversation stopped when they came in. All eyes turned to them, assessing and curious.

Babs seemed oblivious of the attention they were drawing, or maybe she was accustomed to drawing attention. The Malone heiress was probably a conversation stopper in more than one place. She sat down at the counter and Sam couldn't help but notice the way her jeans outlined the sweet curves of her hips. Unfortunately, so did every other man in the place. He was conscious of an urge to drag her out of the restaurant. It surprised him. Possessiveness wasn't his style. But then, none of this absurd adventure was his style.

He sat down next to Babs, dropping his pack at his feet and reaching for a menu. The waitress came over and poured them coffee without asking whether or not they wanted it. Apparently, in this place, there was no question about it. Sam sipped the coffee. It seemed strong enough to etch his teeth but it was hot. Babs took one swallow and then reached for the cream and sugar and Sam hid a grin. She was probably accustomed to fresh ground, drip brewed. This stuff tasted more like it had been boiled, maybe with a few old tires to add body to it.

They gave their orders to the waitress who popped her gum and looked bored. Clearly she'd seen it all. After she left, they stared at the counter, not looking at one another. So much lay unspoken between them that it seemed safer to say nothing.

The door opened with a jangle of the bell. Sam glanced over his shoulder. Caution was an old habit, one he didn't intend to break now. His eyes narrowed. The two men who'd come in looked like they hadn't had a bath in weeks, unless they'd bathed in alcohol. They stood in the doorway, weaving slightly, their bloodshot eyes roaming over the bar. Sam turned back toward the front, jabbing an elbow into Babs's ribs.

She turned to look at him, her eyes ready to fight but he forestalled her angry protest. "Just keep your eyes in front of you."

"I was just looking at them."

"Well, don't. We don't want any trouble."

"You were looking at them."

"But I'm not looking at them now, am I?" He smiled sweetly as he looked into her annoyed eyes. "In case you haven't noticed, you're the only young, moderately attractive female in the place."

"So?" Babs glared at him, put out by the "moderately."

"So, I don't want any trouble. Just keep your eyes in front of you and pretend you're deaf, dumb and blind. Do you think you can manage that?"

Her angry reply was forestalled by a gravelly voice that boomed out just behind her.

"Hello, sugar. Were you waiting for old Luke and me?"

Babs started to turn, her eyes glittering but then she caught Sam's warning gaze and stopped. She might not like it but she had to admit that maybe he knew best in this situation.

The speaker seated himself on the stool next to her, leaning one elbow on the counter. "My name is George and this here is my partner, Luke. We just come clean across the country and you're about the prettiest thing we've seen. Ain't that right, Luke?" Luke nodded.

Sam smiled, leaning forward so that his eyes met George's across Babs's rigid figure. "My lady and I have things to discuss, if you don't mind."

"Heck, we don't mind at all, do we, Luke? But this here is the prettiest thing we've seen." He grinned, displaying a broken front tooth. Sam could smell the cheap whiskey on his breath. George met the chill blue of Sam's eyes and caution seemed to move sluggishly in his pickled brain. He sat back on his stool, giving Babs a little breathing room.

Sam could feel the tension in her leg where it was pressed against his and he wanted to reassure her but now was not the time. With luck, they could eat their breakfast and get out of here without any trouble. The last thing he wanted to do was draw attention.

George sank into a sullen stupor next to Babs and Sam was hoping he'd pass out. Beyond him, his friend Luke seemed comatose. It looked as if everything was going to be all right until the song on the jukebox changed to a fast-paced tune. Dolly Parton's clear voice rang out over the quick rhythms. The music seemed to have the same effect on George that electricity had on Frankenstein's monster. He jerked upright and jabbed an elbow into Luke's ribs. Luke sat up with a startled yelp.

"Dancin' music. That's dancin' music." Sam knew what was coming even before George continued. George reached for Babs's hand. "Let's dance, darlin'."

Babs couldn't have looked more appalled if he'd been an armadillo. Sam couldn't blame her. She jerked her hand away, her expression of contempt getting through even George's alcohol-soaked senses.

"Keep your hands off of me." Even in the midst of what was rapidly becoming a crisis, Sam had to admire the aristocratic sneer in her tone. It took years of practice to be able to sneer that perfectly.

"What'sa matter? You think you're too good for us?" George's slurred voice was taking on belligerent overtones.

Babs looked him up and down and then arched her brows, her upper lip quivering ever so slightly.

"Precisely."

It was perfect. Sam could see Katharine Hepburn looking at a scruffy Humphrey Bogart, Norma Shearer sneering at Clark Gable, Maureen O'Hara and John Wayne. He could also see himself in the midst of a fight.

"Why, you little bitch. You're not such hot stuff." George reached for her arm again and Babs jerked away from him, unconsciously leaning toward Sam. Sam stood up, reaching around Babs, his hand closing over George's wrist.

"Look, my lady and I don't want any trouble. Why don't you just go find a booth and have something to eat?"

But George was not to be placated. He might be drunk but he knew when he'd been insulted and he wasn't going to take that lying down.

"Why don't you go—" Just what he thought Sam ought to do was left unspoken. He swung clumsily, missing Sam by a mile. With a muttered curse, Sam grabbed Babs around the waist, swinging her off the stool and out of the line of fire.

"Stay out of the way." He threw the order at her before turning back just in time to catch George's second punch on the edge of his jaw. The force of the blow sent him back a step but he blocked the next punch with his left arm, stepping into it and burying his fist in George's soft belly. His opponent's breath gusted out. Sam didn't give him time to recover before landing a hard right to the chin that brought George up on his toes. He rocked there for a moment, his eyes glazing over before he fell like a poleaxed ox, collapsing onto the worn linoleum.

Sam didn't have much of a chance to celebrate the quick victory. Luke had apparently come out of his stupor and decided that it was his duty as a friend to help George. Sam blocked his first punch, caught the second one on his cheek. Luke was apparently made of sterner stuff than his friend.

Babs backed out of the way of the struggling men, lifting one hand to press her fingers to her mouth. She'd seen a fight once before. Two cowhands on her uncle's ranch had gotten into a fight over a poker game. She remembered being sickened by the violence they'd displayed as they rolled in the dirt.

The violence of this sickened her, too, but added to that was a small, primitive thrill that she didn't want to admit to. Sam was fighting to protect her. He'd called her his "lady." Not that he had any business using such a possessive term toward her, of course, but there was no denying that he was involved in this fight because of her.

She winced as the two men crashed onto the counter, rolling over it and hitting the floor on the other side. None of the other patrons made a move to stop them. The waitress continued to chew her gum, not missing a pop. The only person who seemed disturbed by what was happening was the cook and no one was paying any attention to his shouted demands that they stop at once.

Someone should do something, Babs thought. Sam might get hurt. She skirted George's prone body and circled the counter, grabbing a pitcher of water on the way. Sam and Luke were still grappling, first one and then the other on top. Babs shut her eyes and threw the water in their general direction, hoping the chill would be enough to break them apart.

There was a startled curse and then dead silence. She cautiously opened one eye and then the other. Sam was glaring at her, his thick hair plastered to his head, his eyes shooting blue sparks. Beneath him, Luke lay prone, his eyes shut, unmoving.

"Did I drown him?" She whispered the question, afraid of the answer.

"No. But you damned near drowned me." He stood up, bracing himself against the counter, still glaring at her. "What the hell was that in aid of?"

Babs looked at him. Water dripped from his hair, soaking the shoulders of his shirt. Luke seemed to be completely dry. She shrugged and set down the water pitcher. "I was afraid you were going to get hurt."

"So you decided to see if I could breathe underwater?" He ran his fingers through his hair, grimacing at the water that dripped from it.

"I'm calling the police." The cook's words made Sam forget his irritation over his damp state. For people who didn't want to draw attention to themselves, they were doing a first-rate job. Looking around the restaurant, he knew there wasn't a man in the place who wouldn't be able to describe both himself and Babs in minute detail. That couldn't be helped but maybe he could prevent an even greater debacle.

"Look, I don't think the police are necessary."

"You may not but it wasn't your place that was torn

up. Look at all the broken dishes. Who's going to pay for those?''

Sam looked at the shattered plates. They'd cleared the counter when they went over it. He reached into his pocket.

''I'll pay for the damages. Would fifty do it, do you think?'' Greed lit the man's thin face.

''Dishes are expensive these days.''

''Okay, let's make it a hundred and call it even. Like I told them, my lady and I don't want any trouble.''

''You in trouble with the law?'' The man backed off a step, clearly wondering if he was in over his head.

Sam forced a friendly man-to-man smile. ''The only person we're in trouble with is the lady's husband. He doesn't like my cologne.''

The man's eyes shifted to Babs and she tried to look like a woman with a husband and a lover. She wasn't sure just what she should have looked like but she must have done all right because the man looked at Sam again.

''Make it a hundred and fifty and I could see my way clear to forgetting I ever saw you.''

Sam kept his smile in place, gritting his teeth together. ''I can give you one-twenty and that's it.'' And that would leave them with exactly ten dollars to their names.

The cook studied him for a moment and then nodded. ''You've got a deal.''

''Get our stuff together.'' Sam threw the order over his shoulder as he counted out the money, begrudging every bill. Still, it was worth it if it helped them avoid any more of a scene than they'd already created.

Babs gathered up his pack and her sack of clothes and was waiting for him when he came around the counter.

Every eye in the place followed them as they walked out the door.

Sam shrugged into his pack, wincing as his battered muscles protested. He was really getting too old for this kind of thing. Grown-ups did not get in brawls in truck-stop cafés. They had gone only a few yards when a voice called out behind them.

"Hey, mister." Sam tensed, turning slowly, wondering what could possibly go wrong now. It was the waitress and she was holding up a paper bag. Warily, Sam walked back to where she stood. Babs trailed behind him.

The woman popped her gum. "Cal really stuck it to you for the dishes. They ain't worth more'n five bucks. I figured the least you ought to get for your hundred and twenty was something to eat. It's just coffee and a few donuts but it's better than nothing."

"Thanks." Sam took the bag from her. His smile caused her to blink and forget to chew her gum for a moment. "I appreciate this."

"Sure. No problem." She dragged her gaze from him and looked at Babs. "You been through here before?"

Babs shook her head, unconsciously edging a little behind Sam. The woman shook her head. "Funny. I could've sworn I'd seen you before. I got a real good eye for faces."

Sam's smile tightened. Great. Just what they needed. A gum-chewing waitress with a heart of gold and a photographic memory. A perfect touch for a perfect day.

"Well, we've got to be going. Thanks again for the donuts."

"Sure. No problem."

Sam turned, keeping Babs in front of him, not giving the woman a chance to see her face again, though it was a little late for that. He kept the pace brisk as they left the truck stop and started down the road.

"Do you think she recognized me?" Babs's voice was breathless with the effort of keeping up with his long strides.

"I don't know. The way our luck has been running, she's probably related to one of the guys who kidnapped you. All I wanted was to go in, have a quiet meal and then leave. A simple enough thing to do. Why is it that nothing is ever simple around you?"

"Wait a minute." Babs grabbed his arm, pulling him to a halt. "You're not blaming me for that mess in there?"

"Well, it wasn't me they wanted to dance with."

"That wasn't my fault!" She glared up at him, shaking her hair back from her face.

"It sure as hell wasn't mine." He matched her glare for glare.

"That's a typical male attitude. Just because a couple of drunks can't control their libidos, I get blamed for it." She might have continued but a sneezing fit took hold of her and, by the time it was over, the argument seemed pointless.

"Here." Sam handed her a handkerchief and she took it from him with a mutter of thanks. Babs blew her nose and stuffed the handkerchief in her pocket before looking at him again.

"Have a cup of coffee and a donut."

"Thanks." Babs took the Styrofoam cup and sipped the scalding hot liquid. "Can we stop for breakfast later?"

"I've only got ten bucks left. We'll have to make do with the donuts. My dad always kept the old place stocked, though. Maybe the new owners have done the same.''

Sam watched her bite into a donut. Powdered sugar clung to her mouth and he had the urge to bend down and taste the sweetness on her skin. Babs glanced up, catching his eye and then looking away. If she could read his thoughts, her own were clearly quite different.

''I suppose you think it's my fault that we're broke. You're the one who paid a hundred and twenty dollars for those tacky plates.''

Sam drew back, only then aware that he'd been leaning toward her. He stared at her, exasperated. She was like dealing with a hedgehog.

''We'd better get going. We've got a long walk ahead of us.''

He pried the top off his coffee and took a hefty swallow of the steaming liquid. It burned all the way down but it didn't do much to chase away the knot in his stomach.

Damn the woman. The thought held more exasperation than anger. Last night she'd been soft and warm, a fantasy come to life. This morning, for no reason at all, she was back to the haughty brat who'd tried to push him off the balcony.

He stalked along the edge of the road, aware of her walking just a few feet behind him. In the intervals between cars, he could hear the crisp brush of her new jeans. She'd been so pleased with herself over those. He softened. Maybe her attitude wasn't so hard to understand after all. The last few days must have been a lot harder for her than they were for him. She'd been kidnapped, rescued, shot at, fought over and then found out that her own family wanted her out of the way—maybe permanently.

She'd been dependent on him for survival and he didn't think she was a woman who took kindly to being dependent on anyone. Guilt washed over him. She was vulnerable and alone and he'd taken advantage of that last night. He should never have touched her, never have made love to her.

But it hadn't felt like he was taking advantage. It had felt wonderfully right. They'd given and taken in equal measure. There'd been nothing one-sided about it. So why was it that he felt like a snake right now?

There was no answer to the question and Sam eventually stopped asking it. They turned off the highway less than a mile from the truck stop, turning onto a narrow, two-lane road that wound slightly upward toward the mountains that loomed in the distance. The weather, which had started out slightly gray and chilly, worsened rapidly. Within an hour of leaving the truck stop, rain started to fall in cold drizzly sheets. Sam cursed, casting a malevolent look at the clouds. He dropped back to where Babs trudged along, loosening his pack as he came level with her. She glanced at him and then looked away.

"Here, put this on." He held his jacket out to her.

She shrugged and kept walking. "I'm okay."

"I don't want you to take a chill."

"I told you, I'm okay."

He caught her arm, jerking her to a halt, his irritation climbing in direct proportion to the miserable weather. Babs turned, shaking back her damp hair to glare at him.

"Put on the damn coat." He bit off the words.

"I don't want the damn coat." She mimicked his clipped tone, her eyes snapping with annoyance.

Sam leaned down until his eyes were on a level with hers. The rain increased, soaking through his shirt, plastering his hair to his head. He ignored it. There was nothing in the world beyond this one incredibly stubborn, exasperatingly attractive woman.

"If you don't put it on willingly, I'll put it on you. It's cold and wet and getting colder and wetter by the minute. For once in your life, why don't you do what you're told without arguing about it."

Babs's jaw set. "It's your coat and you're getting just as cold and wet as I am. I don't see any reason why *I* should have the coat."

"Because I said so and I'm bigger than you are." He smiled, not the bone melting smile she'd seen over the past few days but a baring of teeth that threatened physical force. She didn't really believe he'd force her to wear the coat but something in his eyes made her decide that discretion was the better part of valor.

He took her sack of clothes from her and stuffed it into his pack while she shrugged into his coat. Babs would have died before admitting it, but the quilted jacket felt wonderfully warm. Sam zipped the front for her before she could get her hands free of the long sleeves and it felt too nice for her to protest that he was treating her like a child.

They continued walking, Sam a few feet ahead. He hunched his shoulders against the dampness. He glanced back a few times but Babs wasn't looking at him. Her attention seemed to be on the ground beneath her feet. Not that he knew what to say to her anyway.

A long sloping hill slowed their pace to a crawl but, once on top of it, Sam stopped, waiting until Babs caught up with him.

"There it is." He pointed to a little house about three hundred yards away. A narrow dirt lane meandered off the highway toward the building.

Sam stared at it. The entire day had been a disaster. From start to finish, nothing had gone right. He'd quarreled with Babs when it was the last thing he wanted to do. He'd been in a fight, paid a hundred and twenty dollars for a handful of cheap plates, gone without breakfast and walked for hours in the pouring rain. It was not his idea of a fun time. But the end of the road lay before them. Once inside, they'd be able to rest and decide what their next step had to be. The worst was over.

He turned to Babs and then forgot what he was going to say. She was looking in the direction of the house but her eyes were glazed, slightly unfocused. Her skin was the color of cement.

"Are you all right?" He was reaching for her as he asked the question. It was patently clear that she was not all right.

"I'm just fine." The snap in her voice might have been reassuring if it hadn't been followed by a funny little catch in her breathing. She looked at him, her eyes puzzled. Sam caught her as her knees buckled.

Chapter Nine

"Mr. Stefanoni will be with you in a moment."

"Thanks." Emmet watched as the plump housekeeper left the room. The room she'd left him in was large and airy, decorated in shades of gold with touches of brown—hardly what you'd expect to be the lair of a gangland boss. But then, Stefanoni wasn't your typical mobster. Born and raised in California, he'd gotten control of his empire by shrewd maneuvering. He wasn't above violence but he used it judiciously. So far the police hadn't been able to trace a single illegal act specifically to him. He was, on the surface, nothing more than a powerful businessman.

Emmet stared at a glass display case that was filled with Chinese jade, his hands linked behind his back, his thoughts on the man he was about to see. He hoped Stefanoni would be more interested in getting the real paintings than on getting revenge. As far as Emmet was concerned, Stefanoni was welcome to fit the entire family with cement boots and drop them in the Pacific. All of them except Babs. She was the only one of the bunch worth caring about. It was for her sake that he was here. Whether she liked the family or not, she felt an obligation to them. He'd do what he could to pull their fat out of the fire. For her sake.

The door opened behind him and he turned as Stefanoni stepped into the room. Emmet had seen pictures of the man, photos of him at charity balls or dedicating a hospital wing. Stefanoni's charitable contributions were one of the reasons it was so difficult for the police to get proof of his illegal activities. Too many people were grateful to the man. He looked bigger in the pictures. The man standing before him was below average height and slightly built. His face was narrow, ascetic. His dark eyes watched the world with cool cynicism. He looked more like he belonged in a monastery than in this luxurious house in Beverly Hills.

"Mr. Malone. Sorry to keep you waiting." The two men shook hands. Stefanoni's grip was cool and firm. "Would you like a drink?"

"No thanks."

"I've read your work. You've given me several hours of pleasure."

"Thank you." Emmet seated himself opposite his host, aware that they were skirting the real reason he was here. Apparently they had to get the polite preliminaries out of the way before they got down to business.

"What can I do for you, Mr. Malone? Somehow I don't think this is a social call and I doubt if you're researching a new novel."

"I think we both have a pretty good idea why I'm here. A few weeks ago you bought some artwork from my family."

Stefanoni nodded, his eyes unreadable. "The Caravaggio and several other pieces. Yes, I remember." He reached into his pocket and pulled out a string of amber beads, running them through his fingers. "I hope you don't find such things disturbing.'' His smile was self-deprecating. "I find the worry beads help me think. A habit I picked up in Greece.''

"Not at all.'' Emmet smiled, keeping up the polite facade.

"You came to discuss the paintings?''

"I came to buy them back, if you're willing to sell. Naturally I understand that the value of the paintings has gone up since you purchased them.'' If Stefanoni didn't know that they were fakes, Emmet didn't want to be the one to tell him.

"Ah, you're here to make me an offer I can't refuse.'' The dry wit drew a surprised smile from Emmet.

"I hope you can't refuse it.''

Stefanoni drew the beads through his fingers, his eyes on his guest. "I'm not interested in selling the artwork. I have wanted that particular Caravaggio for some time. I was delighted when your young cousin offered to sell it to me.''

"Lance?''

"Yes. He explained the terms of your grandfather's will so I understood the need for secrecy. It's a disappointment, of course, that I won't be able to show the painting but it's enough that I have it for my own enjoyment.''

Emmet smiled, wondering how he was going to go about explaining that the painting Stefanoni set such store by was a fake. He cleared his throat.

"Well, there's a bit of a problem here.''

"The fact that it's a fake?''

Emmet blinked and then smiled, his expression wry. The man deserved his reputation for shrewdness.

"I'm afraid not all members of my family understand

the value of fair play. You can understand why I want to purchase the pieces back from you.''

Stefanoni nodded, his eyes dropping to the worry beads sliding through his fingers. ''I must admit I was quite upset when I found out that the paintings were not genuine. No one likes to be taken for a fool.'' For just an instant, his face hardened, the mask of polite businessman slipping to reveal something far more dangerous.

''No one need ever know.''

''*I* will know, Mr. Malone. But that's neither here nor there. It's been a good lesson to me. To be taken for a fool by a pack of amateur con artists has taught me not to be too complacent.'' His smile held a feral edge. ''However, I'm not an unreasonable man. If you can provide me with the originals, I'm willing to forget this incident ever occurred.''

It wasn't the deal Emmet had been hoping for but he was willing to take it. Dodie would have a coronary over losing the real artwork but it was better than losing the trust fund. Besides, it served the whole pack of them right. It was about time they faced up to reality.

''Done. You'll have them within the week.''

''Excellent.'' Both men stood up and shook hands. ''It's been very pleasant doing business with you, Mr. Malone.'' Stefanoni tucked the worry beads back in his pocket.

''I'll contact you about arrangements for the paintings.''

''Fine. I've heard that your niece has been kidnapped.''

''That's right.''

''A terrible tragedy. We've met once or twice at social functions. She's a charming young woman.'' Emmet waited. It was clear the man had something more to say. Stefanoni reached out to rub his fingers over a priceless jade figurine.

"The men who kidnapped her—you've heard from them?"

"No. They haven't made any demands yet. Do you know something about them?"

"Perhaps. I have heard rumors that someone hired some very cheap labor. Labor known for doing heavier work than kidnapping."

Emmet felt his stomach tighten as if from a blow. Stefanoni glanced at him, his eyes cool. "I only mention it because you've given me many hours of pleasure with your work and, as I said, your niece is quite a charming young lady. I saw her once put a matron in her place by telling her that if she loosened her girdle, her face might not look so much like a prune."

The half laugh was startled out of Emmet. It was so typically Babs. Stefanoni smiled, sharing his amusement.

"I would hate to see something happen to a young woman of such spirit."

"Do you know who hired this 'labor' and how they contacted them?"

"No. Such people aren't hard to find if you have the money to hire them. They are not the sort I would have working for me." His contempt was obvious.

"Thanks for your understanding and for the information."

"My pleasure."

Enclosed in the quiet of his truck, the radio set to a classical music station, Emmet drove up the coast highway toward Santa Barbara. Sunshine blazed down from a clear blue sky. The Pacific Ocean lay to his left, endless miles of water, calm on this bright spring day. Emmet felt anything but calm.

If Stefanoni was right and the kidnappers were something more than kidnappers, then Babs was in more danger than he'd thought. He'd wondered why Sam hadn't brought her straight back. Even if he didn't want to bring her back to the Malone household, he would surely have been in touch with his mother and Cecily hadn't heard from him. No one had heard from him since he'd called the Malone house and found out the truth about the kidnapping.

So why hadn't anyone heard from him? Or from Babs? The possibilities were endless and none of them were reassuring. If the kidnappers were more than kidnappers, then just taking Babs away from them may not have been enough. If they'd been hired for something more, they might have tried to finish the job.

His fists clenched on the steering wheel. He was talking about someone trying to kill Babs. And not a stranger. Someone in the family. He didn't have much affection or respect for his family but he wouldn't have thought that they'd want Babs dead. He wouldn't have believed that any of them would have the guts to go that far, no matter how greedy they were. But Stefanoni had no reason to lie about this. He had nothing to gain or lose.

Automatically he turned the truck away from the family mansion. He couldn't stand to see any of them now. Not until he'd managed to get his thoughts straight. Without considering it beyond the fact that he needed a peaceful place, he found himself pulling the truck to a stop in front of Cecily Delanian's house. He didn't move for a moment but sat in the truck looking at the neat little home.

Home. Odd that the word came so easily to mind. Home. It was impossible to think of Cecily without thinking of homes and hearths and the scent of baking. Walking up the path, he felt his tension easing, even before she opened the door. Her smile was pure welcome, her delicate skin flushing lightly.

"Emmet. How lovely to see you. I haven't heard from Sam yet, I'm afraid. Have you had any word?" She was holding open the door as she spoke and he stepped in, letting the peace and calm surround him.

"No. I just thought I'd drop by. I hope you don't mind."

"Not at all. You're always welcome in my home. I hope you know that." Her eyes were soothing and offered welcome.

Emmet followed her into the kitchen, inhaling the scent of baking cookies appreciatively. Cecily laughed at his hopeful expression. "They're for the children next door but I suppose they wouldn't miss a few."

She set a cup of coffee and a plate of warm cookies in front of him and then settled herself opposite. Emmet sighed, feeling his tension ease with every minute he was in her company. He'd never known anyone who radiated such peace.

"Have you heard anything new about your niece or Sam?"

"No." He wasn't going to tell her about the conversation with Stefanoni. There was no reason to worry her with that. If someone was trying to kill Babs and Sam was protecting her, that meant that he was in as much danger as she was.

"You know, in all my years of traveling, the one thing I always miss is home cooking. The best restaurants in the world can't match a good home-cooked meal." He bit into a cookie, closing his eyes in pleasure.

Cecily laughed. "Flattery will get you an invitation to lunch. Have you traveled a great deal?"

"Most of the world, I guess. Some of it was research for books. Some of it was just because I was restless. After my wife died, I just couldn't seem to stay in one place."

"I didn't know you'd been married."

"Oh, it was a long time ago. Alice and I were just kids. Actually that's the reason my father cut me out of the will. Alice was 'not our sort.'"

"What sort was she?"

"Sweet, kind, beautiful, a laugh that made you want to laugh with her."

"That sounds like a pretty good sort to me."

"Well, my father didn't agree. He told me he'd cut me off without a penny if I married her. I married her and he cut me off without a penny. One thing you could always say about the old man—he kept his promises."

"Did you ever regret marrying her?"

"Not for a minute. We only had a few years together but they were the best years of my life. Alice is the one who encouraged me to start writing. She died just after my first book came out."

"She sounds wonderful. You must miss her a great deal."

"At first. But time heals all wounds, I guess. Now when I think about her, there's nothing but good memories. What about you?"

"Me?"

"Do you still miss your husband?" He wondered if she could tell how important her answer was to him.

"Oh, now and then. Peter and I were married a long

time. When he died, it left quite a gap in my life. But, as you said, time heals all wounds. I get along all right.'' Her smile held a loneliness he understood. He reached across the table, taking her hand in his, feeling the delicacy of her fingers in contrast to his own work-roughened palms.

"Loneliness can be the very devil."

She smiled, her eyes shining with tears. "Yes, it can. But I've had Sam. I don't know what I'd have done without him. And you've had Babs."

"Yeah, I've had Babs. I just wish I knew where she was and knew that she was all right."

Cecily's fingers tightened over his. "I'm sure Sam is taking good care of her. He won't let anything happen to her."

SAM WIGGLED THE THIN STRIP of wire in the lock, hardly breathing as he listened. The faint click as the lock gave way sounded wonderful. He tucked the wire back into his wallet and turned the knob, breathing easier when the door swung open to reveal the dark interior of the house.

He bent and lifted Babs into his arms. She was limp against him, her skin waxen. His only consolation was that her breathing seemed regular, if a little shallow. He carried her into the house, feeling his way past the furniture. The rain had increased and the heavy cloud cover was bringing darkness on early. Laying her on the bed in the one bedroom, he shrugged out of his pack and dug through it to find his flashlight.

Ten minutes later he'd discovered that there was no electricity but there were oil lamps. There was running water and the water heater must have been gas because there was hot water, though the plumbing was a bit grumpy about providing it. He'd also found blankets in one of the cabinets and there was a supply of canned goods in the kitchen.

He carried one of the lamps into the bedroom, setting it down beside the bed. Babs was still unconscious. He lifted her, stripped off his coat and then the clothes beneath it. She stirred restlessly as he slid the jeans from her but she didn't wake. Sam put his hand on her forehead, his brows drawing together as he felt the heat there. She was feverish but she didn't seem ill other than that. Outside the rain had gone from a steady drizzle to a serious downpour.

If she was seriously ill, she needed a doctor, but there was no phone. That meant he'd have to leave her alone while he walked out to the road and tried to hitch a ride. He felt her forehead again. Was it his imagination or was it warmer than it had been a moment ago?

"Damn." He bundled her into some blankets, hoping that keeping her warm was the right thing to do. She was probably just exhausted. When he thought about it, her life had been a little too full of excitement lately.

Guilt swept over him when he remembered how short tempered he'd been with her earlier. He should have seen how tired she was. Not that there would have been much he could have done about it, but he should have seen it. Maybe they could have slowed down, taken more time to rest. Of course they'd just beat the real downpour as it was.

Sam sat on the edge of the bed and stroked her hair back from her forehead, feeling it slide through his fingers like damp silk. She looked so small, so fragile. The big bed swallowed her. She was so strong, so gutsy that it was easy to forget just how tiny she was. She packed a lot of strength into that small frame.

She stirred, her lashes lifting and then falling, as if the weight of them was just too much for her.

"Babs? Can you hear me?"

"Of course I can hear you." The words were little more than a mumble but they sounded grumpy enough to reassure him. He stroked her hair back, leaning down until his breath brushed across her face.

"How are you feeling? Do you hurt anywhere? Do you feel sick?"

Babs stirred, her head tossing on the pillow. Her lashes fluttered again and lifted, her eyes meeting his. Her eyes were almost black in the dim light of the lantern but she looked rational so the fever wasn't high enough to cause delirium.

"I'm tired."

"Is that all? Are you sure you don't hurt anywhere?"

"I'm all right. Where are we?" Her eyes wandered around the room.

"We're at the farmhouse. You fainted and I carried you here." He was easing his arm behind her as he spoke, lifting her into a half-sitting position. "Here, drink this."

"What is it?" She eyed the cup he was holding to her mouth suspiciously.

"Soup. What did you think it was? Hemlock?"

Babs sipped the warm liquid. It was clear that she resented his assistance and equally clear that she couldn't have managed on her own. She drank almost half the cup before lifting one hand to push weakly at his wrist.

"No more."

"All right." He set the cup down and eased her back down onto the pillows, tucking the covers up around her shoulders. "Are you sure you don't feel sick?"

"I'm fine," she muttered crossly. "Just tired." Her eyes fell shut.

"Okay. You get some sleep." He eased off the bed and Babs's lashes came up, her eyes unfocused but reflecting a vulnerability she'd never have let him see if she'd been fully conscious. She pulled one hand free and reached out, catching hold of his sleeve.

"Where are you going?"

"I'm just going to get us settled in for the night. I won't be far."

"Promise."

She looked like a little girl asking for reassurance. Sam felt his heart melt. "I promise. I'll stay close by." He brushed his hand over her forehead and then cupped her cheek, feeling the softness of her skin beneath his palm.

"Okay." His promise seemed to be all the reassurance she needed. Her eyes shut, her lashes forming dark crescents on her pale cheeks. She was asleep within seconds, her breathing deep and even.

Sam stayed with Babs until he was sure she was deeply asleep, his face wearing an expression of tenderness that would have surprised him if he could have seen it. When he was sure that she was going to sleep for a while, he set about reacquainting himself with the old house.

They had enough food to last for several weeks—not that they were going to be there that long. If he was right and all Babs needed was some rest, they wouldn't stay there for more than a day or two. If there was something more seriously wrong with her... He didn't complete the thought. There couldn't be anything else wrong with her. They were too isolated. It would take him hours to get to a doctor.

There was plenty of wood on the front porch and he built a fire in the fireplace, trying to take some of the damp chill off the small house. He heated the rest of the soup on the gas stove and drank it out of a mug. Babs continued to sleep and Sam continued to worry.

According to his watch, it was well past midnight when his own tiredness finally caught up with him. He banked the fire. Babs was still sleeping and her forehead felt cool. He let his hand linger against her face, studying her in the warm light of the lamp. Funny how just a few days ago he'd been thinking that she wasn't his type. Now he couldn't imagine any other type. Short, slender and shaggy blond hair seemed like the only type. Add eyes the color of milk chocolate and a mouth that begged to be kissed and you had an irresistible package.

She stirred, a slight frown drawing her brows together. Sam's thumb stroked gently over her forehead, smoothing the frown away and she seemed to relax beneath his touch. Last night she'd been wrapped in his arms and her sweet response had been like nothing else he'd ever known.

Today she'd been more like an antagonist than the sweet lover he'd held the night before. He pulled his hand away from her face, his brow furrowing. He couldn't even begin to guess what was going on behind those dark eyes. For now it wasn't important. What was important was that they both needed some rest. Who knew what the next few days might hold.

He arched his back in a bone-popping stretch and then studied the bed. There was more than enough room for two and it *was* the only bed in the place. It would be foolish for him to throw a sleeping bag on the floor and wake up with a backache when there was a perfectly good mattress to sleep on. Besides, it wasn't as if they didn't know each other well enough to share a bed. Over the past few days they'd shared a heck of a lot more than that.

He had a sneaking suspicion that Babs might not view things quite so simply but he was too tired to care. He stripped off his shirt but left on his jeans. The way his life had been going lately, he might have to leap out of bed and do something heroic and masterful. He only hoped that if that were the case, Babs would wake up in time to see it. He didn't particularly want to waste heroics on a sleeping audience. The thought was so foolish that Sam knew he must be more tired than he'd thought.

He blew out the lamp, plunging the room into darkness before lifting the covers. Babs stirred, mumbling fretfully as the mattress sagged beneath his weight. Within seconds she turned toward him. Sam didn't know if it was the tilt of the mattress or his warmth that drew her but she snuggled up to his side as if she belonged there.

He hesitated a moment, knowing that she wouldn't be happy if she woke up to find herself plastered to him. But there wasn't much he could do about it, he argued in his own defense. It seemed logical to make the best of the situation, which he did by putting his arm around her, pillowing her head on his shoulder.

Her small body felt remarkably good, remarkably right. A warning bell chimed somewhere in his head. She felt too good, too right. But Sam ignored it, too tired to care. He felt as if he'd spent months on the run. The old mattress felt like heaven to his battered body and Babs's warmth along his side made it all the more complete. His arm tightened around her as his eyes drifted shut.

In the living room the banked fire flickered. Red and copper embers burned in the grate, casting out more heat than would be expected from their size. The old farmhouse slept, holding Sam and Babs safe and warm.

Chapter Ten

The first thing that Babs was aware of was being warm—wonderfully, deliciously warm. The second thing that registered on her sleepy mind was a steady beat under her ear. Something about its rhythm added to her feeling of contentment. Contentment. That was it. Contentment wasn't something she'd known well. The feeling was as unfamiliar as it was pleasant.

There'd been a time when she'd felt this safe and protected—a long time ago. Still half asleep, her mind wandered. She was lying in her own bed, Mickey Mouse covers pulled over her head. Somewhere in the room she could hear her father prowling about. "Where's Babs?" he kept saying, his voice full of puzzlement. She bit her lip to hold back a giggle, knowing how the game would end. He came closer and closer and she thought she'd burst because of her need to laugh.

She shrieked when he pounced, tugging the covers away from her tousled head, snatching her off the bed and tossing her in the air. "There's Babs, there's my girl. Thought you had me fooled, didn't you?"

She giggled, snuggling her face into his neck, aware of her mother's soft laughter. Aware that nothing would ever hurt her as long as they were there to love her and protect her.

But they weren't always there.

"Stop that noise at once, Babette! You're a Malone. Malones don't cry and they certainly do not scream."

Her aunt's hand closed around her upper arm, the pressure bruising as she dragged her up the stairs. Behind them in the drawing room, the rest of the family sat silent, saying nothing, doing nothing. Babs dragged her feet, pulling back against the hard pressure. Her chest hurt, aching with a pain she was too young to understand, too young to deal with. How could she explain that she was all alone. How could she make her aunt understand that every time she shut her eyes she was back in the car, alone, cold, screaming for her parents—knowing they were never going to answer her again.

"Really, you make me ashamed of you." Dodie thrust open the bedroom door and pulled Babs inside. "Just think about what you've done. Think about the scene you created. You've got to learn that we expect better of you."

"No. Don't shut the door. Please don't shut the door." She threw herself forward as the door closed behind her aunt's implacable figure, but the lock clicked with absolute finality. The sound sent her into a frenzy that she didn't understand, couldn't control. She beat on the door, the wood hurting her small hands. The screams she heard didn't seem to be her own, though they tore at her throat. No one came. She was alone. All alone.

Babs stirred, a frown pulling her brows together. The old pain was still there, surprisingly vivid, still carrying an edge. But she wasn't that child anymore, she was not helpless or alone. She was an adult, able to take care of herself. That was all a long time ago. Right now she was cozy and warm. Wonderfully, deliciously warm.

She snuggled closer to the source of the warmth, her eyes still closed. There was something she should remember, things she should be worried about. She shoved the thought away. She didn't want to wake up, didn't want to give up this marvelous feeling of peace.

A hand came up to stroke her hair back from her face. She was aware of the strength in that hand, a strength she could lean on, depend on. A lightly callused palm slid across her forehead, resting there. She had dim memories of her mother doing the same.

The pillow shifted and she frowned, trying to hold on to it, not wanting to wake up completely. A low chuckle rumbled beneath her ear and then the pillow was gone and her head was resting on something much softer but without the reassuring strength she'd awakened with.

"Are you awake?" The voice was low but it was enough to bring her lashes up.

Blue. Deep, endless blue. She could fall into it and never come out. For a moment all she could see was that wonderful, intense color. She blinked and the blue sorted itself into a pair of eyes surrounded by thick black lashes.

"Sam." Her voice was a raspy whisper, barely audible.

"How are you feeling?" He was leaning on one elbow next to her, his hair falling in tousled waves onto his forehead, his eyes full of concern. His jaw looked dark and dangerous, dark with stubble.

Still half asleep, Babs reached up, touching her fingertips to his jaw, feeling the rasp of his beard. From there it was a short trip to brushing the hair back from his forehead. It slid through her fingers like black silk, warm and alive. Sam reached up, catching her hand in his. Babs watched as he brought her palm to his mouth and pressed a kiss into it. The touch of his mouth on her skin sent tingles through her body, tingles that chased away the last of the sleepy contentment and brought her back to full awareness.

She tugged her hand away, tucking it under the covers as if afraid of what it might do if left free. Sam saw the change in her expression and she thought she saw a flicker of regret in his eyes but she was too busy drawing her defenses around herself to analyze what Sam might be feeling.

"Where are we?"

"We're at my dad's old place. We were headed there, remember?"

"I remember. How did I get here?"

"You passed out like a light and I carried you here."

"Did you put me to bed?"

"Well, I didn't see anyone else to ask." Babs eyed him warily. She had already discovered that she didn't have a stitch of clothing on but somehow it didn't seem like a good idea to protest. Something in his eyes told her that she'd be the loser in that discussion.

She pulled the sheet closer around her body, trying to edge away from him. Did he have to lie there, looking so…so…male? His bare chest seemed to fill most of her field of vision and she didn't like what the sight of all those muscles was doing to her pulse.

"How are you feeling?" Sam reached to feel her forehead and she winced, moved away and then felt foolish when he arched an eyebrow in question.

"I feel fine." She held her breath while he felt her forehead. It was silly. God knows, the man had certainly done more than touch her forehead.

"I think your fever is gone."

"What fever?" It was news to her. The last thing she remembered was trudging along behind him in the rain, putting one foot in front of the other on sheer willpower.

"You were feverish last night. I was afraid you might be coming down with something but I think it was just exhaustion."

Whether he sensed her uneasiness with his nearness or just decided it was time to get up, Babs didn't know, but she drew a deep breath of relief when he rolled off the bed. The breath caught in her throat. Did he have to stand there in those damned jeans and no shirt and stretch like that? She could see every muscle and her memory presented her with unwanted images of how those muscles had felt under her hands. She shut her eyes but that only shut the image in with her.

"Are you hungry?" She opened her eyes, relieved to see him shrugging into a shirt. "The kitchen has a pretty good stock of canned goods. I can't offer you eggs Benedict but I think I can come up with something better than stale donuts."

"Where are my clothes?"

"Don't worry about it. I think you should stay in bed today. You must have been pretty exhausted to collapse like that. You won't need your clothes."

"I think I'm capable of deciding whether or not I'm capable of getting up."

"Maybe, but you don't have to worry about it because I'm deciding for you." The smile he gave her contained enough determination to outmatch her, at least in her current state. There were times when it was less humiliating to concede defeat. She looked away, her face flushing.

"I'd like to go to the bathroom, if you wouldn't mind."

"Oh. Sorry." He rummaged through his pack and then handed her one of his shirts. "The bathroom is through there. I'll just go get started on breakfast. Holler if you need me."

"I think I can manage on my own." She waited until Sam had left, pulling the door shut behind him to give her some privacy. Alone, she dropped the sheet and tugged on the shirt, rolling the sleeves back until she could see her hands before sliding to the edge of the bed and putting her feet on the wooden floor.

She hadn't realized how weak she was until she was actually on her feet. Her knees quivered with the effort of holding her upright. For a moment it was all she could do to stand, let alone walk. After a bit she felt a little more steady, but the short walk to the bathroom almost defeated her.

If the walk didn't kill her, one look at her reflection in the cracked mirror almost did. Her skin looked like an old sheet. There were dark circles under her eyes. Her hair was dull and tangled, showing the effects of getting wet in the rain and then drying without the benefit of a comb.

A splash of cold water on her face and some careful wielding of Sam's comb restored her to the point where she felt almost human. There was nothing she could do about her pallor or the circles under her eyes. Not that it really mattered how she looked. After all there was no one to see her but Sam and it didn't matter what he thought.

Babs stared at her reflection, knowing the thought was a lie. She did care what he thought of her. But she would get over that. She couldn't afford to forget that once Sam was assured of her safety, he was going to collect his fifty thousand dollars and walk out of her life. That was an essential fact and one that would cost her dearly to forget. Sam was in this for the money, pure and simple.

She didn't blame him for it. After all he didn't owe her anything more. They'd made love but that didn't mean anything. They'd made no promises, no vows. Just because waking up in his arms had felt like coming home didn't mean that anything more was going to come of it.

She splashed more water on her face, pretending that it had nothing to do with the tears that burned in her eyes.

When she stepped out of the bathroom a short time later, the bed looked like heaven. It also looked like it was a mile away. She edged her way along the wall toward the rickety dresser and then cautiously braced her weight on it. There was still at least six feet of space to cross over and nothing to hold on to between here and there.

"Need help?" She glanced up, startled, to see Sam watching her. He'd dressed while she was in the bathroom, throwing a carelessly buttoned shirt on over his jeans and putting on his running shoes without socks. A faded kitchen towel was draped over his shoulder, an incongruously domestic touch on his very large, very undomestic frame.

She hadn't heard the door open and she wondered how long he'd been standing there. Her spine stiffened automatically and she shook her head.

"No. I'm fine, thanks." She waited a minute, hoping he would leave so that she could crawl to the bed in peace. He showed no signs of moving. In fact, he leaned his shoulder against the doorjamb as if prepared to wait till doomsday.

Babs threw him a glare that should have withered him where he stood but he didn't seem to notice. She couldn't stay where she was. Just staying upright was taking more strength than she'd ever have believed. The bed wasn't that far away. She could make it that far without falling on her nose.

She stepped away from the dresser, trying to look as though it was no big deal. Her legs shook but held her and she took another step. She might have made it if it hadn't been for the ancient braided rug that lay right in the middle of her path. She took a third step and her foot encountered the slight difference in height. It wasn't much but it was enough to throw off her precarious balance. She gasped and threw out her arms but Sam was there before she hit the floor.

"Stubborn little idiot." The words held an odd note. If she hadn't known it was impossible, Babs might almost have thought it was affection. He swung her up into his arms as if she weighed next to nothing.

Babs lay still against his chest, not looking at his face, trying not to notice how hard his muscles felt. He carried her the few feet to the bed and set her down gently, tugging the covers up over her and tucking the worn feather pillows behind her back.

"Thank you." Babs had to force the words out. She didn't want to depend on him. Not him, not anybody. It wasn't a good idea to depend on people. In her experience, they usually let you down.

"Are you hungry? You didn't answer me before."

"A little." Her stomach chose that moment to growl loudly, belying her casual tone. To his credit, Sam didn't laugh out loud. He didn't even smile but the deep tucks that appeared in his cheeks revealed his amusement. Babs glanced up at him, meeting the dancing blue of his eyes. A reluctant smile tilted her mouth.

"All right. Maybe more than a little."

"How about some canned corned beef hash and some canned corn? I hope you don't mind canned food. It's all we've got."

"Right now anything sounds wonderful, canned or otherwise."

"I don't think we have any otherwise. Stay there." He tucked the covers more firmly around her, stopping her move to get up. "I'll bring it in to you. I want you to rest as much as possible."

Remembering how her last venture out of bed had ended, Babs didn't argue with him. The last thing she wanted was to find herself in Sam Delanian's arms again. The very last thing.

The food tasted wonderful. Babs ate every scrap, balancing a metal tray on her knees. Outside the rain continued to fall, giving no sign of letting up. Sam kept the fire going in the living room and it emitted enough heat to take the edge off the chill air. Tucked into the old bed, Sam's flannel shirt wrapped around her and covers piled over her, Babs felt surprisingly good.

After Sam took the tray away, she lay back against the pillows and stared out at the falling rain, trying to define just what it was that she felt. She felt warm and…cherished. That was it. Cherished.

The thought was enough to dispel the feeling. She sat up, breathing in cool air, banishing the sleepy contentment that was threatening to overtake her common sense. She had to remember exactly what the situation was. Cherishing had nothing to do with it. In simplest terms, Sam was making an investment. His time and care of her in return for the fifty thousand dollars he expected to get at the end of this whole mess.

Sam came and leaned in the doorway, looking disgustingly healthy and male. Babs pulled the throat of his shirt closed, wishing she was wearing something a little more suited to taking charge of her life. It was difficult to be forceful when you felt weak as a kitten and were wearing nothing but a man's shirt.

"Have you had any luck contacting Uncle Emmet?"

"With what? Smoke signals? There's no phone in this place." Sam stretched, looking so imperturbable that she wanted to smack him.

"Couldn't you walk to a phone?"

He looked at her and then looked out the window. "I don't think so. I don't even know where the nearest phone is and I'd be soaked by the time I was ten feet out the door. Besides, I don't want to leave you alone."

"I'm fine."

"Sure you are but I'm still not leaving you alone."

There was no arguing with that tone and Babs didn't even bother trying. She'd have died before admitting it but she wasn't all that keen on being left alone. She yawned, reluctant to acknowledge that she was still tired.

"Why don't you get some more sleep? I'll wake you in time for lunch." The idea had too much appeal for her to argue with it. She slid down under the covers.

The next time she opened her eyes, she was aware of two things at once. The rain had eased to a mere drizzle and she was hungry again. She sat up in bed, stretching her arms over her head and arching her back. She didn't feel like running a footrace but she felt much stronger than she had a few short hours ago.

"Ready for lunch?"

She jerked her arms down, aware of the way that her

breasts pressed against the soft flannel of his shirt. The same awareness was in Sam's eyes but he didn't say anything.

"Must you sneak up on me all the time?" She was immediately ashamed of the petulant note in her voice but it was too late to take it back.

Sam stared at her, one black brow arching. Babs felt her cheeks heat under that mute comment. She sounded like a spoiled brat and she knew it.

"I could try wearing spurs so you could hear me coming. Or maybe a collar with a bell on it?" The image of Sam wearing a collar with a bell on it drew out an involuntary smile from her.

"I shouldn't have snapped. You just startled me."

"Sorry. I'll try to make sure you hear me coming but it's a little hard to stomp in sneakers. How about if I sing an aria from Don Giovanni as I approach the door?"

"Is your voice any good?"

"Well, it depends on how you define good. Pavarotti trembles when I sing but he also clutches at his ears, so maybe it's not fear of my talent. Ready for lunch?"

"Starved."

Lunch was more hash and a can of peas. It was hardly what Babs was accustomed to but she'd learned that hunger had a marvelous way of making everything taste good. She finished her plate. Sam cleared away the tray and Babs was left with nothing to do but stare at the walls. It didn't take long for that to get old. Then she tried sleeping but she wasn't tired enough for that.

"How about a game of rummy?" Babs looked up, ready for any diversion. Sam was standing in the doorway, holding up a pack of cards that looked as if they'd spent their life on the floor of a mechanic's shop.

"Cards?"

"Unless you've got a better suggestion. It's something to pass the time."

She hesitated for only a moment. Her common sense told her that the less time she spent with Sam Delanian, the better. Boredom won out. If she lay here staring at the walls and listening to the rain for another hour, she was going to go stark raving mad.

Sam apparently took her silence for agreement. He crossed the room and settled himself at the foot of the bed. The mattress dipped under his weight.

"We're going to have to be a little flexible."

"Why?"

"Well, this deck doesn't have a ten of clubs or an ace of diamonds."

"That's okay." If he'd told her that they were missing an entire suit she wouldn't have cared. It was still something to do.

They played two hands without speaking beyond what was necessary for the game. Sam won the first hand and Babs took the second. Their playing styles were vastly different. Babs studied the cards carefully, weighing the odds and making her decisions accordingly. Sam didn't seem to pay much attention to what he was doing, relying on luck and intuition.

"Tell me about your family."

Babs jumped, startled out of her concentration on the game. Her eyes shifted from the cards in her hand to Sam's face but he wasn't looking at her. He was rearranging his own hand.

"What about them?" She didn't want to think about her family now. She didn't want to think about anything beyond this hand of cards.

"What are they like?"

"Rich. Spoiled. Naive."

"That sums them up pretty neatly but it doesn't tell me much."

"Maybe I don't feel like talking about them."

"I think we should talk about them."

She tossed her cards down and glared at him. "Do you know how annoying it is to have you constantly telling me what I should and shouldn't do? No one died and made you God so just leave me alone."

Sam's own temper flared to meet hers. "Someone has to point out reality to you once in a while. And reality is that someone wants you dead. Before I take you home, I thought it might be nice to know who that someone is."

"I can't believe that any of my family would want me killed. We don't get along but they wouldn't go that far. It's a mistake of some kind."

"Well, it's a mistake that damn near got us both killed and I don't like mistakes like that."

"Well, nobody asked you to rescue me."

"If I hadn't rescued you, they'd probably be finding your body somewhere right now. I've gone to a lot of trouble keeping you alive so far and I don't want it to go for nothing. You may be a spoiled brat but I'd rather not see you dead."

"Don't call me a brat."

"Then don't act like one."

"Well, at least I don't act like a chauvinistic misogynist with an ego the size of Cleveland."

Sam leaned forward until their faces were inches apart, meeting her glare for glare. The cards lay forgotten between them. The rain had faded to a vague background noise.

"If that's the way you feel about me, would you like

to tell me why in the hell you slept with me?" He bit the question out, his voice fiercely soft.

Babs blinked, feeling her chest tighten. The argument had suddenly become dangerous. She looked away, searching frantically for some safe answer. Her shoulders lifted in a casual shrug.

"It was no big deal."

Sam's irritation climbed to new heights. He wanted to grab her and shake her until her teeth rattled. She was infuriatingly stubborn. She sat there, looking as fragile as a child and then he came up against a stubborn streak a mile wide.

"No big deal?"

She shrugged again, her eyes meeting his and then sliding away. "That's right. I mean, we just slept together. There's no big deal in that."

"Most women consider it a moderately big deal when they lose their virginity."

He heard the catch in her breathing and her eyes swept up to meet his. For just a moment, all the barriers were down and he could see the vulnerability she tried so hard to conceal.

"How did you know?"

"Babs, it wasn't something I was likely to overlook."

"Was I that bad?"

"No. Of course not." He reached out to touch her cheek, his fingers gentle. "It was wonderful. *You* were wonderful. But I don't understand why you did it if you dislike me so much."

"I didn't say I disliked you." She looked away and he could see her drawing her defenses around her like a cloak, shutting herself safely inside and closing him out.

"Well, you sure don't act like you're all that happy about it. So why did you sleep with me?"

She shrugged again, her eyes looking past his shoulder. "I was bored with being a virgin. It seemed like a good time and you were…handy."

"Handy." Sam repeated the word, keeping his tone carefully neutral. "Handy."

"That's right." Still, she didn't look at him.

Sam studied her face, wondering if she had any idea how soft the curve of her cheek was or the way her mouth quivered when she was nervous. Handy. It was so patently ridiculous he couldn't even be angry about it. He nodded as if the idea made perfect sense to him.

"I can understand your impatience overcoming you as we rode along wondering if someone was trying to kill us. I suppose you'd always planned on losing your virginity in the back of a moving van?"

"Of course not." She flushed, her eyes meeting his and then skittering away.

"Then why, Babs? Why did you make love with me?"

"I told you. I—" He gestured sharply, cutting her words off.

"Don't give me that. I don't want to hear that you were bored with being a virgin. If you made it to the ripe old age of twenty-four without giving in to boredom, then it's not too likely that you were suddenly overcome with lust in the back of a moving van."

"I don't know why you're making such an issue out of this. It's really not worth—" Sam caught her chin in his hand, forcing her eyes to meet his.

Babs couldn't look away from the bright blue of his gaze. It demanded so many things she wasn't sure she could give but it refused to let her lie.

"Why, Babs? I want to know. Why me?"

"You make me feel…safe." Her voice was little more than a husky whisper, shaken and half-scared.

Sam's fingers gentled on her face, his other hand coming up to cup her cheek so that he held her trapped. But Babs didn't feel trapped. She felt cherished, protected, cared for.

"You are safe, sweetheart. You are safe." His quiet promise shivered through her, soothing and frightening her at the same time. Frightening because she wanted so badly to believe what he was saying. She needed to believe it.

"Sam, I—"

His thumb pressed against her lips and Babs forgot what she'd planned to say.

"Hush. No more talking. We always get in trouble that way." His smile flickered and then faded as he leaned toward her. Babs forgot how to breathe but it didn't seem important. Nothing was important beyond the bright blue of his eyes.

His mouth touched hers and her lashes fell. Babs thought of keeping him at a safe distance but her fingertips felt the hard muscles beneath his shirt and the idea was gone. He felt so warm and vital.

His mouth tasted hers as if sipping at a cup of heady wine before taking a full drink. She felt her bones start to melt beneath the gentle nibbling of his teeth, coaxing her mouth to open for him. Her breath left her on a sigh of surrender. Her hands slid up his shoulders, her fingers burrowing into the thick black hair at his nape. Sam deepened the kiss, his tongue exploring the sweet softness she'd opened to him.

The cards were forgotten as he leaned forward, pressing her back into the pillows, supporting his weight on his hands. Babs fumbled with the buttons on his shirt, her palms pressing into the crisp hair and taut muscles. Sam's teeth nipped at the sensitive skin behind her ear, his tongue coming out to soothe the sensuous pain.

Outside the rain continued to fall, the heavy clouds smothering the light, leaving the landscape gray and gloomy. But the old farmhouse was snug and warm. Sam explored the soft curve of waist and thigh. Babs rediscovered the hard muscles of his shoulders.

Her skin felt flushed and feverish but it had nothing to do with illness. She was melting in the heat of his touch, in the feel of his mouth. Nothing in the world seemed half so real as the feel of his hands on her body, his mouth on her breast.

Their coupling was completed in one smooth thrust and she arched beneath him, her breath leaving her on a moan of pure pleasure. The passion burned too high to last long. The climax was swift, devastating in its power, leaving them both trembling in the aftermath.

Sam rolled over to the side, taking her with him, holding her close. She'd never felt so comforted, so protected in her life. The thought frightened her even as she pressed closer to him. What was she going to do when he was no longer a part of her life?

Chapter Eleven

Babs didn't have to deal with his leaving yet. For the moment, no one was going anywhere. She spent the rest of the afternoon cuddled in Sam's arms. The rain continued to fall outside but it didn't seem important. They had everything they needed right here.

Darkness came early, the cloud cover hastening the fading light. Babs woke from a light doze as Sam slid his arm out from under her and slipped out of bed.

"Where are you going?" The words came out on a yawn.

The bed dipped as Sam leaned down to drop a kiss on the end of her nose. "Stay here. I'm going to build a fire and light a lamp."

Babs snuggled deeper under the layers of covers, watching sleepily as he dressed. In the near dark he was little more than a darker shadow among shadows. The fading light angled off his muscled shoulders and corded thighs. She felt a pleasantly possessive twinge. He was all hers. In this time and this place, she could lay claim to this man. The thought was surprisingly attractive.

"Stay under the covers until I get the fire going." Sam strode out of the room, still shrugging into his shirt.

At another time Babs might have taken exception to

him telling her what to do. She always made her own decisions. She rolled over, burying her face in the pillow and inhaling. It smelled like Sam—soap and man. For now she'd indulge this heretofore undiscovered urge to be bossed and let Sam take charge.

She lay there, letting her thoughts drift with pleasant aimlessness until Sam came back in, carrying one of the oil lamps.

"I've got the fire going. If you'd like, you can come in and sit by the fire. You're probably sick of that bed."

"Oh, I don't know. It has its advantages." Her husky voice was pure invitation. Sam looked surprised, then intrigued and then regretful.

"Don't tempt me."

"Why not? You're so temptable."

"You're supposed to be resting." He set the lamp on the night table and then leaned down to scoop her up, covers and all. Babs gave a startled gasp. Her arms were tangled up in the blankets so that she lay helpless in his arms. The feeling was new and not entirely welcome. She lay completely still, her body stiff.

"Relax. I'm not going to drop you." She looked up, meeting Sam's eyes, seeing understanding there. Too much understanding. It made her uneasy that he seemed to be able to read her mind. But there was also reassurance. His arms tightened around her in an admonitory squeeze. "I managed to get you here without dropping you, didn't I?"

Was that disappointment she read in his face? Did he think that she didn't trust him? How could she explain that it wasn't him she didn't trust? She made a conscious effort to relax and was rewarded with his smile.

"See, it's not so bad." He turned and carried her into the living room. By the time he set her down on the battered sofa, Babs had to admit that she felt as safe in his arms as she had in her entire life.

A fire crackled in the fireplace, warming the dusty room. Sam disappeared into the bedroom and brought back the lamp he'd left there. Between the fire and the two lamps, the room was bright with soft light. Babs looked around with interest. Since she'd been unconscious when Sam carried her into the house, this was the first look at their hideaway she'd gotten.

There wasn't much to see. A big room that functioned as living room, dining room and kitchen. A few pieces of slightly rickety furniture. Hardwood floors and plank walls, the windows covered with tattered curtains. Not a prepossessing abode but Babs had no complaints. Sam was stirring around in the kitchen, whistling softly between his teeth, the fire cast warmth and light over the room, the door was shut tight against the rain and wind outside. She couldn't remember when she'd felt more content with life.

"This stuff is probably as old as the hills but it's hot." She reached up to take the mug Sam handed her, cradling her hands around its warmth.

"What is it?"

"Tea. I think. It looked a little dusty but it smells like tea and the box claims it's tea. Anyway, whatever it is, it'll warm you up. Hungry?"

"Starving." She sipped at the steaming liquid. It was tea all right or it had been tea in a previous incarnation. It still held some vague resemblance to that beverage, though it also tasted a little like liquid dust. But Sam was right, it was hot and that was reason enough to drink it. She took another sip.

"What are we having for dinner?"

Sam shut a cupboard door and glanced over his shoulder. "Well, I'd like to tell you that filet mignon is on the menu but I'm afraid we're all out of it. How about Spam filets with some sautéed canned potatoes and a side dish of canned peas? And for dessert, we have canned peaches."

Babs wrinkled her nose. "Sounds like a lot of cans."

"Yeah, but it's food. When we get back to civilization, I'm going to have a steak the size of Rhode Island."

Babs couldn't imagine enjoying a steak any more than she did the meal Sam set in front of her a little while later. It was hot and filling. She'd barely been out of bed in the last twenty-four hours but her appetite had never been better. She ate every scrap of it with real pleasure.

Sam stacked the chipped plates in the sink afterward and then came and sat on the sofa beside her. It seemed the most natural thing in the world for him to slip his arm behind her and pull her over to lean against him. Her head fit naturally into the hollow of his shoulder. They sat there for a long time without speaking, watching the firelight and listening to the rain outside.

"Think it will stop raining by tomorrow?" Babs asked.

"I don't know." Sam nuzzled her hair, sounding as if he didn't care if it never stopped raining.

"It's not going to be a lot of fun to walk out of here if it's still raining."

"We're not going anywhere until I'm sure you're rested. And we're not going anywhere until the rain stops."

"I'm fine." She tried to ignore the gentle nip of his teeth on her earlobe. "I don't know why I collapsed like that."

"Exhaustion. And I'm going to make sure it doesn't

happen again.'' His mouth found the pulse that beat at the base of her throat and Babs's head fell back against his arm.

"I'm fine. Really I am." Her voice was breathy, caught somewhere in her throat as he nibbled his way along her collarbone, pushing aside his shirt as he went.

"Let me be the judge of that." Her head spun dizzily, her hands coming up to clutch at his shoulders as he lifted her, laying her on the floor in front of the fireplace, the blankets jumbled beneath her.

Babs stared up into his eyes, losing herself in the bright blue of them. His fingers worked the buttons on the shirt he'd given her, but his eyes never left hers, holding her hypnotized.

"I've always wanted to play doctor with a woman with skin like satin and chocolate-colored eyes." His voice was low, in keeping with the spell he was weaving. The shirt fell open and he laid his hand against her stomach. His thumb rested on the pulse that jumped beneath the skin just above the soft triangle of hair that guarded her most feminine secrets.

"Are we playing doctor?" Babs had to clear her throat to get the words out.

"I'm not playing. I've never been more serious in my life."

His head dipped, his mouth capturing hers, chasing away any possibility of thought. Babs surrendered to the magic he was creating, her arms coming up to circle his neck.

Beside them the fire crackled and popped, but its heat was no greater than the sexual heat they created together. The fire created an orange glow beneath her closed eyelids, adding to the heat. Babs's skin burned everywhere that Sam touched. Her fingers traced the muscles of his back, lighting new fires.

In all the world, there were only the two of them. Nothing else, no one else mattered. Only the here and now and the feel of his strong body above hers.

BY MORNING, THE RAIN HAD STOPPED and only the tattered storm clouds remained. Babs stirred and stretched, aware of feeling rested and more alive than she'd felt in years. Her body ached deliciously, reminding her of last night's passion. Sam had carried her to bed and she'd fallen asleep in his arms. She had no idea what time it was when she woke to the feel of his hands exploring her body, his mouth nibbling a path along her spine. The memory brought a sleepy smile.

The bed was empty but Babs could hear Sam in the kitchen. A slightly scratchy baritone rose over the clatter of pots. Her smile widened. Somehow "It's Not Easy Being Green" was not a tune she'd have expected to hear from Sam. Kermit the Frog he was not.

She threw back the covers and sat up, reaching for the flannel shirt Sam had left draped across the bottom of the bed. Weak sunshine lit the room and she scowled at it. If it wasn't raining, there was no excuse for them to stay here.

She didn't want to leave the old farmhouse. It had been a quiet haven, a break from the madness that had surrounded her life lately. Once they left, she'd have to face the real world again—and deal with what her family had done. She wasn't ready for that. She wasn't sure she'd ever be ready.

She washed her face and combed her hair and then hurried out into the living room. The rain might have stopped but the old house was still cold. Sam had a fire going in the fireplace and the living room was warm and toasty.

"Good morning."

Sam looked up, his eyes sweeping over her from head to foot. Babs felt the look as if it were a touch, warming her, letting her know he was glad to see her.

"Good morning. Ready for breakfast?"

"Sure. What are we having?" She walked to the stove to peek at what was cooking but Sam's hand closed around her nape, tilting her head back for a thorough kiss. By the time he released her, Babs had forgotten all about breakfast. She opened her eyes as he brushed his thumb across her mouth. He was looking at her in a way that made her knees go weak.

"I'm tempted to forget about food and take you back to bed." Babs could only stare at him, her fingers clinging to the front of his shirt. He sighed and pried her fingers loose, pushing her gently toward the living room. "I suppose you need your nourishment. Go sit down and I'll bring your breakfast."

Babs sat on the sofa, carefully avoiding the spring that had broken through the ancient upholstery. Sam brought the food in and settled himself on the floor. She balanced her plate on her knees and stared at its contents.

"Someone must really like corned beef hash."

Sam nodded. "Must have. It could have been worse. They could have liked anchovies."

She took a few bites and then set down her fork. She didn't want to say it. She didn't even want to think it, but it had to be said.

"I guess we'll be leaving after breakfast." She kept her voice carefully neutral, as if it didn't matter at all.

Sam threw her a quick, unreadable look and then

looked down at his plate. He cut a beet up into neat little squares, paying careful attention to the operation.

"I think we should stay here today and start out tomorrow."

"I'm rested enough to go today." Why was she arguing? Nothing would please her more than to stay just where they were. But she didn't want Sam to know how much she wanted to stay here. *She* didn't want to admit how much she wanted to stay.

"Maybe. But I think it would be a good idea to give it another day. You must have been really exhausted to collapse like that. I don't know how far we're going to have to walk before we can get a ride. I don't want to have to carry you to L.A."

"Where are we going to go when we leave here?"

"Well, I figured we'd get to a phone and see if Emmet has shown up. If we can't get hold of him, we'll rent a car. But, one way or another, we're not going anywhere today so why don't you finish your breakfast and relax."

Babs had a million more questions but she didn't ask them. Just for today, she wanted to forget about the rest of the world and pretend that nothing else existed beyond this house and this man.

After breakfast Sam rinsed the dishes and then presented her with a battered copy of an old James Michener novel. He'd found it in the back of a cupboard and the last hundred or so pages were missing but Babs didn't mind. It felt nice to sit next to the fire and read. Sam went outside and she could hear him shifting wood. When he came back in, he was carrying a small piece of oak. He settled himself on a stool near the sofa and began to shave chunks of wood off one end of the stick.

Babs divided her time between her book and watching

him and then gave up on the book altogether and just watched him.

"What are you doing?"

"I'm whittling."

"What are you whittling?"

"I was thinking of doing an oak rendition of Michelangelo's David. What do you think so far?" He held the stick out at arm's length, studying it carefully. Babs looked at it.

"It looks more like Bugs Bunny," she announced after careful consideration.

He threw her an indignant look. "Everyone's an art critic. Obviously it's still in the early stages of creation. It's unfair to judge it before its true character emerges. The wood has a definite message to reveal to the world and I'm trying to set it free."

"I think you'd do better to set it on fire."

"Funny. Very funny." But his eyes held amusement.

It wasn't until after supper that either of them mentioned the future again. Dinner had been eaten and darkness had fallen outside. The Michener book lay forgotten on the floor. Sam's wood carving sat upright on the hearth, resembling nothing in particular. Babs leaned against Sam's shoulder, staring into the fire, letting the bright flames hypnotize her.

"Do you have a will?" The question startled her out of her pleasant stupor. She blinked.

"What?"

"Do you have a will?"

She struggled to shift mental gears.

"Not really. Just whatever provision is in the trust fund. Why? Do you think I might drop dead and leave you without your fifty thousand?" The question held an edge of hurt despite her attempt to make it a joke. She sat up, running her fingers through her hair. Sam's arm fell away from her shoulders, leaving her alone. She didn't like the feeling.

"To hell with the fifty thousand. I don't care about that." He waved his hand dismissively.

"Then why are you asking about my will?"

He reached out and took one of her hands, his eyes intent in the firelight. "Look, I know you don't want to think about this and I don't blame you. But it seems like there's a pretty good possibility that someone wants you more than just out of the way temporarily. They want you dead."

"Why would anyone want me dead?"

"I don't know. But when we leave here tomorrow, it might be nice if we had some idea of who it might be and why. I've given it a lot of thought and the best motive I can come up with is money. You've got a lot of money. If something happened to you, who would inherit your money?"

Babs stared at him, her eyes wide. He was really talking about someone trying to kill her. She'd avoided really thinking about it because the possibility was so horrifying, but he was making it impossible to ignore. Her fingers tightened over his as the realization sank in. Someone wanted her dead.

He must have seen the dawning horror in her eyes because he leaned forward, cupping her cheek with his free hand, his eyes intent on hers. "Nothing is going to happen to you. I'm going to make sure of that."

Staring into the brilliant blue of his gaze, Babs believed him. Those eyes didn't give her any choice but to believe him. Her breath left her on a quick sigh that stopped just short of a sob.

"I believe you."

"Good." His mouth touched hers in a brief kiss before he sat back, his expression serious. "Who inherits the money if something happens to you?"

"The family. I don't remember exactly how it goes. Finney told me about it when I turned eighteen and the trust fund money had started coming directly to me. I guess I didn't listen all that carefully. At eighteen you don't think about dying." She frowned, her eyes focused on the wall behind his shoulder as she tried to remember the conversation with Finney.

"If I die before I'm twenty-five, then I think the money is divided equally among the rest of the family."

"What happens if you die after you're twenty-five?"

"Well, at twenty-five the money is mine so I guess, after that, whatever happens would be what would happen to anyone's money if they died without a will. I guess the courts would decide who gets it."

"So, if you die in the next six months, your family splits the wealth."

She shivered, feeling chilled despite the heat of the fire. It sounded so cold, so final, when he said it. Sam's eyes refocused on her and he gave her a quick smile.

"We're just speculating here. Nothing is going to happen to you."

"I know, but it's pretty scary to think about someone hating me enough to want me dead."

"It probably has nothing to do with you. It's the money. Some people will do anything for money."

"I suppose."

"Tell me about your family."

"God, I could write a book about my family but no one would believe it. What do you want to know?"

"Just a thumbnail sketch of each of them. Give me some idea of who I'm dealing with."

"You're dealing with a bunch of people who haven't figured out that this is the twentieth century. They all belong in the days of servants and lackies. They'd have been happy then."

"What about the aunt who raised you?"

"Aunt Dodie? Well, she'd have made a good drill sergeant or maybe a director at a camp for the damned. Aunt Dodie believes that she was put on earth to manage everyone's lives as she sees fit and to hell with what they want."

"What about money? Does she have any of her own?"

"Some. Her mother inherited quite a bit from my great-grandfather and Aunt Dodie's father managed it pretty well. Uncle Lionel was a lawyer before they were married and he earned a good salary. My cousin Lance never has enough money. He'd probably bump me off in a minute. My aunt has some fantasy about Lance and me getting married—keep the loot in the family, I guess."

"What's Lance like?"

"Spoiled, beautiful, useless. It's a shame, really. He might have turned into a halfway decent human being if Aunt Dodie hadn't drummed it into his head that the world owed him something because he was born into the Malone family."

"So the two of you don't get along?"

She laughed, a short sound that lacked humor. "That's an understatement. We fought like cats and dogs when we were kids. He resented me coming to live with his parents after my parents died. He resented my having money. He resented that I didn't kiss his sleeve as he walked by. He resented me. Period. And I suppose I resented him. It didn't seem fair that his parents were still alive when mine were dead.''

"Okay. So we'll put Lance at the top of the list.''

"Look, we don't like each other but I can't really believe that he'd have me killed.''

"I didn't say he did. But we've got to have a list of suspects. All the best detectives have a list.''

Babs smiled weakly at his obvious attempt to interject a little humor into the situation. What she really wanted to do was shut her eyes and lean against him and pretend that the rest of the world didn't exist. She resented the intrusion into their peaceful little world. But Sam was right. They had to face this sooner or later.

"What about the rest of the family?''

"There really isn't all that much. Uncle Emmet—but I don't think we have to worry about him. There's Aunt Bertie and Uncle Clarence, but they aren't likely suspects.''

"Probably not but tell me about them anyway.''

"Well, neither of them has had any contact with reality since I've known them. Aunt Bertie makes pots and baskets and similar useless stuff. Uncle Clarence collects guns and smokes cigars.''

"Guns? Seems an odd thing to collect for someone who's out of touch with reality. You don't get much more real than that.''

Babs grinned, relaxing for the first time since this conversation had begun. "Well, the story is that in the twenties, Aunt Bertie was quite a flapper.''

"A flapper?'' Sam's mouth turned up, trying to imagine that ditzy voice on the phone belonging to a young woman in a drop-waist dress and beads.

"A flapper. Quite a wild one, too, from what I hear.

Parties, cigarettes and,'' her voice dropped dramatically, ''rumble seats.''

''No. Not rumble seats.'' Sam looked shocked and Babs bit her cheek to hold back a grin. She nodded solemnly.

''Rumble seats. Anyway, my great-grandfather was threatening to throw her out of the family but Bertie was his favorite, his pet, and he couldn't quite bring himself to do it. Just before her behavior became too scandalous, she got married. And not some hole-in-the-wall affair either but a spectacular wedding with the crème de la crème of society. People even flew in from New York, which was no small thing in those days.''

''So she married Clarence and your great-grandfather was happy.''

''Well, not completely. He wasn't real enthused with her choice. Uncle Clarence was supposedly a Chicago gangster with all kinds of unsavory connections. If it had been any of the other children, I'm sure the old man would have thrown them out of the family—lock, stock and rumble seat—but he couldn't bring himself to cast aside his pet so he set about covering up Uncle Clarence's past.''

''A gangster?'' Sam smiled but there was an arrested look in his eyes. Babs caught it and shook her head.

''Don't get any ideas. If Uncle Clarence really was a gangster, it was fifty years ago. I don't even know if the story is true. Naturally, no one will talk about it but that's what I pieced together over the years. Anyway, it was all a long time ago and Uncle Clarence has floated through life ever since.''

''I suppose you're right.'' He leaned over to toss another small log on the fire. ''So it sounds like our top suspect has to be your cousin.''

"I guess. I don't know." Babs stirred restlessly, watching the flames lick hungrily at the new log. "I guess if it has to be one of them, I'd say Aunt Dodie is the only one capable of murder. She might even be able to justify it to herself. She's got a firm belief in her own infallibility. Uncle Lionel might arrange it if she told him to. He does everything else she tells him." She shuddered, looking away from the fire.

"I just can't really believe that any of them wants me dead. There may be no real love lost between us but there's still quite a gap between that and actually killing a person."

The fire found a pocket of moisture in the log, exploding it with a loud pop that punctuated her words. A small lamp that stood on a table next to the sofa exploded at the same moment, showering them with bits of porcelain.

Babs lifted a hand to her hair to brush the glass out of it. Her only thought was that the fire popping couldn't possibly have caused the lamp to explode. Everything seemed to happen in slow motion, like a film slowed down to view frame by frame.

She looked at Sam, her eyes widening as she noticed the look of deadly intent in his eyes as he lunged across the short distance between them. She felt his hands grab her shoulders but it didn't feel real, none of it felt real. She went over backward, feeling the scrape of the braided rug through her shirt, feeling Sam's large frame cover her.

It couldn't have been more than a few seconds that she lay there, counting every heartbeat, her mind refusing to function. Sam's chest crushed her breasts and, after a moment, Babs realized that she wasn't sure which was his heartbeat and which was hers. She drew a rough breath, trying to shake the fog out of her mind.

"What happened?"

"Someone took a shot at us."

A shot. Of course. It wasn't the fire popping that broke the lamp, it was a bullet. And Sam had pushed her down out of the line of fire and covered her, protecting her with his own body. The thought was enough to penetrate the vagueness in her mind. She didn't want anyone taking a bullet meant for her. She moved, trying to shift his weight off her.

"Hold still." Sam hissed the command in her ear.

"Get off me. If somebody is going to get shot, it's going to be me."

"Nobody is going to get shot." He shifted but kept his arm across her shoulders, holding her to the floor. "Stay down and don't move until I tell you to."

Staying close to the floor, he crawled over to the table where he'd set the oil lamp. Babs rolled onto her stomach, watching as he carefully reached up, fumbling a moment before finding the key and turning down the wick. The light dimmed and then went out and the old house was suddenly dark, lit only by the fire in the fireplace.

The flickering light only added to the surrealistic feeling of the scene. It was as if they were playing some silly game where the object was to stay low. Only the consequences of losing this game could be deadly.

Sam disappeared into the bedroom, pulling himself along on his elbows. Babs waited, hardly daring to breathe. She was lying too close to the fire and her right side felt sizzling hot but she didn't move. After what seemed an interminable time, Sam reappeared, still on his belly, dragging his pack behind him.

Glass shattered and there was a dull thud as a bullet buried itself in the wall. Babs caught her breath on a sob and pressed her face against the rug. A light touch on her shoulder made her jump but it was only Sam. She raised her head cautiously.

"It's okay. I didn't bring you this far to let you get killed." Another shot punctuated the sentence. Babs winced but she didn't look away from him. Sam grinned and wrapped his hand in her hair, tugging her forward a few inches to kiss her. It was only a brief touch of the lips but it was enough to make the fear recede a little.

"We're going to get out of this. They're not really trying to kill us."

"They're not?"

"Nope. They just want to keep us pinned down while they work their way closer to the house. They may hope a lucky shot gets one of us but they're not counting on it."

"Lucky for whom?" she muttered.

"Come on, help me pull this rug back." He was tugging at the old braided rug that lay in front of the hearth.

"What for? Is it a magic carpet that will waft us out a window and fly us away?" She rolled off the rug and helped him pull it away from the fireplace. Another bullet zinged overhead and she winced but she didn't stop tugging.

"Good girl." Sam's smile gleamed in the firelight and, illogically, Babs felt better. If he could smile, then maybe things weren't so bad after all. Moving the heavy rug wasn't easy when they didn't dare lift their heads much above knee level but at last it was rolled away, revealing more wood flooring, a great deal of dirt and…a door.

"What's that?"

"It's a trapdoor. There's a tunnel under it that leads to a root cellar in back of the house. When Dad bought the place, the tunnel was collapsed but we restored it. I guess the people who built this place wanted a way to get to the root cellar without going outside. It looks like it used to be big enough to walk through but it's more of a crawl space now."

He was shining the flashlight into the opening as he spoke. The empty black space seemed to swallow the light like a greedy animal. Babs stared into the blackness and swallowed. Then she swallowed again.

"You want *me* to go in *there*?"

"Sure. We'll come out in the root cellar and hike across the old fields to the road. We can find someplace to sleep for tonight and then tomorrow we'll be able to hitch a ride to the nearest phone."

Another bullet shattered a window. Babs looked over her shoulder at the front of the house where killers waited. Then she looked at the yawning black hole, which looked bigger than it had a second ago, as if it were a mouth opening, waiting to be fed. Until this moment she'd never appreciated the true meaning of being between a rock and a hard place.

Chapter Twelve

Babs had never realized just how dark dark could get. This was real dark, as in no light, as in pitch black. Ahead of her the beam of Sam's flashlight was swallowed up by the darkness, its pathetic attempt at lighting the way nullified by the all-consuming black.

The tunnel had settled since Sam had last been through it. His broad shoulders brushed the dirt walls on either side, creating tiny avalanches of soil and pebbles. His bulk blocked any light that might have filtered back to her, leaving her to feel her way along. At least if there were any rats, Sam would encounter them first. She immediately regretted the thought.

Rats did not bear thinking about. On the heels of that thought came another, equally unwelcome. Spiders. She shuddered and inched her hand forward. If she touched something that moved, she would probably pass out and die, stuck in this stupid tunnel. Really, when you thought about it, guns weren't so bad.

"You okay?" Sam's voice sounded muffled.

"Fine." Babs gritted out the word. She wasn't fine at all. She was suffering from an advanced case of claustrophobia, along with acute anxiety regarding any wildlife that might inhabit this awful place. But there was nothing either of them could do about it.

She closed her eyes and then opened them again. It made little difference but, at least with them open, she could just make out Sam's silhouette. There was a scuffling noise ahead and her heart stopped, picturing all the horrid possibilities. Sam was grappling with a rat the size of a small pony, struggling for his life. There was a spider the size of a Great Dane and he was trying to kill it before it could devour them both. He'd had a heart attack and they were both going to die in this damn tunnel.

Before her imagination could present any more scenarios, there was a thud and she realized that Sam's silhouette had disappeared. She stopped, staring into the blackness. He'd fallen into an old mine shaft that went hundreds of feet down.

"Come on." His voice sounded reassuringly close. If he were lying at the bottom of a mine shaft, he wouldn't be urging her to join him. She edged forward again, aware that she could see light up ahead. It was faint but, after the darkness of the tunnel, it looked like heaven. She crawled to the edge of the tunnel and found herself at eye level with Sam. He'd set the flashlight on a shelf and it cast just enough light to give a vague impression of the old root cellar.

"Put your hands on my shoulders and I'll lift you down. I guess the original owners must have had some steps here but there's no sign of them now."

She set her hands on his shoulders and he reached up to grasp her waist, lifting her easily out of the tunnel and setting her on the dirt floor. Babs looked around uneasily. Cobwebs hung from every corner, dust was thick on every surface. In some places there were vague marks that might or might not have been tracks. She didn't want to know.

"Do you think there are rats or spiders or anything in here?" Her voice was hushed as if she were afraid she might wake some of the residents.

"I'm sure there are spiders. I don't know about rats but there might be frogs." Sam was moving away as he spoke.

"Frogs?" Babs took a quick step to catch up with him. "Frogs that jump?"

"Most frogs do." He picked up the flashlight and shone it around the cellar, giving a pleased exclamation when it illuminated a warped wooden door.

Babs stayed right on his heels as he moved toward the door. It was impossible to look in four different directions at once but she was giving it her best shot. Spiders and rats were bad enough but something that might actually jump out of nowhere at you was more than she could take. She had a vague image of large green slimy creatures with big teeth, lunging out of the darkness to attack her. Logically, she knew that wasn't a very accurate picture but she'd left logic behind somewhere in that awful length of tunnel.

"Now, when I open the door, I'm going to go out slowly. Since we don't know exactly where the bad guys are, I don't want to walk into a bullet. You wait here until I signal you. Try to be as quiet as possible. Got it?"

"I got it."

"Good." He wrapped his hand around the back of her neck and tilted her face up to drop a quick but thorough kiss on her mouth. "We're going to be okay. Just wait for my signal."

Sam eased the door open, hesitating as it creaked. He

braced himself and then opened it quickly, wincing at the noise it made. Cool night air flooded the root cellar, banishing years of mustiness. Babs lifted her face, drinking in the fresh air, feeling it banish some of the fear. Overhead she could catch a glimpse of stars. The sight reassured her further.

Sam crouched on the steps, a dark shadow against the night sky. He lifted his hand and she saw starlight glint off steel, silent and ominous. He waited without moving until Babs began to wonder how he could hold one position for so long, and then suddenly he was gone, disappearing so quickly and silently it was as if he'd never been there at all.

Wait, he'd said. She would wait. She would give him thirty seconds and then she was getting out of this place. Bullets or no, she couldn't stand it much longer than that. The skin on her back was threatening to crawl right off at the thought of the creepy crawlies that might be lurking in the darkness behind her.

"Okay." Sam's whisper came just as she was sure she couldn't stand to stay where she was for another moment. "Watch your step. The stairs are rickety."

He reached down a hand and Babs took it, picking her way up the stairs, feeling them creak and moan under her weight. In a matter of seconds, she was standing on firm ground with nothing but sky around her. She could have stood there for hours, just savoring the space but Sam had other ideas.

"Come on." He took her right hand in his left, keeping the gun in his other hand. Babs curled her fingers around his, feeling immediately reassured by the firm strength of his palm.

The old farmhouse was a dark bulk to their right. Sam circled around it, heading toward the road. Babs looked over her shoulder at the house. It was silent now. If the killers were still there, they were no longer making any noise. Sam kept the pace at something just under a run, his hand tugging her along, keeping her with him.

"Hot damn! We're in luck." Babs had turned to look over her shoulder. When Sam came to an abrupt halt, she collided with his back with enough force to rock her back on her toes. Sam barely noticed. He was staring at a small brown car that hardly seemed worthy of such excitement.

"Look at this. Maybe they even left the keys in it." He strode around the front of the car, with Babs trotting along behind him. The driver's door opened to his touch and he reached in, feeling for the ignition switch.

"Damn. No keys." He pulled his hand out of the car and looked around before turning his attention to Babs. In the moonlight, his face was all hard angles and shadows.

"A car could mean the difference between living and dying. I think I can hot-wire this thing but I can't do that and keep an eye out for our friendly neighborhood hit men." He handed her his gun. It was warm from his hand. Her fingers curled around it, testing the weight and grip. "If you have to use it, shoot to kill. It's them or us."

"I know."

Sam's fingers brushed lightly over her cheek and then he bent down to slide into the car, fumbling under the dashboard. Babs kept her eyes skimming over the night dark countryside. It seemed like forever, but could only have been a few minutes, before she heard Sam's triumphant whisper an instant before the engine sprang to life. There was a shout from the direction of the house as the killers heard the sound of the motor.

"Get in!" She didn't need Sam's command to scurry around the hood. He had the passenger door open and she was barely in the seat when he put the car in reverse and stomped on the gas. The tires spun in the loose dirt for an instant before catching. Babs's door slammed shut of its own volition as the car rocketed back up the long drive. There was a sharp popping noise. She ducked automatically, expecting to see a bullet come through the windshield.

The tires bumped from dirt onto pavement and they were out of range. Sam threw the gear into drive and they were roaring down the highway. Within seconds the old farmhouse was several miles behind them. Sam slowed the car to a more sedate speed. To anyone who passed them, they would look like an average couple, driving down a country road late in the evening.

"Where are we going?" Babs reached for her seat belt.

"I think it's time we headed back to Santa Barbara. I can take you to my mom's place and you can stay there. You okay?"

"Sure. I'm fine. I've just been shot at, crawled through a tunnel that was built for munchkins, stood in a cellar full of killer frogs and helped steal a car. I can't wait to see what will happen tomorrow."

"Killer frogs?" Sam threw her a quizzical look.

"You know what I mean." Babs stared out the windshield, her face set. Sam could see her expression in the light from the dashboard and he thought he'd never seen anyone look more mournful.

"What's wrong?"

"I guess someone really does want me dead." There was childlike hurt in the words and he realized how much she'd been counting on it all being a misunderstanding.

"There doesn't seem to be much room for doubt."

"If they just wanted to keep me out of the way for a while, they wouldn't have started shooting like that, would they?"

Babs's tone begged him to tell her she was wrong. Sam would have given anything to be able to give her the reassurance she wanted. It just wasn't possible.

"No, they wouldn't have."

She was silent for a long time. Glancing at her, he could see her teeth worrying at her lower lip, her eyes staring straight ahead, focused on nothing in particular. She looked hurt. She looked betrayed. He wanted to offer some comfort but there was nothing he could say to change the facts.

"Do you think they're all in on it? Do you think they all want me dead?"

"I don't think so. When I spoke to your aunts, neither of them sounded especially happy you were alive. I think it's one of them. We just have to figure out which one."

She was silent again and Sam wished he had some clue to what she was thinking. It couldn't be easy for her to go through this.

"How do you think they found us?"

"I've been giving it some thought," he said. "The only thing I can come up with is our friendly truck-stop waitress remembered where she'd seen you and called your family. Then, whoever it is who—" He paused, looking for a delicate way to phrase it.

"Wants me dead?" Babs's voice held a hard note that revealed her pain as clearly as tears would have.

Sam nodded. "Whoever wants you dead passed the information on to their hired killers. They've got my name. I suppose it wouldn't have been all that difficult to find out that my family used to own the old farmhouse. They must have figured we'd be looking for a place to hide for a while.''

"But how could they have known it was us in there? It might have been someone else entirely.''

"I'm not sure these people care that much if they get the wrong victim. I shut the curtains not too long before they started shooting. They may have been outside watching. Seeing me, they knew it was a sure bet you were with me.''

"What would have happened to us if that awful tunnel hadn't been there?''

"We'd have gone out a back window. We'd have made it.''

She didn't say anything. After a while Sam looked over and saw that her eyes were closed. He didn't think she was asleep but he respected her need for privacy. She had a lot to think about, a lot to try to work out. The road was empty and allowed plenty of time for thinking.

His hands tightened on the steering wheel. The force of his anger surprised him. He was never all that crazy about being shot at but it had happened a time or two before and he considered it an occasional part of the territory. But it was something else entirely for them to be shooting at Babs.

The clock on the dashboard said ten o'clock when he looked at Babs and found that she really was asleep. Highway 5 stretched wide open ahead of him, threatening a case of terminal highway hypnosis. Flipping on the radio, he found a station playing oldies but goodies. It was depressing to realize that some of the songs they were calling oldies were ones he remembered as top-ten hits.

Sometime after midnight Babs roused, stretching and yawning like a child waking from a nap. She looked out the windshield at the empty road and then looked at Sam.

"Where are we?"

"Somewhere between San Francisco and L.A."

"Sorry I went to sleep on you like that."

"No problem. How are you feeling?"

"Okay. You know, I keep thinking about it and thinking about it and it still doesn't make sense. I just can't believe that anyone in my family wants me dead. It's got to be a misunderstanding."

Sam could hear the lack of conviction in her voice but he wasn't going to be the one to make her look at reality. She'd come to terms with it in her own time. In the meantime, he'd be around to make sure she didn't get killed.

"Maybe. But misunderstanding or not, the end result is still people shooting at us."

"True." She stared at the dark countryside as the tires ate away the miles. "You want me to drive for a while? You must be tired."

"I'm okay. You're the one who needs to rest. Whatever is going on, I think we can pretty well bet that it's not going to be a lot of fun. Kidnapping, with or without murder, is hardly an acceptable pastime, even when you keep it in the family."

"I know. I'm not really looking forward to seeing them again."

"Well, you don't have to worry about it for now. We're going to my mother's. From there, we can try to contact Emmet and call the police."

"The police! I don't want to involve them in this."

Sam reached over and caught hold of one of her hands. "We've got to at least call and tell them that you're all right. They think you've been kidnapped, remember?"

"Of course. You're right." She took a deep breath, her fingers curling around his. "Do we have to tell them my family was involved? If the press gets hold of that, they'll have a field day with it. It's bad enough being the 'Malone heiress' without adding this to it. Couldn't we just tell them that you rescued me and leave it at that?"

Sam's response could not lessen the quiver in her voice. "I suppose that's enough. For now. But if we find out we're talking attempted murder, I won't help you cover that up."

"I'm sure it's all a misunderstanding."

"Some misunderstanding," he muttered but he didn't argue any further. They both knew it wasn't a misunderstanding but he understood her need to keep that hope alive. He wouldn't take it away from her.

IT WAS JUST AFTER FOUR O'CLOCK in the morning when Sam stopped the car in front of his mother's house. The quiet neighborhood slept, though there were lights on in one or two houses, a reminder that, for some people, it was time to get up and go to work.

Babs woke from a light doze and stretched sleepily. She looked so vulnerable that Sam wanted to catch her up in his arms and take her as far away from her demented family as possible.

"Are we here?"

"We're here." He reached into the back seat and grabbed his pack before opening his door. "Come on."

"Won't your mother mind us getting her up at this hour? Maybe we should wait a while."

"Mom won't mind. She's used to me showing up at weird hours. Besides, it's too cold to hang around out here."

Babs lagged behind him on the short walk to the porch. He knew she was uneasy about dropping in on a stranger at this hour but he also knew he could depend on his mother to put her at ease. He pulled his keys out of his pocket and found the one that fit the door. It felt strange to be doing something so totally normal as opening the front door of the house he'd grown up in.

He pushed open the door and then stood to the side, waiting for Babs. She hung back. "I don't think this is such a good idea. What if she thinks we're burglars? I don't want to scare her."

"We aren't going to scare her." He reached out, catching her arm and tugging her into the small hallway before shutting the door behind them. "Stay there and I'll find a light."

"Sam? Is that you?"

"It's me, Mom. Sorry we woke you." There was a click and Babs blinked in the sudden flood of light. She had a vague impression of floral wallpaper and hardwood floors but her attention was focused on the woman coming down the stairs. Sam went forward to greet her, meeting her at the foot of the stairs and putting his arms around her, swinging her off her feet.

"Beautiful as ever, I see." His mother laughed, a sweet, youthful sound.

"Put me down, hooligan, and let me look at you." He set her on her feet and she looked up at him, studying him with a mother's eye. "You've got a bruise on your cheekbone, which probably means you've been in a fight, and you need a shave. I was beginning to worry about you.''

"I'm okay. We're both okay." He smiled at Babs over his mother's head and Cecily turned.

"You must be Babs. It's so nice to meet you." Babs came forward slowly, wondering whether she should hold out her hand or just smile. Cecily appeared to think that neither of those was appropriate. She held out her arms, enveloping the younger woman in a quick hug. The gesture was warm and genuine, a welcome Babs had never received from her own family. She returned the hug awkwardly, blinking back tears.

Cecily stepped back, putting her hands on Babs's shoulders. "You're much prettier than your pictures. Even prettier than your uncle Emmet said you were."

"You've talked to Uncle Emmet?"

"Has he been here?"

The two questions ran one on top of the other but Cecily didn't seem to have any trouble sorting them out.

"Yes, I've talked to your uncle and yes, he's been here." She tightened the belt of her long velour robe and ran her fingers through her hair, smoothing it into casual gray waves. "I bet you're both hungry. Why don't you come into the kitchen and I'll make some coffee and some breakfast. You can call Emmet from the phone in there."

She linked her arm through Babs's. "Emmet has been very worried about you."

"What did he tell you?" Sam asked the question as the three of them stepped into the huge kitchen.

"He knows your family arranged the kidnapping and he knew about Sam's call to say he'd rescued you, but then the two of you just disappeared. We didn't know what happened."

"It's a long story, Mom. If you don't mind, could we wait until Emmet gets here so we only have to tell it once?"

"Of course. His number is right there next to the phone. That's the hotel he's staying at. He refused to stay with the family."

"You want me to call him?" Sam asked Babs quietly.

"Would you mind? I think I'd start crying." She smiled but her mouth quivered and he knew she wasn't far from tears now.

"Come on, sit down and have a cup of coffee and think about how nice it is that nobody's shooting at us." He reached out and brushed her hair back from her face, his fingers gentle. Babs turned to rest her cheek against his palm for just a moment, drawing strength from the contact.

Cecily watched the exchange, her eyes narrowing. She couldn't see her son's face but she could see the girl's. Her expression was revealing and Cecily wondered if Babs had any idea just what was written there. An even stronger question in her mind was whether Sam saw the same thing and how he felt about it.

By the time Emmet arrived, Sam and Babs were working on their second cups of coffee and Cecily was halfway through preparations for a breakfast of bacon and eggs and hash browns. When the doorbell rang, Babs set her cup down with a thud, slopping coffee onto the table top. She didn't even notice. Cecily looked at her, her eyes warm.

"Why don't you go answer that?"

"Thank you." Babs hurried from the room. Sam watched her leave. His mother watched him.

"She's very pretty."

"Yes, she is."

"She seems sweet."

"She can be." Sam reached for a napkin and mopped up the spilled coffee. "She can also be quite a spoiled brat."

"That's not surprising, growing up with all that money." She chopped potatoes into neat cubes. "The two of you must have gotten to know each other pretty well."

"I suppose."

"I've heard it said that you can get to know a person's true colors when they're under stress. Babs seems to have come through this in good shape."

"She's got guts." Sam's tone was deliberately non-committal.

"Amazing how close you can get to someone when you're alone with them for days on end."

Sam's smile held a weary edge. "Look, Mom, if you're playing matchmaker, give it up. You're about as subtle as a steamroller. Besides, it's a ridiculous idea."

"Why?"

The simple question seemed to throw him off balance and he stared at her for a minute without speaking. "Why? For a million reasons. Several million, in fact."

"Her money? Don't be ridiculous."

"It's not ridiculous. Besides, this whole discussion is irrelevant. Babs and I have managed to get along just fine because we had to but we have nothing in common. Once this whole mess is settled, we'll go our separate ways and that will be the end of it."

Cecily hadn't been a mother for thirty-five years without learning when to drop a subject. She lifted her shoulders in a slight shrug as if to say that Sam might be right. She slid the potatoes into hot oil and set a lid over the pan before glancing at her son. He was staring at his coffee, his expression brooding. Sam could say what he wanted but she knew what she'd seen in his eyes when he looked at Babs.

When Emmet and Babs entered the kitchen, there were tearstains on her face and his eyes were a bit brighter than normal. Sam stood up as Babs slipped out from under her uncle's arm. Emmet stopped and held out his hand.

"I suspect I've got a lot to thank you for, Sam. When we parted company in Mexico, I never would have thought we'd meet up again quite like this." He shook Sam's hand, the fierce pressure expressing his gratitude.

"I'd like to tell you it was no big deal but, starting with Babs trying to push me off a balcony, I'm afraid we've both had a bit more on our hands than either of us wanted."

"Tried to push you off a balcony, did she? Well, I'm sure she had a good reason. So, tell me what's been going on. We haven't heard a word from you in days. I was beginning to think you'd decided to kidnap Babs yourself."

"Breakfast is just about ready. Why don't you all sit down and we can talk while we eat."

"It smells wonderful, Mrs. Delanian."

"Call me Cecily. I certainly plan to call you Babs. I've got lots of food and I have a suspicion that it's been awhile since the two of you had a good hot breakfast."

Well, we almost had one a couple of days ago but Babs started a fight and we never got to eat." Sam threw Babs a teasing look and she grinned.

"*I* didn't start that fight. George started it. I was just minding my own business."

They bickered back and forth while Cecily dished up food. Emmet and Cecily watched them, noting the easy camaraderie, the way their eyes met, holding so many memories. Emmet glanced at Cecily, a question in his eyes. She smiled and shrugged lightly, denying any positive knowledge but the faint smile that quivered around her lips gave her opinion. Looking from one to the other, Emmet's mouth curved. Maybe Sam Delanian was just what Babs needed in her life. This whole kidnapping insanity might not turn out to be such a bad thing after all.

It took over an hour for Sam and Babs to tell their story. In between bites, they took turns talking, telling the whole adventure, starting with the kidnapping itself, through Sam's rescue, the fight at the motel, their travels in the moving van and finally, their escape from the farmhouse.

By the time the story was told, the food was all gone and they were lingering over fresh coffee. While they talked, the sun had come up outside and was spilling cheerful spring light into the big kitchen.

"So what was happening here while we were gone?" Babs asked the question of her uncle. "How did you find out about the kidnapping? Did the family tell you about the paintings?"

"I found out you'd been kidnapped the same way the rest of the world did—I read about it in the paper. I don't think they'd have told me a thing but Bertie let the cat out of the bag. At least enough of the cat that they had to tell me the rest of it.

"They honestly thought they could get away with cheating a man like Stefanoni, and with kidnapping you. I don't think the lot of them has touched base with reality in years. I talked with Stefanoni and he's willing to forget the whole thing, as long as he gets the real paintings."

"I bet Aunt Dodie liked that."

"She just about had a heart attack but I didn't give her much choice. Anyway, that end of the mess is straightened out. Now all we've got to worry about is whoever has been taking potshots at the two of you."

"I'm sure it's a mistake of some kind." Babs's tone was more pleading than firm. "We may not get along but I can't believe that any of them would actually kill me."

Emmet shrugged and said nothing, letting the comment lie as if he might agree with it. But meeting his eyes, Sam knew he didn't believe it any more than Sam did. Someone in the Malone family wanted Babs dead. The question was: Who?

Chapter Thirteen

"I really don't want to intrude."

"Don't be silly, Babs. I'd love to have you and Sam stay here with me." Cecily's warm tone could not be mistaken for anything other than sincere welcome. Still, Babs hesitated.

"I really think this will be the best thing," Emmet said. "It will give me a chance to find out what's going on. I can dump the car you stole so you can't be traced from that. You and Sam can stay here for a couple of days until I've made a few inquiries and have found out who's behind the shootings."

Babs looked from her uncle to Sam, her eyes questioning. Would he mind her staying with his mother? She wanted to stay. The last thing in the world she wanted to do was to go back to that mausoleum the rest of the family called home. It had never been a home, not in the real sense of the word. But she didn't want to stay here unless Sam wanted her to.

"I think it would be a good idea, Babs. You'll be safe here until we know what's going on. It's only for a couple of days. You can stand me that much longer, can't you?" He grinned but there was something in his eyes beyond humor. There were questions there, uncertainties that mirrored her own.

Everything had changed so quickly. When it had been just the two of them, struggling to survive, things had been fairly simple. Now, wrapped in the cozy warmth of his mother's home, everything had shifted in some subtle way—and she couldn't put her finger on it.

Babs turned to Cecily. "I'd like to stay, if you're sure you don't mind."

"Not a bit. Why don't you come upstairs with me and I'll show you where you'll be sleeping and where the bathroom is. I bet a hot shower would feel nice."

"Heaven. Hot water has been in short supply over the past few days."

Sam's eyes followed the two of them, his expression unreadable. When they were out of sight, he looked at Emmet.

"So, what do you really think? Is there someone in the family who's capable of murder?"

Emmet ran his fingers through his hair, ruffling it into iron-gray waves. His eyes were worried. "I don't know. It's hard to say what people will do when money is involved. There's not a one of them that's worth a plug nickel and they've never quite gotten over Babs having the money to buy and sell the whole bunch. She never held it over them and she's bailed them out time and again, but that just made them resent her more."

"So what do you think the next step should be? Do we call the police?"

"I suppose we'd better call and let them know Babs is no longer a kidnap victim. I still have some friends on the force. I think I can convince them to keep this quiet, at least for a day or two. When it was just a matter of this ridiculous kidnapping scheme, I was willing to try to keep the family out of it. But if one of them is trying to kill Babs, then they'll have to take their chances just like ordinary mortals.''

''Well, those were definitely real bullets they were shooting at us and the guys who jumped us at the motel looked real serious about their work.''

''I'll see what I can find out. I want to thank you for what you did for my niece.''

Sam shrugged. ''I just did what had to be done.''

But now that it was done, where did that leave him and Babs?

IT WASN'T AN EASY QUESTION to answer—for either of them. Sam lay awake that night, in the room that had been his when he was a boy. Just across the hall was the spare bedroom where Babs was presumably asleep. It was strange to be so close to her and yet separated by closed doors. He was only just now realizing that, since climbing over the balcony, there'd been hardly a moment when they weren't in sight of each other.

He stared up at the ceiling, hands under his head. It was late. He'd driven all night the night before. He should have been sleeping, not lying awake pondering how quickly life could change. The quiet neighborhood slept, full of suburban serenity. Sam only wished some of that serenity would rub off on him.

Soon this would all be over. Emmet had dumped the car they'd taken from the killers. He'd talked to a friend on the police force who'd agreed to give them forty-eight hours and then the police were going to start official questioning. Emmet hadn't told him about the apparent murder attempts, only that the kidnapping had been a sort of bizarre family joke that had gotten out of hand. It was unlikely the police department would be amused.

In Sam's considered opinion, the entire Malone clan deserved to be hung by their thumbs. Not just for this madness, but for all the years they'd ignored a lonely little girl and all the times they'd used her. But that wasn't his problem. He had to keep reminding himself of that. In forty-eight hours or less, this whole mess would be settled, either with or without the police. His part in it was all but over.

They'd find out who wanted Babs dead, they'd turn them over to the police and he'd be able to go back to his own life and forget all about the demented Malone family. Only he wasn't sure it was going to be that easy. Something told him that Babs wasn't going to be easy to put behind him.

The next thirty-six hours were unusual. After all the danger and adventuring they'd been through, neither Sam nor Babs quite knew what to do with themselves when no one was shooting at them or chasing them. They also didn't quite know what to do with each other.

Sam found himself avoiding Babs and then missing her when she wasn't in sight. It didn't matter how many times he told himself that he was glad this mess was almost over, he couldn't convince himself that he was going to be able to walk away at the end of it. Something pulled him to Babs even as he backed away. Something stronger than just the bonds of two people who'd gone through a dangerous time together.

It was crazy. They had nothing in common. She probably thought nothing of vacationing in St. Moritz, he was more inclined to backpack into the Sierras. He was eleven years older than she was and centuries older in experience. He, better than anyone, knew what her temper could be like. But he found himself thinking of the way her face lit up when she smiled, the way her mouth softened under his and the way her body curved to fit his.

"Sam. What do you think?"

Sam blinked and shook his head, aware that his mind had been miles away from the conversation. He glanced across the table at Emmet and smiled ruefully.

"Sorry. I was thinking of something else."

"So I noticed."

Sam didn't think it was coincidence that the other man's eyes rested on Babs for a moment. Sam looked at her, trying not to notice the way the early morning sunshine caught in her hair, picking out golden highlights. Her eyes met his, questioningly, and he wondered if she had the same questions he did, the same confused thoughts.

He looked away from her and picked up his coffee cup. "So, what did you say?"

Emmet pushed his plate away and leaned back in his chair, reaching for his pipe. "I've arranged to get the whole family together tomorrow around noon. I figure the best way to find the rotten apple is to get them all together and shake them up a bit. Then we can find out who's trying to kill Babs."

"I still can't really believe that they'd actually want me dead." Babs shook her head, the small movement stirring her hair, reminding Sam of the silky feel of it in his hands, against his body.

Cecily reached out and took Babs's hand where it lay on the table, squeezing it gently. "Perhaps you're right and it's just a terrible misunderstanding."

Babs looked at her, still a bit shy with this woman

who seemed to be the embodiment of all her childhood fantasies of what a mother should be.

"I hope I'm right."

"Well, I hope you are too, muffin." Emmet pulled out his tobacco pouch and unzipped it. Before he could reach into it, Cecily had taken both it and the pipe from him. Her slim fingers packed tobacco into the pipe in neat little chunks, tamping it to just the right firmness before adding another layer. Emmet took it from her with a smile, touching his fingers lightly to the back of her hand. "Thanks. You've certainly got a magic touch with pipes."

"Flatterer." Her smile lit her eyes, making her look years younger.

Sam stared at them, his eyes narrowing slightly. He couldn't count the times he'd seen his mother perform the same little task with his father's pipe. He felt a surprising twinge of resentment that she was doing it for another man. But the resentment didn't last, not when he saw the sparkle in her eyes. Anything that made her look that happy was okay with him. It just might take a little getting used to.

"So, what do you think, Sam?" Emmet lit the pipe, filling the room with a sweet, spicy scent.

Sam had to drag his mind back to the question at hand. There seemed to be so many questions lately that it was hard to remember which one he was supposed to focus on.

"Sounds good to me. I've always wanted to be in on an Agatha Christie-style interrogation. Too bad we can't do it at midnight. We could add a few candles for atmosphere."

"Not a bad idea but nothing short of an act of Congress could get Dodie to stay up past ten. She believes that late hours have contributed to the decline of western civilization. Noon will have to do."

"It'll do. Just what do you have in mind?"

"Well, nothing specific. I figure maybe we can just try to shake them up a bit and see what falls out."

Babs shuddered and Sam reached out automatically, putting his hand on her shoulder. "It's just to scare out the killer—*if* there is a killer."

"I know. But this whole thing is a little gruesome."

"Don't worry. I'm not going to let anything happen to you."

"I know." There was absolute confidence in the words. If Sam said he'd protect her, she believed him. Sam looked into her eyes, seeing things there he couldn't quite define—things he wasn't sure he wanted to know about. His hand dropped away from her shoulder and he looked away, breaking the odd little spell.

"So, what's next?" If anyone else had noticed the strangely intense exchange, they didn't say anything.

"Well, I think the two of you should continue to lay low here until tomorrow. I've got a meeting with Stefanoni today. He was so pleased to get the real paintings that he offered to find out who hired the men who kidnapped you. He may be able to find out what their orders were. It would make it a lot easier if we knew exactly what we were up against." He looked at his watch and sighed. "In fact, I'd better hit the road now."

Emmet left and Sam stood up, carrying his plate to the sink and handing it to Babs. "I thought I'd go clean out the garage," he mumbled. "Give me something to do."

Babs sighed as she watched him leave. It was pretty clear that he was avoiding her.

"Don't worry about it. All men go through that phase." Cecily gave her a reassuring smile.

"I thought it might be something I'd done."

"No. Sam's just got a lot to think about right now."

"I suppose." Babs reached for a towel. As Cecily washed and rinsed a plate, Babs took it from her and dried it, her movements a little clumsy. After all, a Malone wasn't expected to do anything as mundane as dry dishes.

"You're fond of Sam, aren't you?" Cecily's question was light and nonthreatening but Babs found herself throwing up barriers automatically.

"He saved my life—more than once."

"He seems to think you held up your end pretty well."

Babs shrugged, trying to ignore the little glow Cecily's words created. The idea that Sam thought she'd held up her end was appealing. Maybe too appealing. She had to remember that they'd been together under some pretty extraordinary circumstances. She couldn't lose sight of the fact that they had little in common. They were back in the real world now and, in the real world, their lives ran along very different paths.

"We don't really have anything in common." Cecily didn't seem to have any trouble following the seemingly irrelevant comment.

"You know, I've always thought that people put too much importance on having things in common. You don't have to like the same foods or the same movies to make a relationship work. Sam's father and I didn't have all that much in common when we married and we were very happy together. It all depends on how much you want it to work."

Babs set down a plate and reached for another, a faint

frown creasing her forehead. "But what did you talk about?"

Cecily laughed. "Anything and everything."

"Didn't you argue?"

"Some, but in the long run there was nothing more important to us than our marriage so we always found a way to compromise." She paused, glancing sideways at Babs. "Do you and Sam argue?"

"Constantly. Well, not really." Babs flushed delicately and stared at the plate she held in her hands, the towel still. "Sometimes we talked. He's really pretty easy to talk to."

"He's a good listener. He always has been, even when he was a boy."

"What was he like when he was a boy?"

Cecily laughed again, her eyes alight with memories. "An imp and an angel. Like all children. There were times when I was sure he was a changeling—no human child could be so mischievous—and then he'd turn around and do something sweet and I'd forget all about the mischief. His hair would never stay combed, the knees of his jeans were always torn and the house was full of strays that he'd found and just had to bring home. His father threatened to make *Sam* sleep in the garage if he brought home one more lame animal to take care of but, of course, the next time, Peter was out there helping Sam set a broken leg for a mongrel pup he'd found."

"It sounds like you were a close family." Babs wasn't aware of the wistfulness in her tone but Cecily heard it and her heart melted.

"We were." She reached out and brushed a lock of hair back from Babs's face, the gesture automatic. It wasn't until she saw the startled look in the younger woman's face—the yearning—that she realized how strange the casually affectionate gesture was to Babs. She felt a burst of anger against the people who'd let her grow up so untouched. The anger didn't show in her face.

"You know, it sounds silly but, somehow I kind of think of you as family. Ever since Emmet showed up, I've been thinking of you with Sam and hoping you were both safe. And Emmet talked about you a lot so I feel like I know you."

Babs laughed self-consciously, her fingers twisting in the towel. "You can't believe everything Uncle Emmet tells you. He only had me in the summer so he probably doesn't know me as well as he thinks."

"Oh, I think he knows you pretty well. He said you were sweet and full of spirit and courage. I think that's a pretty accurate description."

Babs stared at her for a moment, her eyes dark and vulnerable and then she looked away, struggling for some light comment. It wasn't there.

"Thank you."

"You're welcome." Cecily's smile was like a balm, soothing years of emptiness. The two women looked at one another for a moment, sensing the beginnings of a bond that lay outside Sam and his relationships with each of them—a bond to be treasured.

It was Cecily who broke the quiet moment, sensing that things might be moving too quickly. "I was going to make some cookies. Would you like to help?"

"I don't know. I've never made cookies."

"Then your education has been sadly lacking, my dear. Everyone should know how to make cookies. When Sam was little, he argued quite seriously that cookies should be the fifth basic food group, coming right after milk."

"Did you talk him out of it?"

"Certainly not. I happen to agree with the theory." Cecily grinned, her eyes sparkling in a way that made Babs think of Sam. Funny—a lot of things made her think of Sam.

THE SUN WAS SETTING out over the Pacific but it still cast a warm glow of light over the coast. Sam leaned his shoulder against the pole that supported the back porch and stared out at the hillside that sloped up out of the wide backyard. It was a tangle of brush and chaparral. When his father had been alive, he'd kept the slope cleared. Sam felt tired just remembering hours of back-breaking labor in the warm sun, rooting out weeds.

Looking at it now, he realized how overgrown it had become. He really should clear it out before summer arrived. As the sun dried out the twisted shrubs, it turned them into living tinder, just waiting for the smallest spark to set off a fire. He'd have to get to it soon. Maybe this next week. After tomorrow he'd have nothing better to do.

Tomorrow the Malone caper would be settled and life would go on. He frowned. The thought didn't give him the satisfaction it should have. He should be thrilled to be out of this mess without a bullet in his hide. He *was* thrilled. Having people shooting at him was not his favorite occupation. It was over. He was happy. So why was he scowling?

"Hi." Sam swung around. Babs was standing a few feet away, the screen door just closing behind her. The muffled thud as wood met wood seemed to emphasize the quiet evening. A scrub jay screeched raucously in the live oak that spread its branches over the yard.

"Hi."

"Were you thinking about something vital?"

"No. Nothing in particular." His eyes skimmed over her, taking in the snug jeans and loose cotton shirt. He wanted to reach out and test the fit of her jeans with his hands. He wanted to feel the silky skin beneath the soft shirt. Instead, he smiled.

"Has Mom taught you everything you always wanted to know but were afraid to ask about the fine art of cookie baking?"

"Just about." Babs took a few steps forward, wrapping her hand around one of the trees and leaning against it. "I think we baked just about every kind of cookie known to man. We may have invented some new ones. I had no idea it could get so messy."

"So I see." Sam reached out to brush a faint dusting of flour from her cheek. It was a casual gesture, certainly not out of line between two people who had been lovers. But neither of them expected the electricity that arced from the simple touch.

Babs's gaze swept upward, her eyes deep brown pools of uncertainty. Sam's hand lingered, his fingers cupping her cheek, his thumb brushing across her lower lip. Her lips parted slightly, her tongue coming out to moisten her mouth. Sam couldn't drag his eyes away, his thumb touching her again, lightly, ever so lightly, feeling the dampness. She leaned forward and he knew that it would take only a touch, a whisper for her to be in his arms. His body ached with the knowledge.

He drew a shuddering breath, his hand dropping to his side, the fingers still tingling. He saw her expression change. Disappointment? Relief? It was impossible to tell. How could he read what was in her mind when he didn't understand what was in his own?

"I guess it will all be settled tomorrow." He looked

out over the yard, seeing nothing, his every sense tuned to the woman beside him.

"I guess so. It's going to be pretty horrible if it turns out that someone is really trying to kill me. I wonder what Uncle Emmet found out from Stefanoni."

"I don't know. When he called, he said he was going to see someone who might have some information. He'll be in touch as soon as he knows something."

"I know. But the waiting is hard."

"Waiting always is." He looked at her and then looked away. Did she know how tempting she was? "Still, it's better than being shot at."

Babs laughed, the sound low and husky. "Just about anything beats being shot at."

"True. You know, you really handled yourself very well. A lot of people would have fallen to pieces."

Why don't you just say what you really mean, you idiot. Tell her how you feel.

"I was…impressed with how cool you stayed under fire."

Wimp. That's not what you want to say and you know it. Tell her.

How could he tell her when he didn't know himself? He didn't want to lose track of her. He didn't want everything to end between them tomorrow. He knew what he didn't want but he wasn't sure what he *did* want.

He looked at Babs, reading the same questions and desires and uncertainties in her eyes. She'd never looked more desirable and she'd never looked more dangerous. His life was turning upside down. Too much, too soon. He looked away, staring out at the nearly dark hillside. The porch light cast a bright circle onto the lawn and Sam wished that a light would go on in his mind, casting equal light on his confused thinking.

"I guess what I'm trying to say is—" Whatever he was trying to say was destined to remain unsaid. From behind him, he heard Babs giving a funny choking little sound at the same moment that he heard a muffled thud.

He spun around, every sense on the alert, reaching for Babs even before he consciously realized that she was falling. His arms caught her as her knees buckled, a terrifying red stain spreading over the pale pink of her shirt. Sam dropped to his knees, his body hunched protectively over hers. He threw one look at the dark hill, knowing that was where the shot must have come from but that wasn't important now. The only thing that mattered was the frightening amount of blood soaking her shirt.

He grabbed the front of her shirt and tore it open, sending buttons flying. The screen door squeaked as it was thrust open and he threw one look upward, seeing the shocked horror in his mother's eyes.

"Oh, my God! What happened?"

"She's been shot. I need some towels to stop the bleeding. Call 911. Tell them we need an ambulance." Cecily disappeared back into the house and Sam returned his attention to Babs. She looked up at him, a bewildered look in her eyes.

"I think I've been shot."

"It's all right, sweetheart." Sam used the tail of her shirt to wipe away the blood, searching for the entrance wound. Half-formed prayers floated through his mind.

"I *have* been shot." She seemed more incredulous than anything else and Sam knew she was still in shock. The pain hadn't reached her yet. But it would. He'd have given anything to be able to take the pain and make it his own.

He heard a door open and reached up without taking

his eyes off Babs. A wad of soft towels was thrust into his hand as Cecily knelt beside him.

"I called 911. They're sending an ambulance. How is she?"

"Fine. She's just fine." His tone dared anyone to argue with him. He pressed a towel to the wound high on her shoulder, lifting her slightly to press another towel underneath where the bullet must have exited. The small movement broke the fragile web that had been shielding her from the pain and Babs gasped, what little color she'd had leaving her face.

"Sam? Am I going to die?"

"No. You're not going to die. I'm not going to let you die." Her eyes started to glaze and he reached down to catch her hand, lifting it to his mouth, his eyes fierce on her face. "Hang on, honey. You're going to be all right. You have to be. I love you. Do you hear me? I love you."

But she was beyond hearing anything. Her body had taken charge, sending her into unconsciousness as a protection from the shock she'd sustained. Her eyes closed, her breathing was barely perceptible. Sam felt a terrible fear press against his chest.

"You can't die. I love you. I love you." In the distance, he heard the wail of a siren, the sound growing closer.

Cecily put her hand on his shoulder, squeezing it. He looked at her, his eyes full of wild despair. "She can't die. I love her. She can't die."

Tears filled Cecily's eyes and slid down her cheeks. Just as Sam would have given anything to make Babs's pain his own, so would his mother have done anything to take the agony from his face.

"She'll be fine."

''She has to be.'' There was absolute finality in the words, as if he couldn't conceive of anything else.

Cecily looked at Babs's still figure, the blood soaking through the thick towel, her face as still as a waxen doll. She prayed that Sam was right. Please God, let him be right.

Chapter Fourteen

"I don't understand why Emmet insisted that we all be here like this." Dodie fussed irritably with the sleeve of her severe gray blouse, tugging it down over her bony wrists.

"Remember, he said it had something to do with Babette." Lionel's helpful comment earned him a scornful look.

"Of course I remember what he said. I'm neither deaf nor senile, unlike some members of the family." The contemptuous look she threw at Bertie and Clarence went right over the old couple's head, as did most things in life. "I just don't see why he insisted on this foolish gathering. After all, we don't know where the wretched girl is. It was Emmet's friend who had her last. Maybe he's calling us together to tell us that the man has demanded a ransom. It would be just like Emmet to know an adventurer without ethics."

"I don't know. I have a feeling it may be something else." Lionel's brow furrowed and he tugged at the beard that concealed his weak chin. "I hate to say it but perhaps we made a mistake in hiring those men to kidnap Babette. Things do seem to have gotten rather out of hand."

"Don't be ridiculous." Dodie's strong voice canceled out any possibility of a mistake. "Everything would have been just fine if this wretched acquaintance of Emmet's hadn't interfered. He can hardly blame us for that."

"Oh, I don't know, Mother. It seems to me that Emmet probably takes a pretty dim view of the whole operation. He's strangely fond of Babs. God only knows why." Lance lifted his glass and downed a healthy swallow of cognac, his beautiful features set in a sullen cast.

"Babette was always a very sweet child." Bertie's voice was unexpectedly strong, raised in defense of her great-niece. Clarence patted her hand, his round little face set in its usual expression of vague confusion.

"Sweet but willful, my dear. Don't forget how willful she always was."

Dodie ignored him, as usual. There were few people she didn't ignore. "Well, I just wish Emmet would have the good manners to be on time. I had to tell the cook to postpone lunch. If he's going to insist that we be here, the least he can do is not keep us waiting."

As if the words were a command, the huge library door swung open and Emmet strode in. Any reproach Dodie might have uttered died unspoken. The look on his face was grim enough to discourage even her acid tongue.

"I'm glad you're all here. Saves me having to track you down."

"Your wish is our command, cuz." Lance lifted his glass in mocking salute. Emmet barely glanced at him.

"I'm going to come straight to the point. I want to know who hired the men you paid to kidnap and murder Babs."

"Murder?" Lionel's eyebrows threatened to disappear into his hairline.

"Don't be absurd, Emmet. They were to kidnap her. No one said anything about murder. I think you owe us all an apology, coming in here and treating us like common criminals." Dodie tugged at her sleeves, her mouth pulled so tight her lips all but disappeared.

"That's a big strong, cuz. The Malones may be willing to indulge in a little larceny and kidnapping but we've always drawn the line at murder." Lance finished his cognac and set the crystal glass on the mantel.

"Murder? Poor little Babette? Really, Emmet, I don't know where you got such an extraordinary idea." Bertie's voice fluttered with distress, her knitting needles becoming hopelessly entangled in the shawl she was making.

"Quite right, my dear. Extraordinary idea. Extraordinary." Clarence patted his wife's hand.

"If you're worried because we don't know where Babette is, I think you should look to your friend, Mr. Delanian." Dodie's voice was filled with righteous indignation. "After all, he's the one who interfered with our simple plan and took Babette away from the men we hired. If you're concerned about her welfare, I'd look to him. Perhaps he's holding out for a larger reward."

"As a matter of fact, Dodie, I've been in contact with Sam for quite a while now. He's been protecting Babs, trying to keep the men you hired from killing her. We've both been looking after her. The problem is we didn't do a very good job."

There was a long silence and then everyone began to talk at once.

"What do you mean you weren't successful?"

"Oh dear, has something happened to Babette?"

"Now, my dear, don't worry about it. I'm sure Babette is just fine."

"I'm afraid not, Clarence. She's not fine at all." Emmet's grim tone cut through the babble like a hunting knife through silk. Before he could say anything more, the door behind him was pushed open and Sam walked in. His tousled hair seemed even blacker than usual against the pallor of his skin. A dark growth of beard shadowed his jaw giving him a lean and dangerous look. But it was the state of his clothes that drew a stunned silence. The gray shirt he was wearing was coated with a rusty substance that was horribly, unmistakably blood.

He looked at no one but Emmet, his eyes burning a bright, agonized blue. "I just left the hospital. She didn't make it."

There was a horrified gasp and then the questions broke out again.

"Who is this man?" Even Dodie's stern manner failed her in this moment.

"My God. Are you saying what I think you're saying?" Lionel mopped nervously at his brow.

"Babs? Dead?" Lance reached for the cognac bottle, his face pale, his eyes shocked.

"Babette? Oh, dear." Bertie stared at Sam as if she couldn't believe what she was seeing.

Clarence cleared his throat and patted his wife's hand. "There, there, my dear, I'm sure it's all a terrible mistake."

Emmet's gaze settled on the old man as Sam came up to stand beside him, the gore on his shirt a silent accusation.

"If there's been a mistake made, you made it, Clarence. This is Sam Delanian."

Clarence looked at Emmet, his eyes showing a surprising streak of shrewdness. "I don't know what you're talking about, my boy. The shock you know. Perhaps I should take Bertie to lie down. We were always so fond of young Babette."

Sam moved to block the door, his eyes never leaving Clarence. The old man looked at him and then looked away from the burning rage in those eyes.

"You're not going anywhere. Give it up. We know it was you who hired the kidnappers. You called on people you'd kept in touch with for years, people from the old days when your life wasn't quite so respectable. It was you who had the idea of kidnapping Babs and you were the one who made the arrangements. But kidnapping wasn't all you had in mind."

"Don't be absurd." The voice had lost the quavering quality that had always marked Clarence's speech. "Why on earth would I want Babette dead?"

"Try several million dollars. And two hundred thousand in gambling debts. Money you borrowed on the understanding that you were soon going to come into a large sum of money."

"Prove it." Clarence stood up, facing his accuser. The feeble old man had disappeared. A ripple of shock ran through the company at the change. Gone was the slightly batty old character they'd all taken for granted. This was someone else. Someone much stronger. Someone capable of murder.

"You understand that we didn't know a thing about any of this, Emmet." Lionel rapidly mopped at his brow now, his eyes darting back and forth. "Legally, we can't be held responsible for any of this."

The look Emmet threw him was full of contempt. "Shut up. You may not have planned the murder but I don't think any of you would have been too upset when the money rolled in.''

"You can't prove any of your accusations," Clarence challenged.

"We caught one of the men you hired. Do you really think he's not going to name names?"

Something terrible sparked in the faded old eyes. He reached inside his coat and drew out a small pistol, aiming it unwaveringly at Emmet. Suddenly, fear had joined the shock that already filled the room.

"I waited sixty years for that damned money. I should have had it years ago. The old man was supposed to leave it to Bertie, only he tied it up so that I couldn't get my hands on it. I tried every way I could to get it but he did too good a job."

"So you decided to kill Babs?"

"I didn't have a choice. It was the only way I could get the money. The people I borrowed from were getting impatient. I'm too old for meetings in dark alleys. And I'm too old to spend the rest of my years in prison. Now just get out of my way, like the smart man I know you are. No one else has to get hurt."

"Even if he got out of your way, Uncle Clarence, you'd have to go through me and I don't think you want to kill me in front of so many witnesses."

Sam's head jerked around, his eyes narrowing on Babs's slim figure. She was leaning in the library door and he wondered how she'd managed to get by the police stationed outside. She was wearing jeans, with a hospital gown flapping over them, her feet bare. Her hair was a wild cap around her pale face, her eyes looking too big for her head.

This time the shock wave that rippled through the room was more subdued. There's been so many surprises in the past few minutes. One more hardly made an impression.

"Babs, what are you doing? You shouldn't be out of bed." Sam started toward her but she waved him away.

"I had to be here. I wanted to look him right in the eye."

Clarence stared at her, his face pale, his eyes wild. All his plans were dissolving around him. Nothing was going the way it should have.

"They said you were dead."

"I guess they were a little premature." Babs stared at him. "Why? If you'd come to me, told me you needed the money, I'd have given it to you. Why?"

His face changed, hatred twisting it into a caricature of the dotty old man they'd all thought they knew. "*Ask* you for it? Why should I ask you for it? It was mine. I put up with this family for sixty years, your snobbery and stinginess." He gestured with the gun and Dodie cringed back in her chair. Lionel looked as if he might pass out and Lance quickly finished off another drink.

"Sixty years. No one in this family ever thought I was good enough to be a Malone because of what I was."

"But I never felt that way. Never." The pain in Babs's voice cut through Sam, making him hurt for her.

"Maybe not but if it hadn't been for you, I would have had the money years ago. When your parents died, half of it would have come to Bertie. I wasn't greedy. Half would have been enough. You should have died with them and then this wouldn't have happened. But you didn't die and I couldn't risk another accident."

Emmet's harsh exclamation drowned out the sharp gasps and murmured words of shock. "You killed Earl and Lenore? All these years and no one ever knew. My God.''

Clarence waved the gun again. "I was a professional. Of course no one knew, but she should have died with them." Madness glittered in his eyes. "She ruined everything when she survived the crash. It's all her fault."

Sam tensed as the gun wavered between Babs and Emmet. Babs clung to the doorway, her strength clearly ebbing, the last traces of color gone from her face as she absorbed the news that her parents' accident had been a murder.

"All her fault." Clarence appeared to settle on a target and the gun focused on Babs's slumped figure. Sam braced himself, prepared to lunge forward and block the old man's aim. "All her fault. All her—" The insane litany ended abruptly but not in the way any of them had expected. Instead of a gunshot, Clarence's shriek of pain filled the room. His gun jerked upward, burying in the ceiling the bullet he'd intended for Babs.

They'd all forgotten Bertie, as usual. She'd been sitting on the sofa, wrapped in her shawls, the usual pile of tangled knitting on her lap. She'd listened without speaking as her husband admitted to murder and attempted murder. No one had even thought to wonder at her reaction. They'd been too absorbed in the life-and-death drama unfolding in front of them to worry about a batty old woman. That turned out to be Clarence's fatal mistake. The point of a knitting needle applied to the soft skin of his side had been painful and unexpected.

Sam and Emmet both moved simultaneously. Emmet lunged forward, grabbing Clarence's upraised arm and wresting the gun away from him with little effort. Sam crossed the few feet that separated him from Babs, catching her in his arms as her knees gave way completely.

He knelt on the floor, his body shielding her from anything that occurred in the room behind him.

In a matter of seconds, Emmet had the gun in his own possession and Clarence was standing sullenly in front of him, a broken old man. Emmet glanced over his shoulder to make sure Babs was all right and then looked at Bertie, who was still sitting on the sofa.

"Good work, Aunt Bertie."

Bertie drew her shawls closer around her narrow shoulders and stood up, looking down her short nose at the man who'd been her husband for nearly sixty years.

"I was raised to think divorce a sin. And I was determined to prove Papa was wrong about you. If I hadn't been so stubborn, I'd have been rid of you years ago. I hope they put you away for a very long time." Clarence didn't lift his eyes as she left the room, unconcerned by the armed police officers she passed on the way out.

In a matter of minutes Clarence had been handcuffed and led away. They'd all be expected to make a statement but it was agreed that they could have a little while to recover from the day's events.

Sam was seated in a big leather chair, Babs cradled protectively across his lap. Emmet crossed to the bar and poured himself a healthy drink. Lance picked up the decanter as Emmet set it down, the Waterford clinking against his glass in time to the shaking of his hands. Dodie sat rigidly in her chair, not looking at anyone and Lionel mopped constantly at his forehead, his face flushed and his eyes darting nervously about.

"Well, I guess that's settled," Lionel laughed nervously. "Quite a surprise. Who would have thought it?"

"This was a disgusting spectacle." Dodie's voice quivered with indignation. "I hope you're proud of yourself, Emmet."

Emmet swirled the amber liquid in his glass and nodded. "Yes, I am rather proud of myself. My only regret is that the rest of you aren't going to pay for your parts in this. I'd like nothing better than to be sending the whole lot of you postcards in San Quentin."

Dodie glared at him and then her eyes shifted to where Babs and Sam sat, his arms protectively around her. "I suppose it didn't occur to any of you to handle this in a more discreet manner. Do you have any idea the scandal this is going to cause?"

Babs lifted her head from Sam's shoulder and looked at the older woman, seeing the narrow face and the deep lines of bitterness as if for the first time. It hadn't occurred to one of them to ask how she was or to apologize for their part in all of this. Their only concern was how it was going to affect them.

"You know, Aunt Dodie, I sincerely hope the papers have a field day with this. If I'm lucky, they'll dig up the fact that you sold paintings to a known mobster and then Finney will get to take everything away from you. And, if that happens, I wouldn't advise any of you to come to me for help. I've finally realized that Uncle Emmet is absolutely right: None of you is worth a plug nickel."

She let her gaze move from Dodie's pinched expression to Lionel's nervous face to Lance, who at least had the grace to look away. They were all shallow, unhappy people and perhaps that was their punishment. She let her head fall back against Sam's shoulder, her strength draining away.

"Take me home, Sam. I'm tired."

Sam stood up, cradling her against his chest, his expression full of tenderness. "I'll take you back to the hospital where you belong. As soon as you're well, I'm going to kill you for this stunt.'' But the threat didn't hold much impact when he was holding her as if she were the most precious thing in his life.

BABS PUSHED HER THUMB along the edge of a pea pod, feeling a sense of real accomplishment when the shell popped neatly open and the peas inside fell into the bowl in her lap. She tossed the shell into the basket beside her. Cecily said the empty pods were going into the compost pile, which was another mystery to Babs. It was funny how she'd managed to go her entire life without shelling a pea or seeing a compost pile.

She leaned back in her chair and reached for another pea, her eyes focused on the hillside that rose up from the backyard. In the month since the shooting, Sam had stripped the vegetation from it and was in the process of terracing the steep hill. It was as if he were doing penance for her injuries. If the hill hadn't been so overgrown, the killer wouldn't have been able to hide there. Babs had pointed out that Sam couldn't hold himself to blame. The man would simply have found somewhere else to hide. She might as well not have spoken. He'd continued to work doggedly, stripping every shred of cover from the sloping land.

Cecily had stopped her when she would have argued further. This was something Sam needed to do. Besides, she'd always wanted the hill terraced anyway. She'd smiled but Babs could see the worry in her eyes as she watched her son tear into the vegetation as if it were a malevolent presence.

She sighed. A month. It seemed like it had all happened in the dim and distant past. Her memories of the shooting were vague and unfocused, like images from a bad dream. Her memories of the confrontation with her family were more vivid but they'd taken on a surreal quality. Perhaps it was the only way her mind could deal with the hurt.

She hadn't seen any of her family since the day the police had taken Clarence off to jail. Aunt Bertie had taken a trip to Europe. Babs had received one letter from her, apologizing for the things Clarence had done and saying that perhaps when she returned, Babs wouldn't mind seeing her. Babs held no grudge against her great-aunt. It was hardly Bertie's fault that her husband was a killer.

Clarence was awaiting trial. Emmet had been wearing a wire and the police had a complete tape of Clarence's confession, both to attempting to murder Babs and to killing her parents. The judge had set the bail high and no one had seen fit to pay it. When the time came, Babs knew she'd have to testify but that lay in the future.

Right now it was the present and the very near future that concerned her. Her shoulder was healed. The bullet had managed to go through without doing much damage. There was some residual stiffness and the doctors had warned her that it might be months before that faded completely. She flexed it. There were still twinges of discomfort but not enough to worry about.

"Does it hurt?" Babs looked over her shoulder, smiling at Cecily as the older woman stepped out onto the porch.

"Just a little stiff."

"You're sure?" Cecily laid her fingers on the injured shoulder as if she could tell by touch alone whether or not Babs was in pain. Babs shook her head, feeling a warm glow at the other woman's concern. Over the past few weeks, they'd grown close but Cecily's concern always surprised her. Since her parents' death, there'd been no one in her life to fuss over her. Emmet cared and he took care of her but it wasn't in his nature to fuss. Cecily fussed in the nicest possible way and Babs savored every moment of it.

"I was just thinking that it was about time I stopped pretending I was an invalid and got out of your hair."

"Don't be silly." Cecily sat down in a chair next to Babs and reached for a handful of peas, shelling them with quick efficient movements. "I've enjoyed having you here."

"You were very kind to ask me to stay here when I left the hospital."

"I *wanted* you to stay here. And so did Sam."

Babs looked away, her eyes showing a shadow of pain that had nothing to do with her shoulder. "I think Sam felt guilty about what happened and that's why he wanted me here."

"Sam wanted you here so he could keep an eye on you."

"Well, he's been avoiding me ever since." The words were out before she could call them back. She hadn't meant to say anything but the hurt went deeper than any physical injury.

Cecily reached out, touching the back of the younger woman's hand, her fingers light and gentle. "Men can be very peculiar. Sam has a lot to work out in his own mind but don't give up hope. My son may be a little slow but he's not stupid. He'll come around. Just be patient."

Babs picked up a pod and pried it open, lifting out each pea individually and dropping them into the bowl one after another. "I just wonder if he doesn't wish he'd never met me."

"Of course he wishes it." Babs's head jerked around

and Cecily laughed gently. "He wishes it because you've disrupted his life and things can never be the same. Men are inherently resistant to change. But underneath the urge to hide his head and pretend everything is the same as it was, he knows just how much better his life is going to be with you in it. Just have a little patience."

"I hope so." Babs glanced at her, noticing a gleam in Cecily's eyes. "You look pleased with yourself."

To her surprise, the other woman blushed, the color tinting her cheeks a soft shade of pink. The peas were forgotten. Babs turned her full attention on her friend.

"What's going on?"

Cecily's smile deepened, her eyes soft and glowing. "Last night Emmet asked me to marry him and I said yes." She rushed the words, as if afraid they might not get out unless she hurried them.

"That's wonderful!"

"Do you really think so? We haven't known each other very long and I was afraid it might seem like we were rushing things."

"I think the two of you are perfect together. Uncle Emmet has been alone a long time. I can't imagine anyone more perfect for him than you."

"Thank you."

"Have you told Sam yet?"

"Just a little while ago."

"What did he say?" Babs toyed with the basket of peas, the task forgotten.

Cecily laughed, her happiness reaching out to light everything around her.

"Well, once he'd recovered from the shock, he said he was very happy for me. Poor Sam. I'm afraid he's had to make a lot of adjustments in his life." Cecily looked at her watch and stood up. "I have an appointment with the hairdresser in half an hour. Emmet is taking me out to dinner tonight so you and Sam will be on your own."

"Where is Sam?" She hoped that the panic she felt at the thought of being alone with him didn't show in her voice.

"He went for a drive. He said he'd be back before dark."

Babs thought about what Cecily had said while she dawdled over the peas. Be patient, give him time. Patience had never been her strong suit but she wouldn't have minded if she was sure that there was something to be patient for. Did Sam feel something for her? She knew what she wanted from him. She wanted his love. She wanted him to love her as much as she loved him. Wholly and unequivocally.

She stared out at the late afternoon sunshine, her eyes thoughtful. Was his mother right? Did he care for her or did he just feel guilty because she'd been shot? She wanted more than guilt from him. Lying in the hospital, she'd had nothing to do but think. She'd thought about her life, the death of her parents, her family. And she'd thought about Sam. He'd dominated her thinking, pushing his way into her mind. She wasn't sure she'd dealt with the issue of her family, and there was still an ache inside when she thought about her parents, but she'd come to several conclusions about Sam Delanian. He was stubborn, bossy and annoyingly male—but she couldn't imagine life without him.

The question was—did he feel the same way about her?

Babs had no idea how long she sat there, staring out at nothing in particular, the basket of pods sitting unshelled in her lap. The click of the screen door opening brought her out of her thoughts and she looked over her shoulder, feeling her heart skip when she saw Sam.

"Hi."

"Hi." She had to clear her throat before she could get any sound out. She resisted the urge to smooth her hair or tug at the sleeves of her shirt.

"How are you feeling?"

"Fine. You know, you don't have to keep asking that. The doctors said I was going to be fine."

He shrugged, coming out onto the porch to lean against the railing.

"Habit. I guess I've gotten used to worrying about you."

"Well, you don't have to worry about me anymore." She busied herself with the neglected peas.

"I guess not." He didn't sound all that happy with the idea and Babs risked a glance up at him. He was staring out at the stripped hillside, his expression brooding. The sun was just starting to go down, throwing long shadows across the yard, leaving his face in shadow.

Babs felt a surge of irritation. Be patient, Cecily had said, but Babs didn't feel patient. She felt anything but. She wanted to know one way or the other. If Sam didn't care for her, she had to know. Maybe a little judicious prodding was in order.

"Your mother told me she and Emmet are going to be married."

"Yeah, I know."

"I guess she'll be doing a lot of traveling with him."

"I guess."

She snapped a pod in half and dropped it into the bowl, oblivious of the fact that she had taken the peas out of it. She could have gotten more conversation out of one of the fence posts.

"You know, I've been thinking about it and I think it's time I moved back home." Sam's head jerked toward her. "I mean, my shoulder is basically healed and your mother is going to have enough to do around here without worrying about a guest."

"I wouldn't think you'd want to live in the same house with the rest of your family. Not after what they did."

"Oh, it's only temporary. I think it's time I got a place of my own. Don't you?" She snapped peas in half, tossing them back into the bowl or into the pile for compost without paying any attention to where they were going. She didn't lift her head to look at Sam. Was he relieved at the idea of her leaving? She couldn't bear to see it if he was. The silence stretched until she was sure she could count her every heartbeat.

"You know, I've been doing some thinking about it too." There was an odd note in Sam's voice and she didn't dare look up. "It seems to me that you're not really fit to be on your own."

Her heart sank. All he cared about was her shoulder. How could she explain to him that it wasn't her shoulder she was worried about, it was her heart? Maybe he didn't want to know.

"My shoulder is fine." She leaned forward to set the basket of peas on the floor, blinking to hold back the tears that threatened to flood her eyes. If he didn't love her, he didn't love her. There was nothing she could do about it. "I think I'll go up and wash my hair before dinner."

It was the first excuse that came to mind. Something to get her away from him before he could see her hurt.

She stood up but Sam's hand caught her wrist as she turned away.

"Your hair looks fine and I wasn't talking about your shoulder." She stopped, not lifting her eyes from the floor, not breathing, not daring to hope.

"You weren't?"

"No."

"Then what were you talking about?" She looked up at him, wondering if what she felt was showing in her eyes, not even caring if it did.

"It seems to me that you need a full-time keeper. I don't think you're safe to be let out on your own."

His smile was gentle, his eyes bright with an emotion she was afraid to put a name to.

"Are you…are you applying for the job?" She could barely get the words out past the tightness in her throat.

"I might consider it but I've got some pretty tough requirements."

Her smile shook around the edges. "I could probably meet just about any requirements you might have."

"You probably could." He caught her other hand, drawing her forward until she stood between his out-spread legs as he leaned against the railing. He set her hands on his chest and Babs thought she'd never felt anything more wonderful than the steady beat of his heart under her palms.

"I love you, Ms. Malone." His hand came up to cup the back of her neck and Babs closed her eyes.

"I love you, Mr. Delanian." She opened her eyes and smiled at him, her face alight with happiness. "I thought you were sick of me."

"Never. I've been trying to convince myself that this wasn't crazy." His thumb brushed across the dampness on her lashes and his expression grew more serious. "I could be a fortune hunter, you know."

Her smile told him how ridiculous that idea was. "If you're a fortune hunter, then I'm glad I've got a fortune to hunt."

His mouth caught her smile, tasting her happiness. Her arms slid around his neck and she leaned into the strength of him, letting him support her.

Sam dragged his mouth away, dropping kisses across her face. "You know I'm only doing this to keep you out of trouble. If I didn't look out for you, who knows what might happen."

"I know." His tongue traced the curves of her ear and Babs felt her knees melt.

"It has nothing to do with the fact that I can't bear to let you go."

"I know." His hands tightened on her back, pulling her closer as if trying to absorb her into himself.

"It's just that it would drive me crazy to think of you going around getting kidnapped and starting fights and some other poor sucker having to rescue you. That's all it is."

"I know." His mouth caught hers in a long drugging kiss. He drew back and looked at her, his eyes full of so much love that Babs thought she would surely die of happiness.

"I love you."

Her smile trembled. She reached up to cup his face in her hands, her eyes dark with emotion.

"I know."

And she did know. He loved her, forever and always. It was all she wanted.

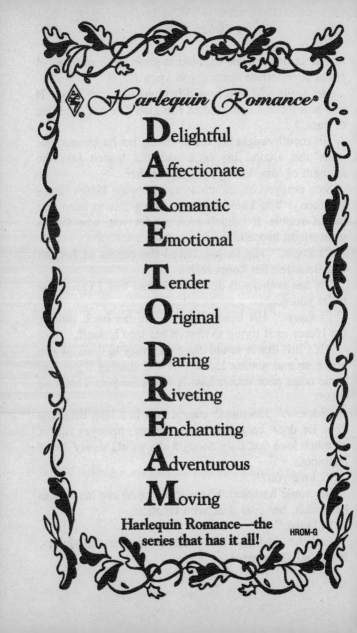

Harlequin Romance®

Delightful

Affectionate

Romantic

Emotional

Tender

Original

Daring

Riveting

Enchanting

Adventurous

Moving

Harlequin Romance—the
series that has it all!

HROM-G

Harlequin® Historical

From rugged lawmen and
valiant knights to defiant heiresses
and spirited frontierswomen,
Harlequin Historicals will
capture your imagination with
their dramatic scope, passion
and adventure.

Harlequin Historicals...
they're too good to miss!

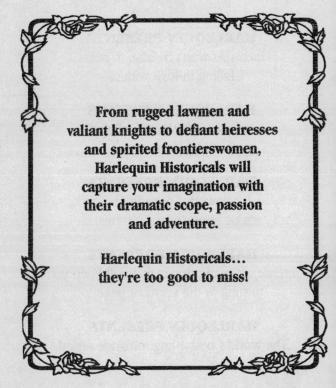

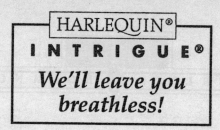

LOOK FOR OUR FOUR FABULOUS MEN!

Each month some of today's bestselling authors bring
four new fabulous men to Harlequin American Romance.
Whether they're rebel ranchers, millionaire power brokers
or sexy single dads, they're all gallant princes—and
they're all ready to sweep you into lighthearted fantasies
and contemporary fairy tales where anything is possible
and where all your dreams come true!

You don't even have to make a wish...
Harlequin American Romance will grant your every desire!

Look for Harlequin American Romance
wherever Harlequin books are sold!